Also by Ellen Crosby
Moscow Nights

THE
MERLOT
MURDERS

A Wine Country Mystery

ELLEN CROSBY

S C R I B N E R
New York   London   Toronto   Sydney

SCRIBNER
1230 Avenue of the Americas
New York, NY 10020

SCRIBNER and design are trademarks of
Macmillan Library Reference USA, Inc., used under license
by Simon & Schuster, the publisher of this work.

For information about special discounts for bulk purchases,
please contact Simon & Schuster Special Sales:
1-800-456-6798 or business@simonandschuster.com

DESIGNED BY LAUREN SIMONETTI
Text set in Bembo

Manufactured in the United States of America

1   3   5   7   9   10   8   6   4   2

Library of Congress Cataloging-in-Publication Data

Crosby, Ellen.
The merlot murders : a wine country mystery / Ellen Crosby.
p.   cm.
1. Vintners—Fiction. 2. Virginia—Fiction. I. Title.
PS3603.R668M47 2006
813'.6—dc22   2006042255

ISBN 978-1-5011-8843-5

For André

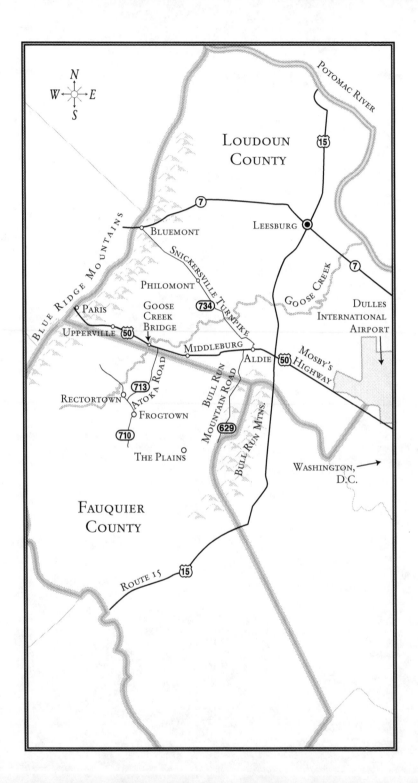

MONTGOMERY ESTATE VINEYARD

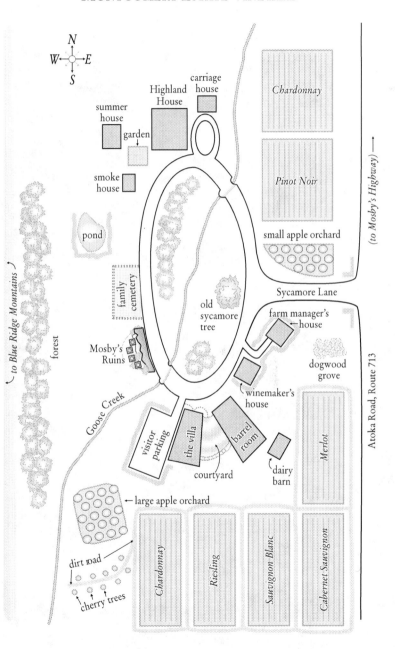

THE
MERLOT
MURDERS

It has become quite a common proverb that in wine there is truth.

—Pliny the Elder

CHAPTER 1

I have always been fascinated by alchemy, though I draw the line at black magic. My family owns a vineyard at the foothills of the Blue Ridge Mountains in Virginia and I am sure there is both magic and chemistry involved in transforming grapes into wine. Not as impossible as changing lead to gold, but nevertheless, no mean feat, particularly if you believe—as I do—in Galileo's definition of wine as sunlight held together by water.

As a child I read the stories of the philosopher's stone, how only a small quantity could convert a massive amount of worthless metal to gold and, supposedly, when added to wine or spirits, it became the mythical "elixir of life"—a potion that would cure illness, restore youth, and even grant immortality. Two years ago I moved to Grasse, the perfumed city in the south of France where my mother grew up, to recover from injuries sustained in a near-fatal car crash. I was twenty-six at the time and neither immortality nor eternal youth were much on my mind. All I wanted was to walk again. So I brought my own "elixir of life" hoping it would hasten my cure—bottles of wine from home.

Philippe, my live-in boyfriend, refused to drink any of it with me. A wine snob and a purist, the only wines he liked were listed in the *Guide Hachette*—and they were all French. So I drank my family's wine when he wasn't around.

Like now. This time he had to go to Italy. Another vague story about business and no idea when he'd be back. When he was home—an increasingly rare occurrence—he stayed up most nights talking on the telephone, smoking pack after pack of Gauloises. He never mentioned those conversations. I knew not to ask.

I seem to have a habit of getting involved with men who don't sleep at night. A bartender, a paramedic, a law student moonlighting as a cabdriver—and now Philippe. There was a time when I slept deeply and soundly the minute my head touched the pillow— "sleeping on both ears," the French call it. But the men who have drifted through my life have gradually turned me into a sheep-counting insomniac.

What kept me awake this night was the mistral—the dry, cold wind that began blowing from the north sometime after midnight. At sunset altocumulus clouds shaped like giant cuttlefish had turned blood red, a sure sign the winds would come that night. Tomorrow the late-August sky would be the luminous blue of a Van Gogh painting and windsurfers would flock to the beaches in droves. Tonight the mistral brought—as it always did—a raging headache.

I switched on the light and swung my feet out of bed, reaching for my cane, which was propped against the wall, where I always left it. I pulled on one of Philippe's shirts, which was draped over a chair next to the bed. It smelled faintly of his cologne. His scent was about all that was left of our relationship.

The cracked marble floor was cool against my bare feet. When I got downstairs I took a bottle of Montgomery Cabernet Sauvignon from the wine rack, grabbed a glass and corkscrew, and let myself out the kitchen door into the garden.

I brushed against the large rosemary bush outside the door on my way across the terrace to the old stone swimming pool. The massive bank of lavender along one side of the pool was dark and dense against a blue-black sky filled with windblown stars.

Wine is inevitably linked to a place, tasting of the seasonal vagaries of sunshine and rain, the particularities of the soil, the differences in the taste of oak that hint at which forest yielded the trees for the fermenting barrels. I sat on a low garden wall by the pool and breathed deeply, getting quietly drunk on the calming smell of lavender and the velvety smoothness of the wine. But even the heady fragrance of the garden couldn't overwhelm the scent and taste of Virginia as I drank, dissolving time and space, until the wine finally seeped into all the hidden paths that led to my heart.

Though I'd become comfortable and easy with my life in France, I wanted to go home again and rebuild my car-wrecked past. Through the open kitchen window I heard the phone ringing. At this hour it would be for Philippe.

I let it ring.

The caller was persistent. Finally I went inside, bringing the nearly empty bottle and my glass. I sat in a high-backed rush chair and picked up the phone mid-ring.

A man's irritated voice said in English, "God, there you are. It's about time. I've been calling for twenty minutes. How come your machine didn't kick in? What took you so long to answer?"

"It wasn't twenty minutes. You know we don't have a machine. I was outside. Nice to talk to you, too, Eli," I said to my older brother, glancing at the kitchen clock. It read two thirty-five A.M. Not the usual hour for a social call, even if he was phoning from America.

"I have some news, Lucie." His voice was slightly less sharp.

"What is it?" I poured the last of the wine into my glass. To get through this conversation, I'd need it.

Eli and I have not been on the best of terms lately, so we don't spend much time on chitchat. In fact, we don't spend much time on anything. The last time I spoke to him was three or four months ago . . . or five. The fact that I have been living in the south of France for the past two years has made this chasm something we can blame on the Atlantic Ocean, pretending it's physical distance, not an emotional divide that accounts for the estrangement.

"It's Leland," he said. "He was out hunting. There was an accident."

"How bad?" I asked. But it was very bad, obviously, or he wouldn't have called.

"He's dead." My brother's heroes came from all the violent action movies he watched as a kid, full of emotionless men without tear ducts. Armageddon could be looming but they could handle it no sweat because they were tough. Just like Eli was acting right now. So I was surprised when he added gently, "I'm sorry, Lucie."

"What happened?" I reached for my glass with an unsteady hand and almost knocked it over. I caught it just in time.

"He was alone, out in the vineyard. He had his shotgun with him so he was probably taking out a few crows. No one's really sure what happened, but we're thinking the heat might have gotten to him," Eli said. "He passed out and the gun somehow went off."

I tipped my head and drank the blood-red wine, wiping my mouth with the back of my hand. No way. Even I knew that guns don't "somehow" go off. You have to pull the trigger.

Besides, despite his record on everything else, Leland Montgomery was never careless when guns were involved. He had his share of bizarre habits, like making his children call him "Leland" instead of "Dad" or "Pop" or "Father," but he took no chances when it came to firearms.

"Who found him?" Eli's story didn't quite ring true.

The silence on the other end of the phone lengthened beyond the boundaries of a normal conversation as though the line had gone dead. It happened from time to time especially on international calls, so that on more than one occasion I'd ended up chattering into the flat blackness of a severed connection.

"Eli? Are you still there?"

For the first time his voice seemed to falter. "Hector. He was out with his dogs."

Hector, our farm manager, had been with my family for decades. Next to Jacques, our winemaker, he was the second most important person in the vineyard. He took care of the crew, the equipment, and just about anything else that needed doing.

"Oh God. Poor Hector."

I suppose I should have said, "Poor Leland," but it wasn't the first thing that came to mind. There is a French proverb that goes, "In water one sees one's own face, but in wine one beholds the heart of another." I stared into my wineglass and did not behold Leland's heart. To be honest, he hadn't often shown that he had one.

"He'd been out there for hours. Christ, I never saw so much blood . . ." Eli spoke in that tight emotionless voice again, but this time I heard a fine crazing in the veneer. "Then Bobby Noland showed up."

"Bobby came?"

"Yeah, he just got a promotion. He's not doing patrols anymore. I think it's crime scene investigations or something."

I'd known Bobby Noland since I was in the second grade and he was in fourth. By the time we got to high school, the principal at Blue Ridge High pegged Bobby as the type who'd be getting into trouble with the law when he grew up. He never figured Bobby for being the law. Frankly it surprised a lot of his friends when he stuck around home and joined the Loudoun County Sheriff's Department.

Eli cleared his throat. "Look, I can buy your ticket for you if you want."

"My ticket?"

"Come on, Lucie, don't tell me you don't plan to come home for this, either."

The "either" referred to his wedding. I hate being baited. He knew as well as I did that I couldn't fake an excuse this time. Not for Leland's funeral. "Don't be ridiculous. Of course I'll be there. I'll get my own ticket."

"Suit yourself."

It was hard to tell if I'd hurt his feelings or he was genuinely relieved that I wasn't putting up an argument. "I suppose we ought to start making arrangements," I said.

"They're made."

"Oh?"

"Well, sure. We're not really having a funeral, anyway. A wake tomorrow night and a graveside prayer service on Thursday. You know what a waste of time Leland thought going to church was. No point making him go now."

"I guess not." I swallowed the rest of the wine. "So you and Mia planned the funeral, did you?"

There was a short pause before he said, "Actually Leland planned it himself. He told Mason what he wanted one night when they were driving home from one of the Romeos' weekly poker games. As for Mia, your sister isn't taking this any better than she took Mom's death. She won't talk about it."

Mason Jones was our lawyer and the Romeos were Leland's drinking and poker buddies. The name stood for "Retired Old Men Eating Out." They had regular tables at most of the local restaurants and cafés and their faithful patronage kept more than one place financially solvent.

"Poor kid," I said. "Do you think she'll be up to going to this funeral? I don't think I could take a repeat of what happened when Mom died."

"I haven't exactly asked her. She's been spending a lot of time with a new friend so I don't see her much."

"Oh?" When he didn't elaborate, I added, "Were you joking about Leland planning his funeral after a poker game?"

"If it was anybody else you know I would be, but we're talking about Leland." Eli paused, then said with some bitterness, "Figures, his kids being the last to know what he wanted. You can imagine how I felt, hearing it from Mason."

"I hope he didn't want anything too weird."

"Nope. We got off easy. It's all pretty normal except for the bagpipes. His Scottish blood must have been surging."

Or maybe it was the post-poker Scotch. "Bagpipes, hunh?"

"'Amazing Grace' as the opening hymn and 'Taps' at sunset— since he was a veteran—as his coffin is lowered into the ground," he said. "Sunset's at seven forty-two on Thursday, by the way."

Eli would know a detail like that. He owned one of those radio-

controlled atomic watches that's never wrong. I could hear him rif-
fling pages. Probably his Filofax, which he usually wore chained to
his wrist. He didn't trust electronic organizers.

"Why does it have to be Thursday?" I said. "I'll never get there
in time for the wake. As it is, I'll barely make it for the burial."

"Give me a break, Luce. Of course you will. With the time difference, you'll arrive practically before you leave France. Sleep on
the plane and drink a gallon or two of water. You won't even be jet-
lagged."

"Why can't you delay it? Something's going on that you're not
telling me. I know you."

"Don't be an ass." He sounded annoyed.

"I'm *not* an ass. Don't be crude. You didn't answer my question.
Why can't you postpone the service another day or two?" I repeated.

"Because it's all arranged. That's why."

"What would be so hard about unarranging a wake and a prayer
service?" I persisted. "Where are you going to get someone to play
the bagpipes on such short notice, anyway?"

"I don't see the need to unarrange anything. I've got everything
under control."

The floor was becoming quite littered with all the gauntlets he
was throwing down. "Fine. Don't tell me," I said. "As soon as I get
back I'll find out from someone else."

"You will *not*." It's hard to understate the overbearing and right-
eous sense of entitlement my brother genuinely felt because he
happened to be born first.

I had just spent two years without him bossing me around. I
didn't plan on getting used to it again.

"Give me one good reason why not," I snapped. "And I'll do
what I want."

There was shocked silence, probably while he dealt with the
new phenomenon of my defiance, then he said angrily, "All right,
you want to know? You couldn't let it wait until you got home,
could you? It's your goddamn godfather. Satisfied?"

"What are you talking about? *Fitz?*"

"You heard me."

Besides being my godfather, Fitzhugh Pico was my parents' best friend and the owner and chef at the Goose Creek Inn, a local restaurant known for its romantic setting, eclectic menu, and discreet waiters. It was the perfect place to propose marriage—or end one, keeping a sly tryst under the radar. Soon after my parents planted our first vines, Fitz and my mother collaborated to produce two private label wines for the inn. Not only was he nearly family, he was part of the family business.

"I don't understand . . ." I began, but Eli cut me off, still furious.

"He's telling anyone who'll listen that Leland's death wasn't an accident. No one can get him to shut up, either."

"Why would he do that? What do you mean, not an accident?"

"Oh, for God's sake. Use your head. Work it out for yourself, Luce."

I sat silently, picking at a strand of loose bulrush on the edge of my seat and thought. Until now I hadn't noticed the whistling sound of the wind as it came through the still-open kitchen door. A pair of moths zoomed frenetically around the overhead ceiling light. One of them smacked into the glass shade and dropped to the floor.

"Oh my God," I said slowly. "Suicide. Leland killed himself and you don't want anyone to know." My voice rose. "You should have told me from the beginning, Eli! Why did you tell me it was an accident?"

"Because it *was*." Eli yelled. "And you're wrong. He didn't kill himself. But I've got goddamn Fitz telling everyone and his goddamn grandmother that Leland was goddamn *murdered*! Okay? Now do you understand?"

This time I did knock the wineglass over. It shattered into silvery slivers on the marble floor.

Murders don't happen in Atoka, Virginia. People don't even litter there. Thelma Johnson, who owns the general store, leaves the side window unlatched so the delivery boy from the bakery can climb through to leave his fresh-baked muffins and doughnuts if he gets there earlier than she does. The town is as wholesome and all-American as Mister Rogers' Neighborhood.

"What was that noise?" Eli asked.

"A glass . . . fell over. Eli, did somebody murder Leland?"

"No one murdered Leland. It was an accident, just like I told you." He was no longer yelling, but he sounded tense and edgy.

I massaged my forehead, which was now throbbing not just from a mistral-induced headache, but from this surreal conversation. Eli's story still didn't sound right. He'd left something out. "What aren't you telling me?"

"I am not going into it over the phone. We'll talk when you get here."

"Eli!"

"I've got another call. I've got to go. Call me and let me know when your flight arrives. I'll come get you. We'll discuss the rest of it then."

I said, "The rest of what?" to dead air.

I stood up and reached for my cane. In the dim light a large shard from the broken wineglass glimmered faintly. I bent to pick it up and saw the blood on my finger before I felt the knifelike edge slice my skin. It was a superficial cut, long and shallow, but the kind that bled like a geyser. By the time I made it from the kitchen to the bathroom in search of a bandage, a red Rorschach trail spattered the cream-colored marble of the stairs and the hallway.

I got to the toilet just before I threw up. Afterward, I sat in the dark on the cool floor of the enormous old bathroom and leaned my head against the wall, pressing on my finger to stop the bleeding. My head still ached.

Eli's brusque, abbreviated account of Leland's death was more disturbing than if he'd told me every detail. My imagination, left to run riot in the complete darkness of a lavender-scented night, conjured scenes from horror movies. Hector's dogs yapping next to Leland's blood-soaked body, lying there for hours in the blistering late-summer heat. Had he suffered? Had he known he was dying?

I stood up and found bandages in the medicine cabinet. Then I packed my bags.

Later I replayed in my mind that phone conversation with Eli. He'd been more than a little opaque about the details of Leland's death. And he wanted to get the funeral over with as quickly as possible.

Odd that he couldn't—or wouldn't—tell me why over the phone.

Was my brother trying to cover up our father's murder?

CHAPTER 2

I always ask for a window seat on an airplane so I can watch cities, mountains, forests, and rivers shrink to toylike size, distilled to their most intense colors and compact shapes. From the air, the sun-bleached city of Nice is sand and terra-cotta, its patina-worn limestone buildings with their bright orange roofs densely packed along the beaches at the Promenade des Anglais. The plane's shadow moved like a bird across the tropical water of the Bay of Angels, which shifted from aquamarine to amethyst and finally to iridescent azure in the strong Mediterranean sunshine.

The last time I'd seen it like this was when I'd arrived, intending to stay for a month or two after I got out of the hospital. But the healing process—both physical and emotional—would not be hurried. I remained, as the months lengthened into seasons and finally, two years passed. Slowly I fell in love with the south of France.

Who wouldn't? Life was endlessly pleasurable, even a bit hedonistic, on the sun-drenched, sensual Côte d'Azur. It moved slower here. It was uncomplicated. I'd found a job as an English language tour guide at the International Perfume Museum in Grasse. Pleasant and undemanding, it suited me fine. I moved slower, too, and I understood, finally, that it was going to be like that for the rest of my life.

When I left Virginia, Leland had given me the keys to the farmhouse we'd inherited from my mother's family. He might have warned me that it was now a shambles, but of course he didn't. One look at the place and I knew he'd stopped paying our caretaker, Jean-Luc, who used to keep the eighteenth-century *mas* and its gardens immaculate. No doubt he'd diverted the man's salary into one of his fringy business deals or used it to pay off debts.

The first time I slept there during a rainstorm I discovered how badly the roof leaked. The plumbing dated back to Napoleon. The electrical wiring had a short somewhere, which meant that switching on a light or turning on the toaster could produce a life-threatening shock. I was forced to assert my ownership against the assaults of territorial and incontinent birds that dwelled in the eaves. In short, I inhabited a ruin.

I advertised for a handyman, offering somewhat steady work in return for room and board and that's how Philippe came into my life. Before long, he moved into my bedroom. They say you get what you pay for and he came free of charge, but in those days I didn't care. In the beginning, it was all bliss.

Before I left for the airport I'd written Philippe a note, which I taped to a bottle of champagne in the refrigerator, explaining what had happened. It was one of the two places I knew he would look when he finally returned to France. I'd taken my wallet with me. Philippe would drift home when his money ran out.

As Eli predicted, I slept on the trip across the Atlantic. When I woke, we'd left the gray-blue ocean behind and the plane was starting its descent. We moved inland and the landscape unrolled in pale green and clay-red checkerboards anchored by farmhouses, barns, and silos with silver domes that flashed like lighthouses when the sun caught them. In the distance the hazy sweep of the low-slung Blue Ridge Mountains bracketed the view.

My family owned nearly five hundred acres near the small village of Atoka in the heart of Virginia's affluent horse and hunt country. As the crow flies, it was about fifty miles from Washington, D.C. Our land had belonged to a member of the Montgomery family for more than two hundred years, a grant to my ancestor

Hamish Montgomery for service to his country in the French and Indian War. He'd called it Highland Farm in honor of his regiment, the 77th Highlanders, whose exploits in that war were legendary.

The farm was located in an area that straddled Loudoun and Fauquier Counties, a part of the Old Dominion romantically famous not only for great scenic beauty but also as a history-haunted place of glory and tragedy. The streets of Middleburg, the town next door to Atoka, were named for the patriots who founded the country—Washington, Madison, Hamilton, Jay, among others—a number of whom had lived locally. It was also the site of some of the bloodiest battles of the Civil War, or as we preferred to call it, "The War Between the States."

Twenty years ago my parents decided to try planting vines on a few acres—my mother's passion, mostly. Before her death six years ago she had talked unceasingly about Virginia as the first place in the New World where anyone had tried to produce wine. She believed that what we were doing now was part of a historic continuum begun at the Jamestown settlements and spurred on by Thomas Jefferson, who had done much to foster a wine industry in the Commonwealth. I still remember her studying his vineyard notes from Monticello like some kind of Bible—Jefferson was considered the patron saint of Virginia vineyards—and that faraway look she'd get in her eyes.

Then she would take me out in the fields where she taught me about the cycle of *véraison,* or ripening, as the grapes developed into mature fruit. Though she could have given me a complex scientific explanation for what was happening, she chose instead to tell her young daughter that the sun and the rain gave the grapes an indefinable quality known as *goût de terroir,* which means literally "the taste of the land." No other grapes in the world—and no other wine—she assured me, would taste like ours. Never forget it, she'd said.

I hadn't.

Eli was waiting for me, as promised, when I pushed my luggage cart through the double doors into the main part of the international terminal. He hugged me in the stiff-armed way brothers and sisters do and murmured in my ear, "I can feel your ribs. You're a walking X ray, Luce."

Spoken by someone who'd lost sight of his own ribs some twenty pounds ago. At least. He had the beginning of a small, self-indulgent paunch. I pinched his new set of love handles. "I can't feel yours."

So much for the greeting.

"Yeah, well, I added a few pounds but it's all muscle. I play a lot of tennis now. Come on. Let's get out of here." He commandeered my luggage cart. "Can you manage? We could get a wheelchair, if you want."

The first time he'd ever treated me like I was handicapped. "Why would I need a wheelchair? I can manage just fine, thanks."

"Don't be so touchy, babe. Just asking."

It was also the first time he'd ever called me "babe."

I'd been expecting the brother who once went a month without brushing his hair to see what it would look like. The Eli who used to wear whatever he found on the floor in the morning, retrieving it from where he'd dropped it the night before as long as it didn't smell too nasty. Instead I got a GQ model, dressed in a pale pink Lacoste polo shirt, khaki shorts, sockless in doeskin-soft Italian loafers with tassels. Someone who clearly understood the difference between mousse and gel and cultivated a regular relationship with a blow dryer.

We emerged from the terminal into the sizzling white heat of a late-August afternoon. Eli whipped on a pair of Ray-Bans and I blinked in the hard light.

"It's a hundred and two," Eli said, staring at his watch.

"Degrees? Don't tell me that watch is connected to the National Weather Service, too."

"I wish. I heard it on the radio driving here. I'm just looking at the time. We're forty-two minutes behind schedule."

"This is as fast as I go, Eli."

He looked surprisingly uncomfortable. "Oh. Sorry."

He stopped behind a black Jaguar XJ so shiny I could see my reflection in it. The license plate said Eli 1.

I'm not a car person. If it moves when you turn the key in the ignition, I'm happy. Two years ago Eli drove a beat-up Honda with a dented front fender.

"New car?"

He gave me the dumb-question look and hit the button on his key to turn off the alarm and unlock the doors. "Yup."

In the old days I would have razzed him about his new toy and the hair and the clothes. He would have retorted with something in kind in the ego-deflating way siblings have of keeping each other humble. But these were the new days so I said nothing.

The Jaguar purred toward the tollbooth and slid onto the highway. Office buildings in various stages of construction sprouted like weeds after rain on both sides of the road. Red gashes in the clay soil looked like open sores where the earth had been bulldozed and flattened. Two years ago this had been farmland. Maybe if I'd seen the destruction unfold gradually it would have seemed less brutal.

"When did all this happen?" I asked.

"All what?"

"All this building. Why do they have to do this?"

"Do what?"

"Destroy everything."

"While you were away," Eli said, and I knew that any sentence beginning with those words was going to end in some kind of indictment, "progress happened." He emphasized the word "progress."

"I don't think this is progress."

"That's because you spent the last two years in France in a fossilized village, where they have laws to protect every stone or patch of ground because Joan of Arc or DeGaulle might have walked on it. Look, Lucie, the world didn't stop just because you weren't around to watch it change."

"Don't start."

"Don't you."

"Say what you want, these buildings are ugly. Look at them. All the same. Who builds this stuff?"

"As a matter of fact," said my-brother-the-architect, "we do." He pointed to a building striped with pink stone and blue-mirrored glass. "My firm built that one. We won a design award for it."

Frankly he could have turned off the air-conditioning after that remark. The temperature in the car verged on glacial.

"I'm sorry," I said, finally. "I didn't mean to insult your building."

"You're entitled to your opinion."

"I said I'm sorry."

"Forget it."

I stared out the window. After a while I said, "What was it you wouldn't tell me on the phone?"

He sighed noisily. "Oh God. Where do I start? It's Fitz. I want you to talk to him and tell him to knock off spreading these crazy stories about someone bumping off Leland. You're his goddaughter. He'll listen to you."

"What if they're not crazy stories?" I asked. "You wouldn't be covering up something, would you?"

He looked at me over the top of the Ray-Bans. "Don't be an ass."

"I'm *not* an ass. I just don't believe Fitz would say something like that if there weren't some truth to it."

"I hate to burst your bubble," he said cruelly, "but Fitz is a barely functioning alcoholic. Catch him late enough in the day and he doesn't know if he's on foot or on horseback. Get it now? The elevator doesn't make it to the top floor anymore. The porch light's on but nobody's . . ."

"Stop it!" I yelled, covering my ears with my hands. "Please stop it!"

He drove in silence for a while, but a muscle worked in his jaw and I knew we weren't done.

"Just suppose," I said after a few minutes, "that he's right. What about some of Leland's business partners? What do we know about any of them, except that most of them probably live under rocks? What if Leland owed someone money and he couldn't pay it back?"

"And some hit man took him out." Eli looked at me curiously.

"That's a hell of a theory for you, Luce. You, ah, wouldn't be in financial trouble yourself, would you?"

"Of course not. I'm fine. I got money from the accident settlement, remember?" What little I'd hung on to that Philippe hadn't spent. Mostly in Monte Carlo.

I still had nightmares about the midsummer's evening we'd left the casino—he'd won, for a change—when two men wearing ski masks forced us off the Route de la Moyenne Corniche near the medieval mountaintop village of Eze. The view of the Mediterranean was spectacular from that height, especially at sunset. I wasn't the only one who appreciated it. One of the men held a gun to Philippe's head and told him in vulgar terms that he would be seeing the water from a much closer vantage point unless he handed over all his money.

After they pistol-whipped him they took his belt and bound my hands tightly to the steering wheel of his Porsche. It took a long time before Philippe came around. When he did, my wrists were bleeding and I was still trying to untie his belt with my teeth. I wanted to go straight to the hospital and the police but Philippe said it was too dangerous. They'd find out. They'd come back for us.

That's when I knew it hadn't really been a robbery. He owed someone that money. I realized, then, how much he was like my father, a charming façade masking a complete fake—the kind of man who'd swear over the phone he loved you while making the call from another woman's bed.

"Look, sweetheart," Eli was saying as if he read my mind, "Leland's so-called business partners were flakes who sold stuff like extraterrestrial real estate. Not the mob. I'm talking condo developments on the moon. Buy early for the best view of Earth. Losers. Like he was."

"You know, Eli, you've changed."

I saw the muscle twitch in his jaw again. "Let's just say I got sick of watching Leland blow all of Mom's money. I don't know why you're defending him, anyway. What did he ever do for you?"

I stared mutely at my hands folded in my lap. Like mother, like daughter. And Eli didn't know about Philippe.

"Now you see what I mean, don't you?" he said. "That's why I need you to get Fitz off this crazy theory of his and make him stop talking. Come on, Lucie, you've been gone two years. It's payback time. You owe this to the family and you're the only one he'll listen to." He emphasized each word like he was talking to a child or a slow-witted person.

"Hell, the gossip's already started," he added. "When I stopped by the general store this morning, Thelma was up one side of me and down the other. I told her Bobby said it was an accident. She clucked around for a while then said, 'Poor old Lee. I guess we just ought to leave him lay where Jesus flang him.' I told her that's just what we intended to do. So now I want you to tell me that you're with us on this. Got it?"

Too bad those Ray-Bans were opaque. I couldn't see Eli's eyes at all. Though probably if I could, all I'd see would be my own reflection. No window on the soul there. If he still had one.

"Us," I said. "You mean Mia agrees with you?"

He said tersely, "She'll do whatever I tell her."

That figured. Though she hadn't always been so compliant.

Mia had been fourteen when our mother was killed one fine spring day, six years ago. The two of them had gone riding together. The child had returned to the stables alone hours later, barely coherent, as she tried to describe where Mom's horse had stumbled, for no apparent reason, while jumping one of the low Civil War–era dry-stacked stone walls that rimmed the perimeter of the farm.

She never regained consciousness. A small mercy. She died that evening. The doctor in the emergency room said later that she might have lived if she'd gotten medical care sooner.

No one told Mia about that conversation, but still she had been too unwell to attend the funeral. Afterward Leland, whose interest in fatherhood had been borderline nonexistent when Mom was alive, escaped home as often as possible. It didn't take long for Mia, left to her own devices while Eli and I were away at our respective universities, to acquire a tattoo, a boyfriend with a slow wit and a fast car, and a pack-a-day habit. When Jacques caught her and her boyfriend soused to the gills in the woods by the winery, even Leland agreed it was time to do something.

Surprisingly he was the one who thought of asking our cousin Dominique to come stay with Mia. The daughter of my mother's sister, she was studying in Paris to be a chef. Leland persuaded Fitz to offer her a job at the Goose Creek Inn and promised free room and board in return for "keeping an eye" on Mia. He said it would be a great opportunity to perfect her English, along with the chance to work with a top American chef.

Dominique told me later he'd described my sister as a sweet child with the morals of a Girl Scout who needed a "mother figure" to give her gentle guidance. It took less than twenty-four hours to figure out what he'd really meant was that she needed a Mother Superior-cum-parole-officer and a short leash. Mia hadn't been overjoyed to report her comings and goings to her cousin after so much unsupervised hell-raising, but eventually she seemed to settle down and we were less worried about the road to perdition.

"Well?" Eli said. "You didn't answer me. We need to present a unified front on this. As a family."

The statement was freighted with so much latent irony that, for a moment, I thought he might be joking. But he was peering over the top of the Ray-Bans again. He was dead serious.

I hadn't had much sleep in the last twenty-four hours and my head still ached. Eli could be relentless when he wanted something, like a dog with a bone.

"Okay, okay. I'll talk to him," I said. "I'll see what I can do. Can we change the subject now, please?"

"Of course. Actually, there is something else we need to discuss before we get home." He paused. "The bad news."

He waited while that sank in.

"Well," I said wearily, "glad we got the good news out of the way first."

"It has nothing to do with Leland."

He had turned west onto Route 50 and the scenery was all farm-land now. The Indians made the path for this road three hundred years ago when they were following the trail for buffalo, which probably accounted for its gentle twists and turns. Here, at least, nothing had changed. Miles of low stone walls that were pre–Civil War lined the sides of the road. Horses grazed serenely on stubbly brown fields and the corn was late-summer high. The traffic had petered out to a single John Deere tractor motoring amiably down the middle of the road. The driver gave way to let Eli pass, waving as we zoomed by.

"So, what is it?"

"Greg Knight moved back home. He's living in Leesburg."

There was a long silence before I said, "When?"

"Six months ago."

"How come no one told me?"

He cleared his throat. "I don't know."

He did know. "You might have warned me when you called last night," I said.

Eli looked over at me the way you look at a grenade after some-one just pulled the pin. "You never would have gotten on that plane."

"Don't be an idiot," I said. "I just would have liked to know before I got here, that's all. What's he doing here, anyway? Bartending again? I thought he had some big radio job in New York. With CBS."

"It was ABC," my brother said, "and he did."

"What happened? They fire him?"

Eli shrugged. "How should I know? We don't talk anymore, not like before. Like I said, he's living in Leesburg. He's got a job work-ing as a deejay at WLEE. With his own nighttime call-in show. Plays jazz in between talking to insomniacs or whatever weirdos are awake at three in the morning." He cleared his throat again. "Not that I listen."

For once it was my turn to look at him. "At least he won't be at the funeral. I'd rather not see him right now and I can't imagine he'd have the nerve to show up."

"Actually," Eli said, "you will and he does. There's something else." He gave me the grenade pin look again. "He's seeing Mia."

He knew better than anyone it was the last thing I expected to hear. "What, as her baby-sitter? He's ten years older than she is."

"He's, ah, sleeping with her."

"Very funny."

He said nothing, just worked his jaw like he was trying to loosen a piece of food that got wedged between two teeth.

"He's not really sleeping with her," I said finally.

"Don't tell her. She thinks he is."

"Oh God, Eli! How could you let that happen? What happened to Ringo? Or Rocko . . . whatever his name was?"

"Who?"

"That guy she was dating. The one with the teeth."

"Oh. Him. He's at some military academy in Pennsylvania. On probation."

"I don't understand . . ." I said. "There's something you're not telling me."

"You haven't seen your sister in two years, babe. She's changed."

"Well, if she listens to everything you tell her, why can't you put a stop to this?" I banged a fist on the wide console between our seats.

He should have been as upset as I was. He and Greg had been best friends since first grade. Then came the rain-wrecked night two years ago when Greg's car slammed into the stone wall at the entrance to the vineyard. He'd actually gotten out and walked away, though he'd returned to watch while the Rescue Squad cut me free with the Jaws of Life. His friendship with Eli and our torrid summer affair had disintegrated into more pieces than a wall of Humpty Dumpties.

He came to the hospital to visit me precisely once during the months I was there. A mumbled apology as though he'd forgotten to pick me up for a movie date. That was it. Those fifteen minutes were acid-etched in my memory, marking the absolute nadir of the Great Depression—mine, that is—during the era when the doctors said I might never walk again. Then I heard that he moved to New York.

Eli wiped at a nonexistent smudge where I'd whacked the console. "Take it easy, will you? That's hand-stitched leather. As for talking to Mia about Greg, it's not that simple. Anyway, they're consenting adults."

Amnesia would have been convenient just then. Too many images of what Greg and I had done together flashed behind my eyelids. "Maybe I could talk to her . . ."

"Forget it, Luce. She'll think it's sour grapes. Look, do you honestly think he's changed? He's still the same Greg. Still with chicks hanging all over him, stuffing their phone numbers into his pockets, willing to cook him dinner or have his baby. Don't ask me how the guy does it."

I closed my eyes again. I didn't have to ask. I knew.

"So is he . . . faithful . . . to her?"

"What do I look like? Dear Abby? You think he tells me he's screwing around on my sister?"

We were taking a little stroll through land-mine territory. The rumors were that Greg had turned his predatory attention away from his affair with me for a brief fling with Brandi, Eli's then-girlfriend and now my beautiful but vapid sister-in-law. He denied everything, of course, but Brandi finally told Eli after Greg went to New York that he'd practically raped her during what she said was a "friendly little drive." Eli believed his wife.

I didn't believe either of them. Not that any of it mattered anymore.

"So you don't have a problem with this, then?" I asked. "Come on. You remember what happened that summer. *All* of it."

He said nothing and just concentrated on the road, though he'd really goosed up the speed while we were talking. He took the left-angle turn at the Snickersville Turnpike so sharply the tires squealed.

I grabbed the armrest. "Eli, slow down, will you? You're driving like a madman."

"I can drive this road with my eyes closed." But at least he let up slightly on the accelerator.

"Well, open them. You didn't answer my question."

"There's nothing to say. Look, I'm sorry, Luce. I don't want to go over ancient history. We can't relive the past."

I leaned back in my seat. For the second time, he was avoiding something. He'd gotten Mia to go along with him and now he wanted my silence, dressed up as family unity. He started worrying his tongue against his bottom lip again, lapsing into a brooding silence.

I stared out the window at the well-loved landscape of home. My days of exile in France were over. I was back for good. Eli was right that we needed to pull together, as it fell to the three of us now to run the vineyard. I had no intention of reliving the past but we had to lay some things, finally, to rest. There would be no sweeping the details of Leland's death under the carpet, either.

The late-afternoon sun streamed in through the glass of the Jag's tinted windows, refracting everything outside to a lovely liquid clarity that almost hurt my eyes. Inside the car, the murkiness was pervasive.

In vino veritas. In wine there is truth.

About time I got some.

CHAPTER 3

We passed the Wild Bird Sanctuary sign at the edge of the town of Middleburg. Route 50 narrowed and became Washington Street, an elegantly pretty tree-lined main street of small shops and cafés, where park benches lined the brick sidewalks and American flags hung limply from poles on the street lamps.

"I hate to rush you," Eli said, breaking the silence, "but as soon as we get to the house you've got to change so we can get over to the funeral home. Brandi and Mia are already there. Dominique will be along as soon as she sees to a retirement party at the inn. Some senator's throwing a bash."

"It's Leland's wake. Can't she leave that to someone else? I thought she had help."

"Of course she does. But let me tell you, if she'd been around when God created the world, she probably would have insisted on supervising to make sure He didn't screw up."

"Dominique? Oh, come on. If she was any more laid back, you'd want to take her pulse to check for signs of life."

"Not anymore. Now you just want to check it to see if she's human. That catering company of hers has grown so much she's bringing in almost as much money as the inn. So her spring is, shall we say, just a tiny bit overwound," he said. "Then there's the matter of her wanting to run the whole caboodle on her own after Fitz retires."

"I didn't know he was thinking about retiring." I said, surprised.

"He's not. She's thinking about him retiring. You should see him at the inn these days when he joins his guests for happy hour. Like I said, for him happy hour never stops. Dominique is getting more and more pissed off about it, too. He's an embarrassment, Luce."

"Why do you always have to be so crude? He opened that restaurant before either of us were even born. It is what it is today because of him."

"Will you calm down? It's not like the guys in white pajamas are going to show up and haul him off tomorrow, though some time drying out is probably just what the doctor ordered. Anyway, all future plans about Fitz and the inn are on the back burner while the festival is on."

"What festival?"

He glanced over so I could see his eyebrows raised above the frame of the Ray-Bans. "You mean you don't even know about that? Our festival. The First Annual Montgomery Estate Vineyard Summer Festival."

"Since when do we have a festival?"

"I just said it's the first one."

"I mean, how come we have a festival? We're just a mom-and-pop vineyard."

"No fooling," he said. "But these days, everyone's got one. So now we do, too. The only difference is most of the other vineyards don't think they have to put on a production that would rival the opening ceremony of the damn Olympics."

"Where do we get all the people to pull off something like this?"

"Where do you think? Dominique roped everyone in the family into it. And Joe, of course."

"I thought that relationship was over."

"Nah, he's still crazy about her even if she thinks he's about as ambitious as a slug. Hell, he'd hang the moon some place different if she wanted it. She'll probably get around to asking, too. She's got him doing just about everything else."

The family had long since stopped placing bets on when Joe Dawson, a history teacher at an elite private girls' school in Middleburg, would get up his nerve to ask Dominique to marry him. Now it was *if* he'd ask her.

"Like what?"

"She's got some theater company coming in to do *A Midsummer Night's Dream* this weekend at Mosby's Ruins."

The burned-out tenant house we called Mosby's Ruins had been the temporary Civil War headquarters of Colonel John Singleton Mosby, the leader of what was probably the most famous guerrilla combat group of the Confederacy. It was thanks to his notoriety that Atoka got its name on the map.

Mosby's nickname was "the Gray Ghost" because of the surprise commando raids he and his partisan Rangers used to stage on Union soldiers. They'd steal Union supplies, then disappear, hiding out in barns or smokehouses or behind the miles and miles of dry-stacked stone walls that checkerboarded the landscape. Our tenant house had been one of his many bolt-holes until Union men burned it.

As kids we played there even though it was unsafe, reenacting Civil War battles where the Confederacy always won. We used the crumbling weed-choked brick walls as ramparts and scared each other with sightings of Mosby's ghost, who was said to appear on moonless nights, still looking for Union soldiers. Later, Greg and I used it as a secret place to make love.

"It's been refortified since you left. We turned the main floor of the house into a stage for concerts, plays, performances." He looked at me. "The place where you and Greg used to do it is a storage room now. We keep the scenery, lights, and equipment there."

I turned red as he smirked. "How nice," I said coldly.

He turned off Route 50 onto Atoka Road. We drove through the town of Atoka—which consisted of the general store with its two gas pumps out front, the farrier, and the Baptist church—and headed toward home. Though it had been less than an hour since we sped away from the airport and the new high-tech construction lining the highway, here the mailboxes still had the same names on them they'd had for decades and the homemade signs stuck in front yards advertising fresh peaches, tomatoes, and 'lopes were the same ones folks used every year.

Eli slowed the Jag, for once obeying the twenty-five miles per hour speed limit, as though recalibrating to the gentler, more languid pace I remembered. "Opening night for the play's been canceled on account of Leland's funeral," he said, after a moment. "Switched to Friday instead. Along with the pig roast."

"Pig roast?"

"You heard me. Dominique wants everyone to dress up in Elizabethan costumes to serve the guests. It'll be a cold day in hell before she gets me to prance around in a pair of tights and some velvet doubloon."

"Doublet."

"Whatever. I'm not wearing it."

We had come to the split-rail fence that marked the beginning of our land. Out my window was a long, clear vista all the way to the layered Blue Ridge Mountains. In front of us were the Bull Run Mountains, a sixteen-mile truncated spur of hills that always made me think of an old man's worn down set of teeth.

The first thing I saw, marking the beginning of our Chardonnay block, was my mother's Peace rosebush, which had exploded into a profusion of velvety yellow flowers the size of small cabbages, against glossy dark green foliage. The French planted roses with their vines for centuries because both were sensitive to the same pests and diseases. If the roses were suffering, it meant the vines would soon be in trouble, too, and in need of preventive measures against bugs or black rot or whatever else ailed them. Now with all the modern equipment we had for monitoring the soil and vines, the roses were there for beauty, and because my mother loved them.

Farther down another of her favorite hybrid tea roses, the blood-red Chrysler Imperial, indicated the beginning of the Pinot Noir. The middles, the spaces between the rows of vines, which we usually planted with bluegrass, were deeply cracked and brown. It obviously had been a hot, dry summer, but the vines would have thrived in weather like that.

I kept my face turned toward the window so Eli wouldn't notice that my eyes were suddenly watery, and pretended to look for the smaller of our two apple orchards, which was just beyond the Pinot Noir.

"Hopefully we'll get a good price for the place," Eli said. "Considering the shape it's in."

He spoke in that same casual tone of voice so it didn't hit me right away what he'd just said. When I realized, it was like a physical blow. "You're not talking about the vineyard?"

"What else would I be talking about?" He sounded irritated, like he'd actually expected to have gotten away with dropping that bombshell into the conversation without me noticing. "Of course we're selling. Mia and I certainly don't plan to run it. And you don't either, obviously." His glance strayed in the direction of my feet.

I reddened and smoothed my ankle-length cotton dress, now badly pleated after sleeping in a cramped airline seat, and shifted my bad leg so it was less visible.

So this was what he hadn't wanted to tell me on the phone. I never saw it coming. "You can't be serious," I said.

His lips were pressed together like he was trying to keep his cool and refrain from blurting out some insulting reply. I didn't care what he said. This time he wasn't going to bully me and win.

"You want to sell our home!" I said. "How could you? Our family's owned that land practically since the country was founded. Everyone's buried there . . . Mom . . . Leland . . ."

"The cemetery's not a problem." He cut me off, speaking rapidly. "I've got it all figured out. We'll move them."

He slowed the car and put on his turn signal. A row of cheerful burgundy, white, and green posters with an abstract design of grapes twining around musical instruments was plastered on the stone wall that marked the main entrance to Highland Farm and Montgomery Estate Vineyard. Mia's artwork, almost certainly. She was the only one of us to inherit Mom's artistic talent. The place where Greg's car destroyed part of the wall was still visible, even with the posters covering the seam between the old and new stone, though the demolished stone pillar had been completely rebuilt. Eli turned into the entrance.

"That is an absolutely revolting idea," I folded my arms and stared out the window.

"It is not. I'm not talking about throwing a bunch of coffins in the back of Hector's pickup and carting them off to a landfill or something. There are ceremonies for situations like this. We'll find another site, maybe build a mausoleum. It'll be tasteful." He sounded irritated. "Mia agrees with me, babe. And don't tell me you can't use the money like the rest of us."

So much for family unity. He and Mia were going to gang up on me so it was two against one.

A cloud of red clay dust swirled around us as we drove along Sycamore Lane, the private gravel road that led to the house and the vineyard. The name came from the magnificent two-hundred-year-old tree, which had grown up a few hundred feet from the main entrance, dividing the road like a "Y" into left and right forks. Eli came to the divide and downshifted, pausing briefly in front of the enormous tree with its soaring branches and its crepelike bark, peeling like a bad case of sunburn. It had been here as long as my family and it could easily live another three or four hundred years.

"We're broke, is that it?" I said. "Are you telling me we have to sell the place to pay off Leland's debts?"

He glanced at me as he nosed the car to the right and headed directly toward the main house. No sentimental tour for my homecoming. Had we gone left—the road was an enormous loop—we would have first passed the winery, Mosby's Ruins, the cemetery, and a large spring-fed pond.

"Calm down, will you? And don't turn on the waterworks, either, Luce. I can't take it right now. We're not technically broke."

I wiped my eyes with the back of my hand. "I'm *not* crying. And you sound like a lawyer. Just tell me yes or no. Are we broke or not?"

"It's complicated."

"Tell me. I've got time."

"No, you don't. We've really got to move. We're twenty-one minutes behind schedule. I'll fill you in later."

"It wasn't my idea to have the wake two hours after I got off the plane from France," I said. "And you drove like a madman. You made up for a lot of lost time. We'll be fine."

"We're the family. We *can't* be late."

He pulled the car into the curved drive in front of the house. Highland House, as it was called, was a harmonious mixture of Federal and Georgian architecture built of locally quarried stone. Not a pretentious or grand mansion, it possessed—at least to my eyes—a grace and elegance in its well-proportioned symmetry that made it seem somehow more substantial than it was. Scott Fitzgerald used to attend parties here when he came from Baltimore to visit friends in the area, and FDR dined with my grandparents the day he gave the dedication speech for the newly constructed Blue Ridge Parkway.

When my mother was alive, she'd made frequent pilgrimages to the gardens of Monticello, Thomas Jefferson's home, and to the Pavilion Gardens at the University of Virginia in Charlottesville, which he'd designed. I'd often gone with her on those trips, watching while she read his *Garden Book,* making plans to incorporate into her own gardens the harmony and beauty Jefferson had sought to achieve. Like him, she believed botany ranked near the top of the list among the sciences, and so it had happened that every year our home had been one of the most popular ones on the annual garden tour.

"Oh my God," I said. "What happened?"

I stared through the Jag's tinted window. Everything she had created was gone. The lawn was coarse and scrubby where there weren't rock-hard bare spots. If I hadn't known where the flowerbeds had been, I'd have thought the yard was always this weed-tangled and ugly.

The house hadn't fared much better, for it looked depressingly seedy and run-down. The paint on the shutters, the large paneled door, and the fluted columns had gone mottled and grayish and was peeling in long scales. The moss-covered façade was stained below the bowed bay windows, two of which were mended with duct tape where the glass had cracked. Weeds bloomed in the chipped stone urns which sat on either side of the door. Our family motto, *Gardez bien*—"watch well" or "take good care"—carved in the stone lintel above the doorway was obscured by grime and lichen.

"I'm glad Mom can't see this," I said, when he didn't answer.

He turned off the engine and punched the button to unlock the doors, a bit savagely, I thought. "Knock it off, Lucie. You've got no right to say anything. You left, remember?"

He got out of the car, hoisted my suitcase out of the trunk and headed for the front door without waiting for me. By the time I got inside, he had already vanished up the sweeping spiral staircase. The exterior state of deterioration should have tipped me off to how bad the interior would be, but inside was worse. When my mother was alive the house smelled of lavender and lemon furniture polish and fresh-cut flowers. Now it stank of stale grease, stale air, and stale urine, like an animal might have squatted on the Aubusson rug every now and then. Half the bulbs in the Waterford chandelier were either burned out or missing, so the light was as dingy as the furniture and walls. What most disoriented me though, was the silence. My mother's antique long case clock, whose quiet ticking sound and mellow chimes were as calming and familiar as breathing was stuck at twelve-thirty. How long had it been since anyone had bothered to wind it? It was like the heart of the house had stopped beating.

I heard Eli shout from upstairs. "Hey, shake a leg down there! We haven't got all day." A moment later he appeared at the upstairs railing. "Oh God. I'm sorry . . ."

"Forget it." I walked over to the stairs. Since the accident, I needed to climb stairs the way a small child does, always the same foot first, my good foot taking the weight for the rest of my body. I hooked my cane over my right arm and gripped the railing, pulling myself up.

"Um, can you manage?" He sounded tentative. "I mean, do you need some help or something?"

I stopped and looked up. "With what? Climbing the *stairs*?"

"Uh . . . I don't know. I mean, just checking." He wiped his forehead with a folded white handkerchief he'd pulled from his pocket.

"Look," I told him. "Keep treating me like some kind of cripple and I'll deck you with my cane first chance I get."

He pursed his lips together but it wasn't much of a smile. "Okay, I get your message. I'll shut up. Maybe I'll go call the funeral home and tell them we're going to be eighteen minutes late."

"You do that."

When we walked into the B. J. Hunt & Sons Funeral Home—only twelve minutes late—my palms were so sweaty my cane kept slipping in my hand. Eli took my elbow and murmured in my ear, "You look like you're dressed to go to a hunt club ball. You're bound to scandalize the blue-rinse crowd and knock a few pacemakers out of kilter."

My long black dress, it's true, was more like something to wear to a fancy dress party than to a wake. "It's not like I had any time to shop," I hissed. "It's the only black dress I own." What I didn't say was that all my dresses are long now so my twisted left leg is hidden from view.

"I wasn't criticizing. You don't look too bad in that. It looks kind of . . . French. You know, sexy."

"Thanks. Thanks a lot."

He held the door for me. "There's something else I meant to tell you."

All of a sudden he sounded nervous.

"Now?" I said. "Right this very second? Can't you tell me after I see everybody? It already feels like I'm facing a firing squad. At least let me get through that."

"Well, then you'd know."

I stopped and looked at him. "What would I know?"

"That Brandi's pregnant."

"Pregnant." I stared. "She's pregnant?"

"Umhm."

"So I guess this isn't recent news if I could tell by seeing her."

He tugged on the collar of his shirt like it was constricting his breathing. "Oh, it's pretty recent. We haven't actually known that long ourselves."

"How long have you known?"

"Five and a half months."

"Five and a half months?"

"Well, we waited to make sure everything was okay before we said anything."

Men can be so dumb when they make up excuses. At least he spared me the real reason. I can never have children. It was one of the invisible consequences of the accident. At least he'd been considerate enough to figure it might be a sensitive subject.

We walked toward the elevator and I concentrated on my feet again.

"Sorry about the timing, Luce," he added. "I meant to tell you sooner, but sometimes things don't work out the way we mean them to, you know?"

Something in his voice made me glance up and there was no avoiding what came next. I looked straight into the depths of the get-lost-in-me eyes of Gregory Knight, who had shown up to pay his respects to Leland, and I saw heartache coming my way like a freight train.

CHAPTER 4

I'd thought long and hard about what I would say if I ever saw him again. I'd even rehearsed a speech, which I used to recite to the bathroom mirror while brushing my teeth. A real drop-dead diatribe, delivered in perfect Ice Maiden tones, with a good amount of spitting for effect.

I couldn't remember any of it. For a long moment, the only sound in the room was the too-loud ticking of a grandfather clock that stood in the corner of the dimly lit foyer.

Then Eli said coolly, "Leaving already?"

"I've got to get over to the station. I'm supposed to meet someone before work." Though Greg spoke to Eli, his eyes never left mine. "It's good to see you again, Lucie. I'm really sorry about your father. If there's anything I can do . . ."

I had wondered whether there would be some kind of emotional litmus test when we met so I'd have some clue how he felt after all this time. Maybe guilt or remorse or even the apology he never offered. But there was none of that, only polite concern on a tabula rasa.

He'd moved on. I hated myself that it could still hurt. The Ice Maiden was supposed to be tough as nails. "You can get out of the way. We're late."

I stomped past him, banging my cane, though the effect was

lost on the thick carpet muting all sound as it was meant to.

"I'm sorry," he said, again. "You look very pretty in that dress." I didn't turn around. The outside door closed quietly and I heard his footsteps clattering on the staircase. Eli caught up with me and took my elbow again. "I got a chance to look at the tread marks on his back on his way out. I think he got your message."

I yanked my arm away from him. "I doubt it. And I can manage fine on my own, thanks."

He held the door and let me walk into the Green Room alone. Though it had been only two years, they'd all changed. Brandi, dark-haired and dark-eyed, was as lovely as ever, but now robustly and self-consciously pregnant. She came to me immediately, moving like the QE2 docking at port. She leaned over and kissed the air, missing any part of my anatomy by a good eight inches. "Lucie," she said, "I guess Eli told you about our fabulous news. Isn't it great?"

"Congratulations. It's wonderful."

"I know." She squeezed my arm with her left hand. I glanced down at her large marquise-cut diamond engagement ring and diamond-studded wedding ring. If she flashed those rings in hard sunlight, she could probably send messages in Morse code to extraterrestrials on distant planets. They must have set my brother back plenty.

Dominique stood behind her. Her auburn hair was shorter than I remembered, layered in chunky tufts as though it had been cut with loping shears instead of styling scissors, giving her an untidy boyish look. She'd always been tiny with that indefinable waiflike French chic no American woman had ever successfully copied, but I wondered as I smiled at her if she was flirting with anorexia. There were black rings like bruises under her eyes and her skin stretched taut over her cheekbones. I used to think of her as delicate, like fine porcelain, but now she seemed so brittle she could have been hollow inside. I hugged her carefully.

"Chérie," she said, "it's good to have you home again. You look wonderful." She smiled tiredly and stepped back to look me over. "You've changed."

"I walk now," I said. But I knew she was talking about other things.

"More than that," she replied and left it at that.

"You've changed, too," I said. "You're dead tired. Eli says you're working all the time."

"Bah!" She flicked her hand, like she was shooing away a pesky fly. "Isn't that the American way? Work hard? Get ahead? A chicken in every soup? I have a successful business. I have to work so much."

Though her English had improved considerably since she moved to the States, she'd never really gotten the hang of a lot of American idioms. Get her really upset and the English would go out the window entirely. Some things, at least, were as they'd always been.

Mia was last. Eli hadn't been kidding. She was unrecognizable, changed completely from the kid who used to wear ripped low-cut jeans with skanky little midriff-skimming tops that showed off her butterfly tattoo. I glanced automatically at Dominique, who I assumed was responsible for the transformation, but she shook her head almost imperceptibly. Then I caught the infinitesimal eyelid flicker in Brandi's direction.

Though it was easy to see why my brother was captivated by his wife's smoldering *Playboy* centerfold beauty, what was less understandable—at least, to me—was how he could deal with the fact that she was, frankly, thick as two planks. She once told me the only thing she liked about France was French toast and that she never understood all the fuss about the Mona Lisa, who was, well, rather a dull-looking woman.

But she'd clearly wrought a miracle with my sister, who looked stunning. Dressed in a clinging dark blue silk dress, fresh-faced, tanned, her long blonde hair worn in a sophisticated French twist, Mia stepped forward and held out her hand, like we were strangers. "Hello, Lucie."

I had been moving toward her expecting a hug, but stopped when I saw her outstretched hand. I put out my own hand and shook hers. It probably looked as awkward as it felt. "Hello, Mia. You look wonderful."

"Thanks." She pulled out of my grasp, crossed her arms, and looked away. Her mouth moved and I thought she was going to say something else. Then I realized she was chewing gum. And she wasn't going to say anything.

"Are you all right? How are you holding up?" I knew it sounded lame but I couldn't think of anything else to say, especially with Brandi hovering nearby.

Mia's gaze came back to rest on me. The expression in my kid sister's eyes changed from incredulity to scorn. "Why, I'm fine. Just fine. Thanks for asking. Maybe you ought to go pay your respects to Pop. Everyone else has already done it."

"Maybe I ought to."

I leaned on my cane for support as I knelt down before the closed coffin, breathing the dense mingled odors of roses, gladiolus, and chrysanthemums from the substantial funeral bouquets. I shut my eyes and tried to pray for Leland.

Dominique came over as I pulled myself up, leaning on my cane, and stood beside me. "Don't mind her," she murmured. "It's not you. It's Gregory."

"It sure feels like me," I said. "And what about Greg?"

"They had an argument, just before you came in. Mia wanted him to stay with her all evening. She's very . . . possessive. Or maybe I mean *ob*sessive," my cousin said. "I think she might be jealous because you and Gregory were lovers once."

I groaned. "It's *over*. As for being 'lovers,' come on, Dominique. Name one girl in my high school he didn't come on to. He's just moved to a new generation."

"I don't understand what anyone sees in him. The only person he cares about is himself." She shrugged. "He's certainly not my bag of tea."

"Mine, either. Anymore."

At exactly 7:30 P.M. people began arriving. By 7:45 the room was so crowded I could hardly move. I felt a big, meaty hand grasp my shoulder and turned around. My nose was practically plastered against his chest.

"*Ma chère* Lucie!" Fitz crowed. He was originally from Charleston and spoke with an aristocratic Southern accent that sounded ever so slightly British, so it seemed like he'd just said "my chair Lucie." He'd picked up his French from Dominique and my mother. He had a good mind for the vocabulary, but his pronunciation—with that little drawl—reminded me of someone who'd just left the dentist's office and the drugs hadn't worn off yet.

He took hold of my other shoulder, pulling me to him like he was squeezing toothpaste from the end of the tube. A strong smell of the alcohol on his breath washed over me. "I'm so glad to see you, sugar."

I stepped back to get away from the fog of booze. "I'm glad to see you, too, Fitz."

He had aged. Though he was still portly, still with the flowing mane of white hair combed back and the neatly trimmed beard, there was something newly frail around his eyes which seemed to have shrunk away from his skin, settling deeper into the bones of his face. His breathing was labored.

"Are you all right?" I asked.

"Now, Chantal darlin', don't you worry about me."

"It's Lucie, Fitz. You just called me Chantal."

He released me and stepped back. "Oh, Lordy. I know that. I'm sorry, child. I didn't mean to. I know who you are. But you know, you are the spitting image of her when she was your age." He stared hard at me.

I squirmed. Eli had homed in on the pair of us. I turned slightly so he was out of my line of vision, but I could feel his eyes boring holes through my back.

"Let's go," Fitz said.

"What do you mean?"

"I need to talk to you."

"Right now?" I whispered. "In the middle of Leland's wake? Can't it wait?"

"It can't." He poked me gently. "Now let's skedaddle. No one will notice. We'll be right back."

Eli noticed. I saw his jaw tighten when I glanced at him as we left the room.

Fitz led me outside through the service door. We stood near the back of the house on a wraparound porch. I felt like I was swimming in the suffocating humidity. It was quiet except for the occasional sound of a car driving by and the metallic end-of-summer sound of the cicadas.

I hitched myself up on the railing to take the weight off my aching left foot and propped my cane next to me. Fitz stood in front of me, arms folded across his chest.

"You have a little talk with your brother yet, sugar?"

It was a rhetorical question. "More like a monologue," I said. "I got the 'what you missed' speed-dial version of life in Atoka for the past two years, with a big helping of guilt thrown in because I was gone."

"Meaning he told you he wants to sell the vineyard?" When I nodded he said, "What about you? You gonna go along with that?"

"Of course not."

"That's my girl. I knew I could count on you. We'll hold those people off."

"What people?"

"Whoever was pressuring your daddy to sell the vineyard, Lucie. It's been losing money lately. You know old Lee. He made a small fortune on those grapes. The problem is, he started with a large fortune. Your momma's money."

There was no humor in his voice and, anyway, it was an old joke among vineyard owners. Running a vineyard was an expensive proposition.

"Then someone offered to buy the place from him, except it was a fire sale price. Lee wouldn't sell."

"Eli didn't tell me that," I said.

"I'll bet he didn't," Fitz said. "They were keepin' that kind of hush-hush. And Eli probably told you that I'm an old crackpot, too, didn't he?"

"Eli wouldn't say . . ." I said, but he cut me off.

"Like hell he wouldn't. I'm not sure who it was came around talkin' to your daddy trying to persuade him to sell the place but let me tell you, that so-called 'accident' Lee had was mighty peculiar, if you ask me."

I could just make out the expression on his face in the warm yellow light that shone through one of the windows behind us. True, he smelled like he'd drunk enough to float an ocean liner, but he also seemed in control of his faculties. He was watching me gravely.

I'd been holding on to the railing to keep my balance. My grip on the smooth, worn wood tightened. "You really think someone killed Leland because he wouldn't sell the vineyard?"

"I do."

"Then why kill him? Now he'll never sell it."

"True, my chair. But Eli wants to. And he got Mia to go along with him, didn't he?"

Though the heat was so oppressive it seemed I could chew it, I shivered. "You don't think that Eli had something to do with Leland's death?"

He stared at me, nodding so slightly that it could have been a small tremor brought on by the booze. But it wasn't. He'd filled in the missing piece of the puzzle that Eli hadn't supplied.

"That's murder," I said, raising my voice. He shushed me and I added more quietly, "Not my brother. I don't believe it."

"Child," he said gently, "I'm not accusing Eli of colluding with someone to have Leland murdered. All I'm saying is that whoever wanted to buy the place might have known Eli would sell if Lee wasn't in the picture."

"What about Bobby Noland?" I asked. "He said it was an accident."

He snorted. "What *would* he say? By the time he got there, the site was so contaminated it was impossible to tell what the hell really happened. The workers trampled everything that might have been evidence and what they didn't mess up, Hector's dogs did.

Then there was a power failure at the morgue the night Lee's body
got there."

"Oh God."

He leaned forward. The sultry August heat seemed to intensify
the rank smell of the alcohol so it came through his pores, mingled
with perspiration and the sweet scent of his cologne. "That's why
Eli got the body released so soon and the whole thing's gonna be
hushed up. It was a hell of a break for your brother. Now he's got
the green light to sell the place. Pay off some of that heap of debt
he's sunk into."

There was a small sound in the bushes at the far end of the
porch and I jumped. "What was that? And what heap of debt?"

"Probably a stray cat. That little princess he married is very high
maintenance, sugar." Fitz sounded annoyed. "Don't tell me he
didn't tell you about the palace they're building over near Leesburg?"

I shook my head.

"It's going to be Versailles when they're done. Or the Disney
Castle. I heard she wants a big ol' fountain with swans floating
around right there in the front yard. There's no way can they afford
a place like that on Eli's salary."

"Then he needs the money."

He brushed a strand of hair off my cheek and tucked it behind
my ear. "Exactly. And what he doesn't need is all the bad publicity
from a murder right there in the vineyard if he's trying to put it on
the market. See what I mean?"

I saw. "So do you think Eli's involved with this person? Whoever might have had Leland killed?"

"People do a lot of things where money's concerned. It's a powerful motivator, especially when you haven't got it and you need it.
I don't think Eli had anything to do with this directly, you understand," he said. "But when you lie down with dogs, my chair, you
get up with fleas."

"God, Fitz. Do you know what this means?"

"I'll tell you one thing it means." He leaned forward and put his hands on my shoulders. "Since I'm part owner of the vineyard, thanks to your sweet momma, I get a vote in all this. You and me, we're two against Eli and Mia. Without a majority vote, Eli can't sell."

"*What* are you doing?" Eli's voice cut through the darkness. Both Fitz and I jumped this time, knocking over my cane, which clattered noisily on the porch floorboards.

He was standing in the shadows at the opposite end of the porch with his hands in his pockets. How long had he been there? How much had he heard? We'd been speaking quietly, but our voices could have carried.

"Talking," I said sharply. "What are you doing, sneaking around like that? Good Lord, Eli, you scared the wits out of us."

"Look who's talking about sneaking around. You're the one who left." He sounded irritated. "Do you realize you've been gone twenty-one minutes? People are asking for you. Thelma's here now and so are Joe Dawson and most of the Romeos. You need to come back inside. You have obligations, Lucie. Family obligations."

"Sorry, Eli," Fitz said, picking up my cane. "It's my fault she's here so long. She was feeling a bit woozy, that's all, so we came out for some fresh air. Then we got to talking and catching up on things. She'll be right along in."

"Okay." Eli stood there with his arms folded and waited.

"I'm coming, Eli."

"I'll wait for you."

"You don't have to. I'll be there in a minute."

"I need you *now*. Thelma wants to have a sing-along of Leland's favorite songs." He sounded grim. "I'm counting on you to distract her."

This time we both heard the slamming of the front door as he left.

"I'd better go," I said. "He's pretty upset. Do you think he heard anything?"

"Naw." Fitz took my hand and slipped something small and hard into my palm. "Here. Don't lose it," he whispered. "It was your mother's."

"What is it?"

"A key."

"I know that. A key to what?"

"Possibly a jewelry box."

"Why are we whispering? And how come you didn't say anything about this until now?"

"Your mother didn't want Lee to know. It was among some papers she left me. Private papers. I was . . . going through them re-
cently. This seemed like the right time to turn the key over to you."

"He's dead. Do we still have to whisper?"

"Don't you sass me, child. I did it for your own good."

I stared at him. "Did what? And Mom kept her jewelry box on
the dressing table in her bedroom. She never locked it. When I was
little she used to let me try on the fabulous jewelry she inherited
from Grandmama Bessette."

"You must have been very young to have worn those." He
sounded disgusted. "Because she sold them all, one by one." He
saw the look on my face. "You didn't know, did you? She did it to
bail your poppa out of debt. I'm sorry, my chair. I don't mean to
upset you, but it's time you knew the truth."

"Then what's this for?" I held out the key.

"The one thing that's still left. At least I think it is. Her diamond
necklace. Ever seen it?"

"Oh my God," I said. "Once. She wore it to the White House
when she and Leland went to a dinner for the French Prime Minis-
ter. I never saw it again."

"It's worth a fortune, Lucie," he said in a low voice. "Not to
mention the provenance. Your mother told me it belonged to Marie
Antoinette. It came into the possession of that countess who was
your ancestor. The one who was Thomas Jefferson's friend."

"The Comtesse de Tessé," I said. "Do you think my mother hid
it? Marie Antoinette's necklace?"

"I hope so." He closed my hand around the key. "No one has seen
it since she died. At first I figured Leland sold it, but he swore he
didn't. Maybe for once he told the truth. That's why I never said any-

thing about this key. I wanted to make sure there was something left for you children that Lee couldn't squander. If you sold the necklace now, you'd have enough to pay off the vineyard's debts. I'm sure your momma would understand. You just have to find it first."

He squeezed my fist so tight the key cut into my palm. I winced and he loosened his grip. "Sorry, sugar."

"I don't know how to thank you for this," I said, finally.

"Well," he said, and something in his voice made it clear he was going to tell me precisely how I could do just that, "there is something you could do for me."

I extracted my hand. He sounded vaguely Faustian. "What is it?"

"There's something else that hasn't been found since your momma died. Her diaries."

"My mother never kept a diary," I said.

It had been a family joke that Chantal Montgomery was single-handedly responsible for Atoka having its own post office rather than us being lumped in with Middleburg. I never saw her desk when it wasn't heaped with stacks of writing paper, boxes of note cards, pens with different colored ink, sealing wax, and embossed address labels. During her life she had written thousands of letters, postcards, and notes. But as many times as I'd watched her writing, her head bent over some piece of correspondence or her gardening journals as Edith Piaf warbled "La Vie en Rose" on one of her old records, I didn't ever recall seeing a diary.

Fitz clasped his hands to his chest and for a second, I thought he might be having a heart attack. "I am not *asking* you if she kept a diary. I am *telling* you she did. And when you clean out that compost heap of a house that used to be your mother's pride and joy—and I know you will—you are going to find them. And then . . ." He shook a finger in my face, revving up with the fury of a Bible-belt preacher taking a sinning congregation to task. "And *then* you are going to turn them over to me."

Them. More than one. "Why?"

"So I can burn them. It's what she would have wanted."

My mother baked cookies for every school bake sale, library

fund-raiser, and church social I could remember. She sewed our Halloween costumes by hand and never missed a sports event, dance recital, or school concert. She read the same bedtime stories over and over and decorated elaborate birthday cakes in cute shapes and knitted mittens with animal faces on them.

She was not someone who wrote a diary that needed to be burned. Her life—to continue the metaphor—was an open book.

At least I'd always thought it was.

"What makes you so sure?" I asked. "I mean, I think I would have known . . ."

"Honey." Fitz pulled me to him and stroked my hair. His voice was soft in my ear, a gentle wheeze. "You're gonna give them to me when you find them, you hear me? Let your poor momma rest in peace. I'm asking you."

"Yes," I said, and my voice quavered. "I suppose I am."

"Good." He crushed me in another bear hug. "Now go along inside, like Eli said. They're waiting on you."

"Aren't you coming?"

"Lord, no. I came to see you, that's all. I already made my peace with Lee." He stepped back, stumbling unexpectedly.

"Careful!" I grabbed his arm to steady him and he clung to it, pulling like it was a lifeline. I let go of my cane and wrapped the other arm around a porch balustrade to keep us both from falling. We swayed together until he found his footing.

"Whoops." His chuckled giddily. "Almost lost my step there, didn't I?"

"Why don't you come inside, Fitz? Rest a bit."

"Naw, I'm fine. Besides I need to get over to the winery. We've got a wedding tomorrow afternoon at the inn and the bride and groom ordered some bottles with custom labels. Quinn said he'd leave the cases out for me."

"Maybe you shouldn't be driving . . ."

"Don't you start, Lucie. How do you think I got here?"

"Please, Fitz?" I smiled. "Let me take you to the winery after the wake is over. We can talk some more. Come on."

His genial bonhomie evaporated. "Now you pay attention, you hear? You've been listenin' too much to that brother of yours. He ought to mind his own business for once. I am fine and I know what I'm doing. So stop patronizing me!"

"I'm not . . ."

"Oh yes, you are. And you of all people ought to know better." He stabbed a finger at my chest. "Robs a body of his own dignity when people act like you can't take care of yourself, doesn't it, my chair? It's humiliating."

I was silent, wondering how I'd betrayed myself and let him find the soft place in my shell of invulnerability.

He nodded. "I thought you'd understand. Go inside now." He still sounded cross, but he leaned over and his lips brushed my forehead. "Good night, sugar."

A moment later the darkness swallowed him except for the tapping sound of his receding footfalls and then the noise of a car door slamming.

I went slowly back to the Green Room. Fitz had turned the tables neatly so that now it was Eli's motives I was wondering about. Everything he'd said had made sense. If only he hadn't begun slurring his words right before he left.

Upstairs, I could hear them singing. "You'll Never Walk Alone." One of Thelma's favorites.

Eli met me at the door, scowling. "Just in time to close the barn door after the horse bolted. Thanks a bunch."

"I'm sorry."

"What happened to Fitz?"

"He went over to the winery to pick up some cases of a special label wine for a wedding. Who's Quinn?"

"Quinn Santori. The new Jacques."

Jacques had been both our winemaker and viticulturist since my parents first opened the vineyard. The rootstock for the original vines came with him from France, so in the beginning we produced only *vitis vinifera,* the so-called noble wines made from Old World or European grapes. He had lived in one of the tenant houses on our property, but most of the time he was either in the fields or at the winery.

"Where's Jacques?"

"He had a stroke a few months ago. His daughter came over from Giverny and took him back to France." He took my elbow. "Come on. Maybe we can head her off before she starts 'Climb Every Mountain.'"

"A stroke? When did that happen? Somebody could have told me." At least now I knew why Jacques hadn't answered my last letter.

"I guess we forgot. Sorry, babe." He smiled pleasantly, but his eyes were mocking. One more life event I'd missed during my long absence. He jostled my arm. "Let's go."

I still had Fitz's little key in my hand and it fell, bouncing on the wooden floor. Eli reached down automatically and picked it up. "What's this?"

"My suitcase key."

I didn't intend to lie. But as he handed it over our eyes met. He knew Fitz had just put me wise to what was really going on.

I closed my hand around the key and smiled back. "Thanks."

"Sure. Come on." He turned away and I followed him into the Green Room. I realized then that I didn't trust him.

Though judging by the expression on my brother's face, it was pretty clear that he didn't trust me, either.

CHAPTER 5

———— ∞∞∞ ————

The punishing heat didn't let up for Leland's funeral. The Blue Ridge had vanished, bleached by the haze until it disappeared, blending into the colorless sky. The horizon looked disturbingly flat and closed-in. Eli reported before we left for the funeral home that when Hector's men dug the grave for the coffin, they broke a shovel trying to penetrate the concrete-like clay soil. The drought was reported as the lead news story on the local radio station, instead of being lumped with the rest of the weather forecast.

Once again, everyone in town showed up for the short ceremony, crowding in to our brick-walled cemetery, standing shoulder to shoulder, drenched to the skin in heat-seeking dark clothing. It seemed surreal as all funerals do, the bizarre intersection of time when Leland was and wasn't among us—a lifeless body inside a glossy wooden casket soon to be lowered into the ground. I stared at my mother's headstone, unable to clearly conjure the sound of her voice in my head anymore, however much I might want to hear it again.

The bagpiper played "Amazing Grace," and it was achingly lovely. Next to me Mia sobbed quietly into a handkerchief. I put my arm around her thin shoulders, half-expecting her to pull away and gratified when she leaned against me protectively. I stroked her hair. Eli reached over and took her hand.

Then Reverend Martin said, "Please bow your heads."

After a few minutes I noticed Eli glancing at his watch. His lips were moving.

"Stop it, will you?" I whispered behind Mia's back. "It will be over when it's over. Leland won't come back and haunt you if it doesn't end precisely at sunset. It doesn't have to be perfect."

"It's far from perfect," he snapped. "Fitz was supposed to give one of the eulogies. He's not even here. Mason's doing it instead."

I looked around. "Where is he?"

"How the hell should I know?"

Reverend Martin cleared his throat loudly and Eli and I looked up. He was staring directly at us. Mason Jones, our lawyer, was standing next to him, hands clasped around a Bible. I blushed and quickly bowed my head as my brother did the same. We didn't speak again until after the last note of "Taps" sounded as the sun disappeared, leaving a Technicolor sky behind.

"So what's going on with Fitz?" Eli asked in a low voice. He handed me his handkerchief. "Here. Your mascara's running."

The three of us were standing in an untidy receiving line at the gate to the cemetery with Dominique. Mia was no longer crying but her eyes were red-rimmed and swollen.

I pressed Eli's handkerchief against my watery eyes. If I started to cry, she'd lose it again, too. I tried to keep my voice steady. "I don't know. Do you think he's all right?"

"This isn't like him." Dominique twisted her jet-bead necklace around her fingers until it became a choker. "I can't imagine where he could be."

"He reeked of booze last night," Eli said. "You wouldn't have wanted to light a match near him. Maybe he went home, had a few more belts, and is still sleeping it off." He looked at me pointedly. "You were the last one to see him, weren't you?"

"I suppose I was," I said. "He told me he was coming here to pick up some cases of specially labeled wine for a wedding. I assumed after that he was going by the inn."

Last night's conversation with Fitz in the tropical darkness, his whispered accusations and revelations in the shadowy recesses of that porch, still haunted me. For the rest of the evening I'd felt like a sleepwalker, the jet lag clouding my judgment about what was real and what I'd imagined.

"If he was supposed to stop by the inn, he never made it," Dominique said.

"Maybe somebody should go look for him," Brandi suggested. "But not you, Eli. I need you to stay with me." She folded her arms protectively over her belly. She'd been playing the baby card with a heavy hand ever since I'd laid eyes on her. Last night at the wake she'd had Eli dancing around like a Mexican jumping bean, getting her water, fanning her, massaging her feet. At this rate, by the time the blessed event rolled around he'd probably go into labor for her.

"Are you all right, angel?" He looked worried.

"The heat." She put a hand to her forehead. "I need to lie down."

"We'll go right away," he said. "I brought the Jag. Anyone else want a ride?"

"I'll go with Greg," Mia's voice still shook. "He said he'd wait for me."

I'd noticed him standing with a few of the Romeos next to an ancient oak tree. He'd nodded to me when we gathered for the service, but we hadn't spoken. Mia left us, threading her way through the crowd and ran into Greg's arms, clinging to him. He bent his head and I could see him talking to her. She nodded and began crying again.

I looked away, feeling mildly ashamed like a voyeur caught watching an intimate moment.

"I'll go," Dominique was saying. "I should check on my staff. I need to make sure there's enough for everyone to eat."

"We could feed Lee's Army," I said, "with what the neighbors dropped off before the service. Plus all the catered food you brought, Dominique."

"Well, yes," she said, "but I just hired two new girls and they're a little green behind the ears."

"In that case," Eli said, pulling his keys out of his pocket, "let's go. Come on, Lucie. You're coming with us, of course."

"You go on without me. I need to clear my head. I'll catch up. Maybe I'll go the long way and stop by the winery."

Eli looked irritated. "I don't think you ought to do that."

"Why not?"

"Well, because. For one thing it's going to take you a long time." He saw the expression on my face. "That's not what I meant. What I'm saying is everyone expects you to be at the house."

"I'll be there."

"Leave her, Eli," Brandi said. "Let her do what she wants. Can we please go?"

He turned back to his wife, who looked bored and unhappy. "I'm sorry, babe. Of course we can. We'll go right now. Dominique? You ready?"

Dominique squeezed my arm. "Be careful," she murmured. "And forget about Mia and Gregory, okay?"

The three of them walked toward the Jaguar, and Eli's headlights swept past me a moment later.

There was no one left at the graveside except Hector and two young Mexican workers who were standing about fifty feet from the gate, leaning on shovels. Hector raised his baseball cap in a small salute and walked toward me. The others followed. For an old man, Hector still moved with the compact fluid grace of a panther. I reckoned he had to be close to sixty-five, maybe even older. Now he and Fitz were the only ones left who could remember every one of our harvests.

"You okay, Lucita?" he asked. "Why aren't you going with the others?"

"I'm fine. I just need a little time before I go back to the house."

"Sure, sure. I understand. We'll be taking care of Mr. Lee now." He made the sign of the cross. "We wait until you're gone."

"Thank you," I said. As I walked away I could hear the rhythmic chipping sound of their shovels moving earth from one place to another, which seemed to be amplified in the ovenlike twilight stillness. I walked as quickly as I could down the road toward the winery.

If those cases of wine were still there then Fitz never made it before he disappeared. Maybe a cop had pulled him over for DUI and he'd spent the night in the drunk tank.

Next time, no matter what he said, I'd take his car keys.

The winery was located just past the stone bridge where Sycamore Lane crossed over Goose Creek. I made it to the bridge and sat on one of the parapets, resting my sore foot. In the gathering dusk the deep fissures in the streambed were still visible and there was only a pathetic meandering gleam of water that looked like someone had forgotten to completely shut off their garden hose. That was Goose Creek.

A pair of headlights caught me in their glare. A white pickup truck came down the road from the direction of the winery. The driver tooted his horn and waved a hand out the window as he pulled up next to me. Harmon Animal Clinic and a telephone number were stenciled in black on the truck door.

"Lucie honey, what are you doing here? Are you all right?" Doc Harmon was one of the Romeos, another of Leland's poker and drinking buddies. He'd been at both the wake and the funeral.

He had the sad-eyed long face and countenance of a basset hound, but a pit bull's aggressiveness when it came to treating farm animals humanely. Though his hands were the gentlest of anyone I knew, I'd heard he once punched out a farmer in Philomont after showing up unannounced to look after a sick colt and discovering a cockfight going on for the pleasure of a large group of spectators. Doc made the farmer donate the proceeds of his little side business to the animal shelter.

Besides his practice, which catered mostly to horses, he was on the staff of the Animal Swim Center, which specialized in rehabilitating injured animals. Increasingly he spent time on the road traveling to racetracks or even the Olympics with owners who wanted him available when one of their horses was competing.

"I wanted to walk a little before I went back to the house," I said.

"I was just heading over to the winery. I haven't seen it since I came home."

"You look all done in. It's getting dark, too. Jump in and I'll drive you there." He peered at me. "You feeling all right?"

"Fine," I said. "Hot. I forgot how wilting the humidity can be."

"You could fry an egg on the hood of my truck, if you had a mind to," he said. "You're awfully flushed, darlin'. Let's get you out of this heat."

I went around and climbed into the passenger seat. He took my cane as I did so and propped it between us. "Stick working okay for you? You doing any physical therapy?"

"I was. And a lot of swimming."

He grunted and backed up the truck, heading toward the winery. "Swimming's good. Hydrotherapy. It works wonders for the animals, too, moving around in that water without having to worry about fighting gravity. Keep it up now, you hear?"

I nodded and he barreled down the road, pulling into the parking lot.

"Thanks for the lift, Doc. What were you doing at the winery?"

"Wanted to make sure the truck didn't get caught in that mass of cars you got over at the big house. I'm on call. I got a few minutes, though. Need me to wait for you? Were you going to fetch something? I can run you back there when you're done."

"That would be great, if you don't mind. I just need to check something. It won't take long."

"Take your time." He lifted a mobile phone off a cradle on the dashboard. "I need to call the answering service anyway. This heat's getting to the animals, too."

I climbed down from the truck and walked up the fieldstone path to the winery. The rambling ivy-covered brick building was largely my mother's design. She'd sketched dozens of pictures of ideas until she finally settled on one that harmonized the romantic neoclassical architecture she'd grown up with in France with the simpler colonial style of Highland House designed by Leland's pragmatic Scottish ancestors. The result looked more like a graceful old villa than a commercial structure, which was exactly what she wanted—and what we'd named it.

She originally wanted the villa to be situated on a bluff much like Highland House but the architect she hired advised against it, urging her instead to build into the side of a hill. That way he could design the complex to take advantage of the natural cooling properties of the soil by locating the wine cellar partially underground. They found a place where the view of the Blue Ridge wasn't quite as spectacular as she'd wanted, but the logistics worked for the cellar. Then he showed her a plan for a European-style courtyard and porticoed loggia that would connect the villa, which would consist of a tasting room, offices, and wine library, to the production area, where a crush pad, barrel room, and laboratory would be located. It was also close to the old dairy barn, redesigned as storage for the tractor and the other tools and equipment used in the fields. My mother fell in love with the whole idea.

The place was exactly as I remembered it though it seemed the ivy that grew on the building, extending its tentacles in graceful arcs over the windows, had grown even more lush and thick. In the autumn the leaves would become flame-colored and in winter, the bare brown skeletal vines would look like latticework twining elegantly on the brick façade.

The door was unlocked. I walked inside and flipped on the lights at the bank of switches. The cathedrallike coolness of the tasting room was a sharp but welcome relief from the withering heat. I read once that scientists have discovered the existence of "place cells" in the human brain, allowing us to store maps of locations that have particular importance or meaning. When we return to one of these mind-mapped places, our brain cells react differently, provoked by the potent cues of sight, smell, or sound associated with where we are. I stood in this room, which had been mapped not just in my memory but in my heart.

Even after so many years, it still retained my mother's indelible stamp—her attention to detail, her love of beauty—everywhere I looked. It was a grand rectangular room with a vaulted ceiling and four sets of floor-to-ceiling French doors leading to the fieldstone terrace with its serene view of braided hills, vineyards, and the layered Blue Ridge in the far distance. There was an enormous open working fireplace in the center of the room with sofas and chairs pulled around it on all four sides. Persian carpets from my mother's home in France covered the quarry-tile floors. Her paintings of the vineyard hung on the walls, along with a handmade reproduction of a tapestry from the Musée de Cluny in Paris, showing coopering and wine making in the Middle Ages. The tiled bar was at the far end of the room, with the brilliantly colored mosaic of grape-laden vines and fruits my mother had designed for the façade illuminated by one of the overhead spotlights, making the colors glow like jewels.

Directly off the main room an arched wrought iron gate led to the wine library with its deep leather chairs, wine barrel end tables, and our growing collection of books on colonial and contemporary wine making. A heavy door that always reminded me of the entrance to a monk's cell led to a small corridor and the offices.

I went there first, turning on more lights, to look for the wine Fitz should have collected. It was more likely that it would be here than in the barrel room, which was a bonded wine cellar. We never moved wine out of the cellar until we planned to sell it because we had to pay the sales taxes right away. There was no sliding by that rule thanks to mandatory monthly reports filed with the Alcohol and Tobacco Tax and Trade Bureau.

I must have been expecting to see Jacques's office, with its familiar collection of photographs, awards, vintage silver bottle-stoppers, and the antique map of France during the reign of Charlemagne on the wall behind his desk. Instead the room was bare—a small shock—completely devoid of any personal effects belonging to the new winemaker. Maybe Quinn Santori had decided to use the smaller office next door, which had been my mother's. I looked in and wished I hadn't. The room had been turned into a dumping ground for cases of wineglasses used for tastings, rolls of labels for our various wines, and a half-filled box of corks. There were also several opened cases of wine, but none with customized labels.

Perhaps Quinn had left the wine behind the bar. I went back to the main room and found it.

So Fitz hadn't come here after all. Maybe Eli was right that he went for yet another drink after the wake. Alone, except for whatever inner demons he was carrying around.

I was still behind the bar when the door to the tasting room swung open. The man who entered was probably in his mid-forties, wearing a pair of green and brown camouflage trousers, a loud print Hawaiian shirt, and more jewelry than I was. Two heavy gold chains, one with a cross on it, and a thick gold bracelet on his right wrist. No earring though. His military brush cut was mostly gray and he had "don't-mess-with-me" eyes that were calculating and unnerving.

"Can I help you?" He wasn't really asking. He was probably wondering what I was doing behind the bar.

"You must be Quinn," I said. "I'm Lucie Montgomery. I was looking for some cases of wine that you left for Fitz Pico last night."

"We found 'em," he said. He sounded grim.

"The wine? Isn't this it?" I gestured to the cases on the floor.

"Fitz," he said. "We found Fitz."

"I don't understand."

"He's in the barrel room. Call 911, will you?"

I had visions of Fitz, passed out on the floor of the barrel room since last night. "Is he all right? Doc Harmon's outside . . . I know he's a vet, but . . ."

"Yeah, get him in here, too. I got Jesús throwing up all over the place."

"What are you talking about?"

"The poor kid was in the middle of transferring the Merlot into one of the purged tanks when he realized it wasn't empty."

My heart started pounding like war drums. "What do you mean? What are you saying?"

"I'm sorry, ma'am. I thought you'd know. I'm saying Fitz is deader 'n a doornail. He was inside that tank. Death by almost instant asphyxiation."

CHAPTER 6

Some people can deliver disastrous news as calmly as if they're reporting on the weather, blunting the shock and horror of their words. It took a long moment before I understood what he'd just said.

I said numbly, "There would have been pure carbon dioxide in that tank."

"Yes, ma'am."

"My God, what was he thinking? I need to go to him. He's my godfather."

"He doesn't need anything from anyone anymore." He sounded brusque and businesslike. "Call 911 and get that doc over to the barrel room pronto. My cell phone's dead or I would have done it already. Then I saw this place lit up like a Christmas tree. Now that I know it's only you, I need to get back there."

"I'm coming with you."

He looked up at the ceiling and I could almost hear him count to ten. "Look, I understand how you must be feeling, but I don't need two people barfing all over the place. Help me out here. Make that call like a good girl, okay?" He turned and walked out.

So this was our new winemaker.

I called 911 like a good girl.

Doc Harmon and I were on the lawn outside the villa with

Jesús, who looked pale and scared, when Bobby Noland drove up in a brown-and-gold Sheriff's Department cruiser. Fortunately he hadn't turned on the lights and sirens or it would have alerted everyone at the main house—meaning almost everyone in Atoka—that something was happening at the winery. The place would be a mob scene in no time.

Eli was right behind Bobby in the Jaguar.

I'd switched on the outdoor lights, which included floodlights and fairy lights strung in several of the bushes and trees. Bobby walked across the lawn, caught in the wash of light, still with the swaggering bantam way about him that he'd had in high school. I hadn't seen much of him in the dozen years since he'd graduated.

He started talking from ten yards away. "What happened? The call came in when I was still over at the house. Y'all got enough food there to last you till the cows come home. The dispatcher said someone was hurt bad at the winery."

He and Eli reached our little group. Bobby pointed to Jesús. "This the guy?" He nodded to me. "Hey, Lucie. Didn't get a chance to see you earlier. Sorry for your loss."

Up close Bobby looked like he'd aged more than he should have, but maybe it was the uniform and the holstered gun on his belt. When he took off his cap his sandy hair was short and bristly as a porcupine's. In high school it used to hang in his eyes sheepdog style, which always made him look like he was hiding something. Now I could see his eyes. He wasn't hiding anything, including how tired he looked.

I still had Eli's handkerchief from earlier in the evening, damp again from fresh use. I twisted it around my fingers like a strand of rope. "Thanks, Bobby. It's Fitz. Jesús here's the one who found him."

He'd been unwrapping a piece of bubble gum, which he was about to put in his mouth. He stopped and said, "Fitz Pico? Where is he?"

"In the barrel room."

"What was Fitz doing in the barrel room?" Eli asked.

"I don't know. But he was in one of the stainless-steel tanks. It had been purged. Injected with pure carbon dioxide."

"Oh my God," Eli made a small choking sound and coughed. Our eyes met for a second before he turned away. He looked upset. But not grief-stricken.

"Fitz was in one of those big silver tanks?" Even in the artificial light, I could see Bobby go pale under his dark reddish suntan. He spoke into a microphone attached to a shoulder strap. "Send backup. Montgomery Vineyard." He turned away and muttered again into the microphone. Then he said, "Where's that winemaker of yours? Santini?"

"Santori. Quinn Santori," Eli said as I added, "In the barrel room."

"Shit. He better not of messed anything up." He turned to Doc Harmon. "I could use some help, Elvis."

"Sure thing. You all right, son?" Doc looked at Jesús, who nodded.

After they left Eli grabbed my elbow, dragging me next to a small border garden of red salvia and white impatiens where Jesús couldn't hear us.

"Goddamnit!" A tiny vein pulsed in his temple. "Do you know what this is going to do to our asking price when we put the place on the market?"

I jabbed my index finger against his chest. "Fitz is *dead,* Eli! Do you still have a heart in there or did you swap it for a cash register? How can you be so cold?"

"Cold? Give me a damn break. I feel as bad as you do." He ran a hand through his overgelled hair. "Just because I'm being realistic doesn't mean I'm not sorry about Fitz."

"Sure. I can tell it's tearing you apart."

He had changed from his monogrammed dress shirt and tie into a monogrammed peach-colored polo shirt. There was a time when he refused to wear clothing that had someone's name printed or sewn on it, even his own. And I'd never seen him wear anything peach.

"Knock it off. Don't act so damned sanctimonious, okay? You haven't got a monopoly on grief, Lucie. This isn't only happening to you."

"I never said it was," I said. "But you can at least spend a few seconds mourning him before you start talking about money."

I smacked my cane against the ground as I walked over to Jesús and sat down. We'd scrapped like a normal brother and sister when we were kids. But this was something more. Eli was driven in a way I didn't remember—his concern about money, the designer wardrobe, the palace he was building. How much debt was he in, anyway?

I fanned myself with my hand and unstuck my dress, which clung to me like I'd showered in it. It got this hot in the south of France, but it was a dry heat, cooled and tempered by the mistral and scented with the powerful fragrances of lavender, thyme, and rosemary. Here the air was so thick I could practically see it and the smell was the dank chemical odor of soil and plants and grass decomposing.

An ambulance showed up, along with a fire truck and two other official-looking cars. Though they didn't use their sirens, their red and blue strobe lights pulsed in the nighttime blackness, adding to the surreal feeling that was slowly taking hold of me.

Eli caught up with one of the fireman who walked quickly toward the courtyard to the barrel room. He wore a dirty yellow jacket with orange reflective stripes, overalls, boots, and a helmet. On the back of the jacket, large luminescent letters spelled out "Gleason." He stopped and shoved the helmet off his forehead, listening to what my brother told him. He shook his head and moved on.

Eli saw me watching and strode over. "This is absurd. We're not allowed in our own place."

"Let them do their work, Eli."

He glared at me but said nothing.

It was a while before Bobby finished. Jesús had wandered over to the stone wall by the parking lot, leaning against it and chain-smoking. Doc Harmon left on a veterinary emergency. "Maybe I can save a life somewhere else," he said. "There's nothing I can do here."

Eli and I sat on the villa steps, not speaking. We got up when Bobby finally walked through the courtyard archway carrying a small notebook. He kept clicking his ballpoint pen like he was counting something.

"Well, Santini says there wasn't any oxygen in that tank. It was pure carbon dioxide. He says Fitz would have suffocated instantly."

I shuddered.

"Santori," Eli said. "And he's right. Jacques was strict as hell about not letting anybody work around the tanks without a buddy when they were cleaning them. Climbing into a purged stainless-steel tank is like climbing into a shark tank. There have been accidents just like this out in California." He shrugged. "Making wine has its occupational hazards."

Bobby blew a bubble and popped it. "Jesus, Eli. Are you trying to pass this off as an accident? You think Fitz took a wrong detour and ended up in your tank of wine?"

Eli reddened. "Of course not. But when he showed up at Leland's wake last night he was stinking drunk. He told Lucie he needed to stop here to pick up some wine. I don't know . . . maybe he got disoriented or something."

Bobby opened his notebook and clicked the pen once more. He started writing. "He said he was coming here, did he?"

"To pick up some special cases of wine for a wedding," I said.

"Santini says there's a bunch of money missing from your safe," Bobby flipped back through a few pages. "More'n four thousand bucks. You got some migrant workers here who just show up for harvest. Not the same guys every year. Not the same guys every day, for that matter." He looked at us. "And someone cut the lock to the barrel room door. You'll need to replace it."

"Robbery?" I asked. "You think he surprised someone trying to rob us?"

"Dunno," he said. "We're talking to all your crew. It's taking a while, though, because nobody speaks English. Hector just showed up. He and Santini are doing the translating for us." He blew another bubble. "So when was the last time you all saw Fitz?"

"Shortly before the wake ended," I said. "He left when Thelma started singing."

"Wise move." Bobby chewed thoughtfully. "So what time was that, about?"

"Nine-thirty?" I guessed.

"Closer to nine-forty," Eli said.

Bobby looked up from the notes he'd been writing and frowned. Then his face lightened. "Oh right. You've got that nuclear watch. Must come in handy sometimes. So nine-forty, then." He did some calculating. "That'd put him here about nine-fifty, nine-fifty-five. Kind of late at night to be working, isn't it?"

"Restaurants and vineyards don't work eight-hour day shifts, Bobby. Just like you guys," Eli said.

"That so?" Bobby squinted at us. "So where were the both of you last night?"

Eli looked incredulous. "At Leland's wake, of course."

"I meant afterwards. When did you leave and what did you do?"

There was something different in his voice that changed him from the kid who had a regular seat in detention hall to a cop who had the authority to pry into the details of our lives. He looked at both of us and, when his eyes met mine, they were opaque and unreadable. A cop's eyes.

Eli looked annoyed. "Oh, come on, Bobby. Brandi and I went home. To bed."

"You're saying you didn't spend any time here? This place or the big house?"

"Only to drop Lucie off," Eli said. "Brandi was exhausted. We went straight home after that. To Leesburg."

"Did you drive by the winery?"

"Nope."

"What about you, Lucie?"

"I went to bed after Eli took me home. I had just gotten off a plane from France yesterday afternoon. I was really beat, Bobby."

"Who else was there? Mia? Dominique?"

"Mia stayed with Greg Knight and Dominique slept over at Joe's," Eli said.

"I'll check that out, too." He didn't look up from his notebook, but the bubble he blew this time was lopsided and deflated instantly.

"Yo, Bobby!" Another uniformed officer stood in the courtyard archway. "We need you."

"Coming." The three of us walked toward him. "You two stay put," Bobby said. "I don't suppose I have to tell you that this place is now a crime scene. No one goes in there until we take the yellow tape down. Understood?"

"Your guys shouldn't leave the door open like that. The place is climate-controlled." Eli sounded irritated. "You know, harvest starts next week, Bobby. You can't shut us down."

"Actually, Eli, I'm afraid we can." Bobby was short. "And the place is gonna stay shut down while we go over everything for evidence. So if anybody gets any cute ideas about sneaking back in and contaminating the site before I give the all clear, you'll be hearing about it from hell to breakfast. Understand?"

He left for the barrel room without waiting for an answer, his heavy-soled shoes crunching on the gravel.

"Damnit," Eli said. He picked up a handful of stones and pitched them, one by one, at nothing in particular.

"Why did you have to be so hard on him? Maybe we could have worked something out, if only you hadn't treated him like he was Barney Fife, straight out of Mayberry."

Eli's eyes were cool. "I'm starting to wonder whose side you're on, Luce."

I heard the car coming before it pulled into the floodlit parking lot. A blonde woman driving a khaki-colored Jeep with the top down parked next to Eli's Jag.

"Oh God," Eli said. "What's *she* doing here?"

Katherine Eastman opened the door to the Jeep and climbed out, a large leather purse slung over one shoulder. She was dressed in a black mini-skirt and clingy red tank top that had either shrunk in the dryer or she was kidding herself. She must have gained twenty-five pounds since the last time I'd seen her.

"I came as soon as I heard," she said. She was wearing lipstick to match the fire-engine-red tank top, eye makeup that looked like it had been applied by a road marking gang, and her hair, which had once been a flatteringly warm shade of auburn, was Marilyn Monroe blonde. "Is it really true?"

"You shouldn't have bothered," Eli said. "We could do without the press."

"I'm surprised to see you here, Eli. I didn't realize your leash extended this far." She hugged me. "Hey, kiddo. It's good to see you again. I'm so sorry about your dad."

Kit and I had been friends since we used to play in the sandbox together and she'd been my brother's girlfriend until Brandi showed up. The split between Kit and Eli had been volcanic. Kit told me later that she finally understood the truth in the saying about the fine line that existed between love and hate, that it was absolutely possible to go from loving someone so much you would die for him to hating him so much you could kill him. Two years later it looked like the bitterness between them had hardened to mutual contempt.

"Where have you been?" I asked. "I tried to reach you."

"At my mom's. The home helper was sick. You know we can't leave her alone anymore. She sends her apologies about missing the funeral and the wake. She's having a tough time at the moment."

"Tell her I'll be by to visit, when she's up for it."

"She'd like that." She glanced over Eli's shoulder. "So what happened? Do they know anything yet?"

"About what?" Eli said. "What are you talking about?"

"When the police scanner's not working," Kit said, "we get our information from jungle drums."

She was a reporter with the *Washington Tribune,* an ascending star who'd been working in D.C. on the national desk until her mother had a stroke. From one day to the next she asked to be assigned to the regional bureau in Leesburg to be closer to home.

A lot of people thought it was a demotion, criticizing her for what they said was a self-inflicted wound that was going to stall out her career. Kit told them to go to hell.

"One of our guys found Fitz inside one of the stainless-steel tanks. It had been purged," I said.

"Oh my God." She reached into her purse and pulled out a reporter's notebook. "Put that away," Eli said. "This is a private matter."

"Like hell it is, Eli. Fitz was a nationally prominent chef."

"You're doing a story?" I asked.

"Yeah. For the National desk. Metro's pretty ticked off because they wanted it, but, hey, like I said, Fitz was well known. And, um, cause of death is, well . . ."

"Get out of here, Kit," Eli said. "You're trespassing."

Kit walked over to him and fingered the collar of his polo shirt. "Peach, hunh? New color for you. Kind of feminine, but it suits you."

The sound of the barrel room's large hangar door opening behind us cut off Eli's reply. Two paramedics wheeled out a stretcher with a body bag strapped to it. Bobby walked behind them, looking grim. No one spoke as they crossed the courtyard and loaded Fitz into the waiting ambulance.

I pulled out Eli's handkerchief yet again. Kit put her arm around me and the coil of her reporter's notebook dug into my shoulder.

Bobby walked over to us after the ambulance moved slowly off in the darkness. "Hey, Kit," he said. "You here on business or as a friend of the family?"

"Both."

"Public affairs will have a statement. Probably tomorrow morning."

"I need something tonight, Bobby."

He chewed his gum for a moment, like a cow ruminating. "Sorry. No can do."

She closed her notebook. "Off the record? Come on. Fitz was a friend."

He chewed some more, then said, "Your word?"

Kit nodded.

"I wouldn't tell her anything," Eli said stiffly.

Bobby stared at him, then flipped open his own notebook. "Looks like Fitz might have surprised someone in the middle of a robbery. One of the workers didn't show up today. A couple of the men say he left the camp they have near Winchester and no one's seen him since last night. Santini said he had the payroll money in a safe in that lab he's got next to the barrel room since today is payday. Picked it up from the bank yesterday because he didn't want to mess with it on the day of Leland's funeral. A couple of the guys from the crew were there when he locked it up, including the guy who's missing. Name of Zeus." He looked up.

"So how did Fitz end up in the tank?" I asked.

"I'm getting to that part," he said. "Don't rush me."

"Sorry."

"We think someone might have forced him into the tank," he said. "The guys are checking for prints and going over everything. One of your hammers is missing from that pegboard you got with all your tools. Neat idea to draw an outline of everything so you know where stuff belongs." He sounded approving. "Could be it'll turn up somewhere and someone just forgot to put it back, but we found evidence of blunt trauma to the head. The hammer could have been used as a weapon, but that's just speculating."

"Oh my God," I said.

"Enough of a blow to kill him?" Kit asked. "Do you think he was dead before someone put him in the tank?"

He shrugged. "Dunno. The ME will let us know when they do the autopsy."

"Who would want to do that?" I asked. "Why Fitz?"

"Sounds pretty random to me," Eli said. "Wrong place, wrong time."

"I'm going to Winchester." Bobby closed his notebook and stuck his pen behind one ear. "I'll see you folks later."

"I'm taking off, too," Kit hugged me again. "I'll call you tomorrow. We need to talk. Lunch, maybe?"

After they left, Eli said, "That woman is a parasite."

"You didn't always think so."

"I saw the light." He folded his arms across his chest. "You know, I don't understand you anymore. If she writes some lurid tabloid story, it's going to affect you, too."

"How can you expect this not to come out in the press?"

"Yeah, I suppose we could get ahead of the curve and advertise it ourselves. How about this? 'We'll knock you dead at Montgomery Estate Vineyard. Try our full-bodied Merlot.'"

"That's disgusting!"

"No fooling. That's why I'm trying to tell you that the last thing we need now is more bad press. Do you know what it's going to do to the value of this place now? It's going to tank. We'll probably have to *pay* somebody to buy it."

"We're not selling, Eli."

He looked scornful. "Says who?"

"I do."

"We outvote you, babe. Mia and me. We're selling."

"Family discussion?"

We both jumped. Quinn Santori stood there holding an unlit cigar that he caressed with his fingers. He looked at me the way men in bars stare at women who walk in alone.

"A little chat," Eli said. "We were just finishing. What can I do for you, Quinn?"

He pulled a pack of matches out of a pocket of his camouflage trousers, bent his head, and concentrated on lighting the cigar. After a few puffs he said, "Well, we're shut down, it's harvest, and you got yourself a group of pickers nervous as bunch of barnyard turkeys at Thanksgiving because one of 'em is apparently a prime suspect in a murder. What do you people want to do?"

"It might not be for long," I said.

He looked at me. "Ma'am?"

"I said, we might not be shut down for long. I'm sure we can work something out with Bobby to speed up the investigation so we'll be back in business in a few days."

He stroked his chin with the thumb of the hand that held the cigar. "You think so, do you?"

I couldn't tell if he was being sarcastic or not. "Yes."

He puffed on the cigar. "Well then, I'll need to set up some place temporarily in the meantime. I figure the big house would be the best bet. I'd like to move over there as soon as possible."

"You can move in tomorrow morning," I said. "We can talk about how we're going to handle things then."

"Pardon?" he said. He flicked an ash off his cigar and looked at me like I'd just sprouted another head. "We?" He glanced over at Eli and cleared his throat. "Eli?"

Eli cleared his throat, as well. "Uh, Lucie. Why don't we let Quinn take care of business the way he wants? We don't know what in the hell we're doing here."

"What are you talking about? Of course we do. We've helped with harvest since we were old enough to walk," I said. "It's our vineyard."

"Look, babe," he said, "I'm an architect. I've got a day job that pays the rent and feeds the wife and kid-to-be. I can't work here. Mia doesn't want to work here. As for you . . ." He stopped. If he was going to say something about me being handicapped, he changed his mind. "You've been selling perfume the last two years."

I glanced over at Quinn. He looked relieved, and even a little amused.

"I didn't *sell* perfume," I said. "I worked as a tour guide at the International Perfume Museum in Grasse."

"Okay, so you talked about perfume," Eli said.

"I've spent plenty of time helping out with harvest. I worked with Jacques that last summer before . . ." I didn't finish.

Eli put his arm around me and it felt like a vise. "You'll have to excuse her. She's a bit jet-lagged," he said to Quinn. "I think we'd better finish this conversation back at the house, hadn't we, Lucie, and let Quinn get on with whatever he needs to do?"

If Eli and I were going to have it out, then I didn't want Quinn as a spectator, either. I removed his arm from my shoulder, keenly aware that he had just done a first-rate job of sandbagging me in front of our winemaker.

"There's nothing more to discuss," I said. "See you tomorrow, Quinn."

Quinn's eyes went back and forth between Eli and me. They were hard and black like coal. His voice was hard, too. "You'd better get this worked out, folks. When Leland hired me he promised me free rein to run the place. No one standing over my shoulder and telling me what to do. If you're going to move the goalposts, or if you don't even know where the goalposts are anymore, I want to know it."

"Jacques never had carte blanche to run the vineyard," I said. And he never talked back like this smart-mouthed guy, either. "He and my mother always worked closely together."

"What someone else did is no concern of mine," he said. "You know, this vineyard could have its best harvest ever this year. The drought's been great for the crop and your vines are coming into their peak producing years. Seems to me you've got enough on your plate with no access to your equipment and your wine cellar. If you're going to start fighting among yourselves, then you can also find a new winemaker."

He flicked another ash off his cigar and strode past us to a beat-up Toyota in the parking lot. He couldn't get the engine to catch right away but when it did, he did a rubber-burning three-point turn and zoomed off into the night.

"Well, well." Eli glared at me accusingly. "You certainly turned the old killer charm on him, Luce. I think he just quit."

CHAPTER 7

"He didn't quit," I said. "He threatened to. He's got a hell of a nerve, blackmailing us like that. What made Leland hire him, anyway? He'll never replace Jacques. He's a troglodyte by comparison."

One of the reasons people bought so much wine from us in the past was because Jacques, with his gracious European politesse and elegant manner, could charm anybody into anything. If Quinn was always this abrasive, we wouldn't be able to sell water to someone who'd just come through the desert.

"He came cheap," Eli said. "Leland wasn't offering what you'd call a competitive salary and he was the only taker. He's supposedly a decent enologist and a viticulturist, even if he has a few rough edges. The crew likes him. I'm going back to the house. You coming or not?"

I nodded and we walked in silence over to the Jag.

At least Leland had hired someone who was good at both enology and viticulture. Enology is the science of wine making. Viticulture is the science of grape growing. Larger vineyards have enologists, also known as vintners, who are there only to make and blend the wine. They also have viticulturists who are out in the field with the vines, tending them, testing them, and deciding the optimum time for harvest. But at a small vineyard like ours, the two jobs are generally handled by one person.

"Where did he come from before we got him?" I asked as we got in the car.

"California. Some vineyard in Napa."

"Why did he leave?"

"What is this? Twenty questions? I don't know. He said he wanted to move on. I don't think Leland really looked into it much. He was desperate for someone at the time."

"That's obvious. Mom would never have hired him."

"What difference does it make anymore? The sooner we unload this place, the better. It's been one catastrophe after another lately. I can't take much more of this."

We spent the rest of the short drive down the gravel road in silence. Last night Fitz said that he and I were two votes countering Eli and Mia. Now it was two against one. I glanced fleetingly at my brother's profile and looked away.

He could not . . . *would* not . . . have gone to see Fitz in the barrel room after leaving the wake. He could not be capable of cold-blooded murder.

Or could he? And Leland. Him, too?

We pulled into the semicircular drive in front of the house. A few cars were parked near the old carriage house, which we used as the garage.

I cleared my throat. "Looks like almost everyone's gone."

Eli looked at me curiously. "You gonna faint or something? Your voice sounds weird."

"I'm fine."

We walked into the house. One of the waitresses who had been collecting dishes in the parlor said Dominique had gone over to the inn to see about dinner.

"I'm going to check on Brandi," Eli said, heading for the stairs. "It's warm in here. I hope no one turned the air off."

"Who is going to tell Dominique about Fitz?" I asked Eli after he came back, reporting that Brandi was still asleep. "And I checked. The air-conditioning is still on."

"I'll tell her."

"I'll come with you." We were standing in the large circular foyer. I was holding more plates, still heaped with chicken bones, remnants of dinner rolls, and daubs of color that had once been salads or vegetables.

"You stay here. If Brandi needs anything, you'll have to take care of her. You can do that, right?"

"Eli." I set the plates down by the bust of Jefferson, wiped my hands together, and faced him. "I limp because of an injury to my *left foot*. See these?" I waved my hands. "They work just fine, like they always did. Brain still works, too. Unless Brandi wants me to kick a field goal, I'm probably going to be able to handle anything she might throw my way. Okay?"

He turned the color of a June strawberry. "Jeez, Luce. I get it, okay? But Brandi . . . you don't realize how precarious . . . she nearly lost the baby during her first trimester. It's been a difficult pregnancy. We've got to be very careful." He cocked his head at the sound of a car roaring up the driveway. "Who's that?"

I crossed the foyer and glanced out one of the parlor windows. "Mia. Driving like she stole something. Where'd she get the red Mustang convertible?"

"It's Greg's. He must have let her borrow it while he's at work. Wonder what brought her back here?"

"Does she know about Fitz . . . ?" I began.

The front door opened and Mia burst in. "Know what about Fitz?" She sounded breathless. "They finally found him?"

She had changed from her black funeral dress into a pale yellow lace-trimmed camisole and matching shorts. Her blonde hair was pulled into a ponytail and she'd tucked a daisy behind one ear. When she was a baby, my mother called her *mon ange*—my angel. There was still something fragile and gossamer about her, both physically and emotionally. She lacked the steely stubbornness Eli and I had inherited, and our mental toughness. The news about Fitz—on top of Leland's death—would crush her. Eli and I exchanged glances.

"Let's go sit on the veranda," I said gently. "We'll talk there."

With its worn herringbone-patterned wooden floors, white columns connected by arched latticework, and old-fashioned ceiling fan that whirred like a large dragonfly, the veranda was the place where everyone gravitated to read or nap or daydream—and to watch the vividly hued sunsets with their backdrop of the graceful Blue Ridge.

Not surprisingly it was in the same sorry state as the rest of the house. Planters and urns, which had once been filled with flowers, were moss-covered and sprouted weeds. The white wicker furniture looked scarred up and some pieces needed mending. The paint on the columns was peeling and scaly.

I sat with Mia on the wicker love seat, trying to ignore the stains and worn spots on the cushions made from my mother's favorite Provençal fabrics. Eli sat across from us in the glider, rocking back and forth. Its springs needed oiling.

"He's dead, isn't he?" Mia sounded weary. "First Pop, now Fitz. What happened? Tell me."

I put my arm around her once again and this time her muscles went tense and rigid. "I'm so sorry, honey," I said.

Eli shot me a look before he said, "We think he was trying to stop a robbery at the winery. I'm sorry, babe. Someone pushed him into a purged tank."

She turned white under her suntan and her hand went to her mouth. "I'm going to throw up," she said and bolted.

Eli got to her faster than I did. He held her shoulders as she stood retching into a flower bed that was now nothing but a mass of weeds. "Get some water, will you?" he muttered to me.

The front door closed as I came back through the foyer. I held a pitcher in the hand I didn't need for my cane and had tucked a glass between my elbow and my ribs.

Mason Jones let himself in without bothering to ring the doorbell. He'd changed from the expensive-looking dark gray suit he wore at the funeral to an expensive-looking blue-and-white seersucker suit. In all the years I'd known him, I'd never seen Mason in anything but a suit. His shirts were handmade and had discreet monograms on the pockets and all his ties were silk, ordered from London.

"I came as soon as I found out." He was carrying a zippered butter-soft black leather folder. Also monogrammed. "What are you doing there, Lucie love? Let me help you. You're going to drop something." He came over and extracted the glass. "You all right?"

"We just told Mia," I said. "She and Eli are out on the veranda. She took it pretty hard."

Mason held the door for me as we went outside. Eli had moved to the love seat. Next to him Mia sat with her elbows on her knees, holding her head in her hands.

"Look who's here," I said.

Mia looked up. "Hi, Uncle Mason." Her voice trembled. Eli handed her the glass of water after I poured it.

Mason sat in an oversized matching wicker chair after first checking out the condition of the seat cushion. He put his leather folder between the cushion and the arm of the chair.

"I'm so sorry, children," he said. "I don't know what to say. This is horrible . . . horrible."

"Who told you?" Eli asked.

"I was over at the inn when Elvis Harmon came by," he said. "I was supposed to have dinner with him and a couple of the boys." He shook his head. "We put it off for another time."

"Dominique knows, then," I said. "She's probably devastated."

He smiled sadly. "Aw, honey, you know your cousin. She just soldiers on, no matter what. I stayed with her in the kitchen while she cried, poor thing. Then she pulled herself together like she always does. She was terribly distraught though, on account of the way things stood between Fitz and her before . . ." He faltered. "Well, before."

"You knew they were having problems?" Eli said.

"You know how word gets around, son."

"How about a drink, Mason?" Eli asked. He gestured to Mason's leather folder. "This isn't strictly a social visit, is it?"

Mason's smile didn't make it all the way to his eyes. "As it happens, I do have some business to discuss. I didn't expect to find all three of you here, but since everyone's present perhaps we ought to take advantage of the situation, difficult as it is. And I'll take bourbon and water, if you've got it."

He was an old-school Southern lawyer, silver-tongued and silver-haired, with highly polished manners and old-fashioned gallantry but the killer courtroom instincts of a barracuda. Even though I really wanted to crawl into bed and forget this day, there was something in his voice that implied it was more than a polite invitation. If Mason had something to say, you didn't turn him down. As a kid I'd called him "Uncle Mason" like Mia still did, but that didn't change the fact that he handled all our affairs, personal and professional, as though counters behind his eyes were calculating billable and nonbillable hours. The billable hours bought him a lavish horse farm, where the President and the First Lady occasionally came to ride, and a gorgeous wife who frequently graced the society pages of the *Washington Post,* the *Tribune,* and *Vanity Fair* because of her glamorous fund-raising parties for local charities. There weren't many nonbillable hours.

"Is this about the will? Is there some kind of problem?" Eli suddenly sounded tense.

"Don't you worry," Mason said. "Everything's fine. Let's all have a little drink and then we can chat about it."

"I'll get the bourbon," I said. "It's on the sideboard."

"Stay here. I'll get everything," Eli banged into the glass-topped coffee table in front of the love seat as he stood up. Mason's remark had obviously unbalanced him. He was worried about something. "What are you girls drinking?"

"White wine please," I said. "Whatever's open."

"Nothing for me," Mia said.

While he was inside I lit the citronella torches in the border garden and set an oil lamp on the coffee table. Eli returned with a tray and the drinks—and Leland's best Scotch for himself.

He drank Scotch when he was upset.

Mason raised his glass. "To Lee and Fitz."

After we drank Eli said, "So what's this about, Mason?"

Mason set down his glass and picked up the leather folder. He pulled out a few papers and reached into his inside jacket pocket for a pair of half-glasses. I could tell Eli was squirming and that Mason was going to take his sweet time about this. "Well, Fitz's death changes things, children."

"What do you mean?" One of Eli's nervous tics was a habit of bouncing one foot up and down like his toes were attached to a spring. Right now his right leg was twitching like an electric current was running through it.

Mason looked at him over the top of his glasses. "Leland left the vineyard to the three of you, just like he always planned." He'd switched to his courtroom voice. "But he wasn't sure if y'all would always agree on things, so he named Fitz the director of the corporation that owns it. That would have given him day-to-day control of the business."

"Who runs it now that he's gone?" I asked.

"It reverts to the three of you. You each have one vote, except for the person who owns Highland House. This house. That person gets two votes."

"Who owns the house?" Eli asked.

"Lee couldn't decide," Mason said.

"What do you mean, he couldn't decide?"

"Just that. So he figured rather than play favorites, he would leave it up to the two of you, Lucie and Eli. He wants you to roll dice for it. High score wins Highland House. The other one gets the house in France." He turned to Mia. "As for you, darlin', there's a trust from your momma's family that passes to you. You can't have control of the money until your thirtieth birthday, but you will have an allowance. As custodian I can also authorize payment of certain essential expenses like your college tuition, for example."

"How much . . . is there?" Mia seemed startled. "I never knew anything about this."

Mason consulted his notes. "It's just shy of half a million. You're well taken care of, child."

"This is ridiculous," Eli interrupted. "I mean, I'm glad Mia got the trust money, but everything should be divided equally. I don't believe this."

Mia glanced at him wide-eyed.

"That's not how your daddy set things up," Mason folded his glasses and set them on top of his papers. "He didn't want to have to choose who got which house—and there was no way to divide two houses three ways. So he came to this arrangement—on his own, I might add. You know how Lee liked gambling."

Eli helped himself to more Scotch. "I guess I'd better get the dice."

"Now?" I stared at him. "You want to do it *now*?"

"Why not? You can't practice for this, you know."

"Very funny. I'm really tired."

"Let's get it over with."

I looked at Mason, who nodded. "Just as well."

Eli went back inside the house, the screen door banging noisily behind him.

"Do you want another drink?" I asked Mason.

He reached for the bourbon. "I think I will. You having something, too, darlin'?"

"The white wine must be in the refrigerator. I think I could use another drink, too. Mimi, you change your mind? Want something?"

She was sitting on the love seat Indian style, picking the petals out of her daisy and setting them in a pattern on the coffee table. She looked up. "You haven't called me that in years."

"Old habits."

"Nothing, thanks."

Eli held the dice, clacking them in his hand when I came back to the porch with an open bottle of last year's Chardonnay.

"These are the only ones I could find."

"The Monopoly dice," Mia said. "Where were they?"

"Are those legal?" I asked.

"In the drawer of the telephone table in the foyer," Eli said. "And dice are dice."

"Not necessarily," I said. "Hand them over."

He clacked them together again.

"He had trick dice when we were kids," I explained to Mason.

"I was eight." He slapped them into my open hand. "Oh, all right. Since you've got them, you roll first."

I blew on the dice, closed my eyes, and tossed them. They sounded like pebbles as they bounced on the glass table. Before I could open my eyes, I heard Eli's voice and the elation was unmistakable. "Three! You rolled a three!"

So he'd won, after all. Now he had the legal right to sell the house and the vineyard and there was nothing I could do to stop him. His two votes and Mia's in favor of selling stacked up against my lone vote to hang on to it and run the vineyard ourselves. He'd probably have the FOR SALE sign up first thing tomorrow morning. Sooner, if he could find somebody who'd do it tonight.

"Your turn, Eli," Mason said, after I sat there, mute, staring at my brother.

"Sure." He scooped up the dice and winked triumphantly. If we'd been younger and Mason weren't around, I might have done something to wipe the smirk off his face.

But we were older and I'd just lost my home by throwing a stupid three with a pair of Monopoly dice. Now Eli could have a swan swimming around a big fountain in the front yard of some castle he was building in Leesburg. I picked up my glass and drank long and deep.

The dice cracked against the glass table like bullets before ricocheting off the edge and clattering to the floor.

"Nice move," I said.

"Where'd they go?" Mia asked.

"Over here." Mason pointed under an end table. He stood up and peered at the spot he'd just indicated. "It's too dark. Hand me that lantern, will you?"

Mia gave it to him. "Be careful or you'll get lamp oil on yourself."

He bent over cranelike and angled the light nearer to the floor.

"If that doesn't beat all." He stood up and set the lamp back on the table. "Snake eyes." He pulled a folded handkerchief out of his breast pocket and wiped his hands.

"What?" Eli said.

"A two. You rolled a two." He refolded the handkerchief and stuffed it carefully back in his pocket.

"Lucie *won*?" Mia sounded incredulous.

"A three beats a two," Mason said.

"Are you sure it's a two?" Eli asked. "It's pretty dark."

"Check for yourself, son." Mason looked levelly at my brother and, for a moment, I thought Eli actually might get down on his hands and knees and crawl under that end table. But if he did, it was as good as calling Mason a liar.

He shifted uncomfortably and looked away. "It's okay. I'm sure you're right."

"Well, we'll talk about all this later, children," Mason stood and picked up the folder. "I'd best be getting home now."

"Lucie and I'll be talking about things, too," Eli said, glancing at me.

"What's going on?" Brandi, wide-eyed and alert, stood at the door to the veranda.

"Well, hello there, angel face. Nothing's going on. Mason just stopped by for a drink." Eli had jumped up at the sound of her voice. "Did you have a good nap?"

"I'm hot," she said. "I want to go home."

"Of course, princess. We'll leave right away. I'll bring the car up to the front door so you don't have to walk too much."

If he could have, I'm sure he would have driven it right on to the veranda so princess didn't have to walk at all. I don't know why it grated on me so much, but Eli's transformation into the archetypal touchy-feely sensitive male seemed about as genuine as those publishing house letters announcing you've just won $10 million. He hadn't exactly been in touch with his feminine side when he dated Kit. Back then, his idea of a fun evening was for her to watch him play Formula 1 video games all night with the guys at one of the truck-stop restaurants on Route 29.

As he walked past me, he leaned over and said in a calm, low voice, "You need to be reasonable about all this, Luce. We'll be talking."

"I'm always reasonable," I said quietly, but I could feel the skin prickle on the back of my neck.

"I've got to get something upstairs," Mia said. "Then I'm going, too."

We walked through the ovenlike house to the driveway. Mason got into a silver Mercedes. Brandi nodded a cool good-bye as Eli helped her into the Jag. A moment later Mia bounded outside.

"What did you get?" I asked curiously.

She blushed and discreetly slid a slim plastic case out of her pocket. Birth control pills. "I, um, forgot the other day. I need to start being more careful. See you."

She pulled out of the driveway before the others, the red Mustang churning gravel as she sped down the road. I had nearly shut the front door when I heard Mason's voice. I left it slightly ajar and listened.

"What are you going to do, son?"

"We're selling." Eli sounded completely confident. "Lucie was talking some sentimental crap about hanging on to the house, but I'm sure she'll agree to sell the vineyard. It's too much hard physical labor, especially for someone in her . . . well, you know."

"So she'd still keep the house? You'd have to sell the land in two parcels," Mason said.

"Nah, don't you worry. She'll change her mind. I can talk her into selling this albatross along with the vineyard in return for letting her stay in the place in France. She hasn't got the money or the stamina to maintain it, especially the way it's deteriorated. Hell, Doc Harmon told me she was exhausted when she insisted on walking from the cemetery over to the winery after Leland's funeral. She's real touchy when you bring it up but just look at her. She's a cripple now. She needs to deal with it."

I'd heard enough. Quietly, I closed the door.

It probably wasn't the smartest decision in the world to try to hang on to the vineyard when Leland had left us nearly bankrupt. Our new vintner seemed like the kind of guy you'd hire as a bouncer at a night club. Eli was right that Highland House, neglected for years, needed repairs that were well beyond our bank balance.

The vineyard had not been a business with a bottom line for my mother and Fitz, as Eli now saw it. It had been a labor of love. It was part of the *goût de terroir*—the taste of the land. The blend of the tangible—grapes, soil, and sunlight—and the intangible, which came from the passion and personality of the winemaker who created it. People had been trying to grow grapes in Virginia since the Jamestown settlement when the House of Burgesses, the country's first legislature, required every male over twenty to plant at least ten grape vines. Years later Jefferson wrote that we could make wines to rival the best European ones.

My mother had been excited by the renaissance in Virginia wine making that took place in the 1970s, among the first to see the possibilities of converting some of our acreage from growing hay to growing grapes. To give up now on her dreams, when our vines were just coming into their best production years, was unthinkable.

In France I had learned, of necessity, to take life slower, to measure time by seasons, not deadlines. A life that required me to fit into nature's schedule, and not the other way around, held great appeal. More pragmatically, I had been educated by Philippe, on the rare occasions when he was home, in the useful skills of carpentry, plumbing, plastering, and tilework. On my own, I'd cleared the land around the farmhouse and replanted the gardens. I was not— as my brother believed—completely helpless or useless.

He'd changed since he married Brandi. That was clear. But less clear was how far he'd go to please her, where his loyalties now belonged.

He was still my brother. We shared parents, genes, a life history. To imagine him tangled in some twisted twenty-first-century version of a Greek tragedy so he could have gold-plated faucets on his bathtub was lunacy.

I went back to the veranda and stared at the star-filled night sky. My Chardonnay was tepid. I flung it into the garden and watched the drops sparkle in the yellow light of a citronella torch. Who else, besides Eli and me, had known Fitz was stopping by the winery last night?

Could he have brought Brandi home, then doubled back and confronted Fitz in the barrel room? He had a motive and opportunity—but also an alibi, thanks to his wife.

I blew out the candles and went inside. Eli was right that the house was uncomfortably warm and anyway, I was now too restless to sleep.

The little key that Fitz had given me last night was upstairs in my bedroom. I went upstairs and got it, running my thumb and forefinger over its notched edge. Like most everyone in Atoka, Fitz never bothered to lock the door to his house. Maybe I'd take a little drive over there and have a look around. He might not have told me everything he knew last night about who was pressuring Leland to sell.

Though if I discovered Eli was connected to this business, then what? I might learn soon enough how far he would go to get what he wanted. Now that the house belonged to me.

I'd just moved to the top of the list of people who stood in his way.

CHAPTER 8

—⊷⊶⊷—

I finally located the keys to Leland's Volvo station wagon where I should have looked in the first place. In the ignition. The car probably qualified for antique vehicle license plates and it was clearly on its second trip around the numbers on the odometer. The last time I remember it reading eleven thousand miles, I'd been learning to drive.

Fitz lived just outside Middleburg on Possum Pond Lane. He had ten acres and a charming cottage that had been built in the 1920s. Over the years, he'd renovated and updated the place, especially the kitchen, which now was state-of-the-art professional. What I liked best about his house was that it sat on the edge of a pond he called Little Possum Pond. The pond was shaded by an enormous weeping willow and every year families of Canada geese would come and take up residence for the summer. Fitz fed them with scraps from the inn and fussed over them like they were his children. Word must have spread about the good deal to be found at Little Possum Pond, as the community of geese grew larger each year.

Tonight everything was quiet as I drove up the gravel driveway. The motion-sensor light by the garage came on, which unnerved me. There was no sign that the police had been here yet, which was good—for me. The nearest neighbors were at least half a mile away on either side and the house, which sat well back from the street, backed up on woods. Even if I turned on every light in the place no one would notice I was here.

I went in through the front door, which led directly into the living room. Of all the things I remembered about Fitz's home, the most vivid was how it smelled—as if he'd just finished baking sugar cookies. That achingly familiar scent still lingered in the air.

I went first to the kitchen. It was as immaculate and pristine as always, except for the collection of booze—Armagnac, whiskey, and wine—that had new prominence on a Hoosier cabinet. I opened drawers and cabinets, not expecting to find anything other than what I did: enough kitchen equipment and utensils to send any gourmet cook to gadget heaven.

The living room was pleasantly masculine, the decor a gift from a local interior designer who adored his Double Chocolate Died-and-Gone-to-Heaven Cheesecake. What gave the room its personality, though, were the framed autographed photos on walls and tabletops, of Fitz with the great and near-great.

I walked over to the fireplace. Gloria, his interior designer friend, was probably responsible for the spectacular dried floral bouquet of nandina, holly berries, coneflowers, and black-eyed Susans that sat between the andirons. Fitz's favorite work of art, a reproduction of Da Vinci's *Last Supper,* hung above the photo-filled mantel. Gloria had tried for years to get him to put an original painting that fit more with her "country manor" theme in such a place of honor, but Fitz had ignored her. The aging school photographs of Eli, Mia, and me were tucked between the frame and the glass as they always were, as though we were dining with the Apostles. He'd changed our pictures every year at Christmas until we'd graduated from high school and been immortalized in caps and gowns.

A small pile of mail stuck out from behind a mantel photo of Fitz with his arm around Julia Child. I pulled out the papers and sat down on his leather sofa. His latest phone bill, the electric bill, and an invitation to an upcoming Musicfest summer concert in Leesburg.

The last item was a yellowing envelope on which the heavy impression of a key was visible. I lifted the flap and pulled out a note card, which bore the same key impression. Years ago my mother had reproduced a few of her watercolors of the house and the vineyard, turning them into note cards. She'd sold them at the winery or given them as gifts.

This painting—the original—hung in Leland's office. The weather-etched tombstone of Hugh Montgomery, who had been one of Mosby's Rangers, was in the foreground. The serene sun-dappled Blue Ridge floated in the distance. My mother had often gone to the cemetery to paint, saying there was something particularly special about the light there. She used to take me along for companionship, leaving me to read a book or explore the sun-warmed gravestones of my ancestors, memorizing the inscriptions on the markers while she worked.

The verse inside the note card was written in my mother's graceful penmanship.

> *The purest treasure mortal times afford*
> *Is spotless reputation; that away,*
> *Men are but gilded loam or painted clay.*
> *A jewel in a ten-times-barr'd-up chest*
> *Is a bold spirit in a loyal breast.*
> *Mine honor is my life; both grow in one;*
> *Take honour from me, and my life is done.*
> *Richard II, Act 1, Scene 1*

Shakespeare. She loved Shakespeare. I knew the precise location on the bookshelf in her study where she kept her well-worn copy of his complete works.

I stared at the quote, unable to connect it with the key. Was the reference to "a jewel in a ten-times-barr'd-up chest" a hint about the location of the jewelry box where Fitz suspected the necklace was hidden? If it was, Fitz hadn't found it—or perhaps he hadn't had enough time to look. He'd said he'd only recently gone through her papers.

I slipped the card into the envelope and looked down at the fire-place hearth. Though it was summer, there were ashes in the grate. I moved the floral arrangement to get a better look. A fragment of a blue satin ribbon gleamed faintly among the charred papers. I poked the debris with tongs from a nearby stand. Other than the ribbon, all else was ash and cinder. He must have burned their cor-respondence, except for the envelope with the note containing the key—just like he'd wanted to do with her diaries.

I searched the rest of the cottage, leaving the bedroom suite for last. On his bedside table was a photograph of his parents. Next to it in a dime-store bright brass frame was a picture I'd never seen of Fitz and my mother. She was holding Mia, who was probably not more than a few months old. It was taken at the winery, in the courtyard loggia, probably in summer because a profusion of gera-niums spilled out of a wine cask next to where they stood. Mia, completely toothless, grinned giddily, and Fitz and my mother looked radiant. I picked up the frame and slipped the photo out, holding it so the light from the bedside table lamp reflected off it.

A faint but unmistakable impression of a key. The photo had been in the envelope. Mia would have been too young to know why that picture held such special significance for my mother and anyone else who might know was dead.

I set it back on his nightstand and walked into the master bath-room. Fitz was taking enough medicine to keep a pharmacy in busi-ness. I recognized the drug Leland used to control his cholesterol and another to lower blood pressure, but it was the antidepressant that surprised me the most.

I closed the medicine cabinet and stared at my haunted reflec-tion in his mirror. Alcohol and antidepressants. The worst combi-nation in the world. How long had he been hiding the fact that he was depressed? Had Dominique known?

How could I have let him walk away from me last night?

I drove home and went directly to my parents' bedroom and my mother's dressing table. Her jewelry box, a family heirloom passed down through generations of Montgomery women, had originally belonged to Leland's great-great-grandmother Iona. I found it where it had always been and wiped away the dust with the side of my fist. It was not locked and Fitz's key didn't fit the lock, either. I lifted the polished burled wood lid with its mother-of-pearl inlay surrounding the initials IEM.

Iona Esmé Montgomery's velvet-lined jewelry box, which once held the Bessette family jewelry, was empty. Judging by that coat of dust, it had been that way for a long time.

I slept badly for a second night, despite the lingering effects of jet lag. When I woke the next morning I felt the same muddled lack of clarity I remembered from my days in the hospital, a nonrestful drug-induced slumber that, combined with the oppressive humidity, felt like someone had their foot on my chest. Downstairs a door slammed and I heard male voices.

I looked around the room, disoriented until memory clicked into place. I was home, not in France. I squinted at the alarm clock in the liquid gray light. Just after 5 A.M. Quinn said he was moving the winery operations over to the house today. He hadn't wasted any time.

I got up and showered, changing into jeans and a black-and-white striped tank top. Quinn was in the dining room, pacing the floor, a mobile phone clamped to his ear, restless and seemingly impatient with whoever was on the other end of the line. Every time he passed the china cabinet, he picked up a different piece of my great-grandmother's Limoges or her silver and studied it as he paced. He was still wearing the combat fatigues, but he'd swapped the Hawaiian shirt for a T-shirt with a Harley-Davidson logo on it. He hadn't shaved, which made him look even scruffier than I remembered from yesterday. I went over and took a Sèvres bud vase out of his hand and set it back on the shelf. Then I went through to the kitchen.

I poured coffee and juice and made toast and slowly took everything out to the veranda on one of my mother's hand-painted vintage Tole trays, my cane hooked over one arm. I sat on the stone wall at the edge of the veranda and looked out at the view.

Directly below me was a series of stepped-down terraces heavily planted with azaleas, rhododendrons, dogwood, and cherry trees. The vineyards were off to the north and south, where the terrain was gentler, and weren't visible from here. Our property ended at a private gravel road that led to our neighbors' stud farm. Their barns and the neat pastures outlined by split-rail fences, where a few horses grazed picturesquely, looked impeccable compared to the wilderness on our side of the road. Beyond their farm, the land rose gently again and became a forested ridge of deciduous trees that would turn flame-colored in autumn. Framing everything should have been the soft blue-gray layers of the Blue Ridge, but they had been whited out once again by the heat and humidity.

When people say "old as the hills" I'm sure they mean the Blue Ridge, which have existed since before the Himalayas came to be and were grandfather-old when the Alps erupted. Now they were worn to nubs, a smallish mountain range like a series of dowagers' humps, just under five hundred miles long and not so wide you couldn't hike across them in a day if you were determined.

The screen door banged behind me. Quinn sat down, coffee mug in hand, his legs dangling over the ledge. "I can borrow a few pieces of equipment from John Chappell over at Hogsback Mountain Winery." He sipped his coffee. "When you see Eli, tell him I need to talk to him, will you? The motor on the destemmer's broken. It's going to cost eight hundred bucks, give or take, to get it fixed. I'll need the money today."

I was pretty sure Eli didn't have that kind of spare cash lying around anywhere, after what Fitz had told me about the state of his finances. Nor had I realized the immediacy of our need for money.

"You mean . . . from Eli?"

His eyes narrowed. "I don't care which one of you gives it to me, if that's what you mean. I've been dealing with Eli for financial matters since . . ." He paused. "Since a few days ago. If you want to give it to me now that's fine by me."

"I'll get it to you by the end of the day."

His face was bland but his eyes were skeptical. "Fine, then. I'll call Carlyle's and order the part right now."

The screen door banged shut as he left. I finished my coffee and followed him inside. Dominique, barefoot and wearing an oversized T-shirt from the prep school where Joe taught, was spooning fresh-ground coffee from the grinder into the coffeemaker. She looked up when she saw me and spilled coffee on the counter.

Her eyes looked like two bruises.

"I'll take care of that." I crossed the room and took the scoop out of her hands. "I like my coffee strong after two years in France but you're making paint stripper."

Her pale smile seemed more like a grimace. She reached for a pack of cigarettes on the counter and lit one with shaking hands.

"I thought you quit," I said, wiping up the spilled coffee.

"I did."

"You slept here last night?"

She exhaled a cloud of smoke through her nostrils. "I couldn't stay at Joe's. I wanted to come home. I tried not to wake you."

"Are you all right?"

"Who would do this?" She chewed on a fingernail and her eyes filled with tears. "I don't understand. Who would do such a thing?"

"Someone took the payroll money out of the safe in the lab. Bobby thinks Fitz might have surprised whoever it was."

"I should have gone. I should have picked up those cases. He asked me to go for him and I . . ." She sucked hard on her cigarette. "It should have been me."

I pushed the button on the coffeepot and after a second, it started to gurgle. "How long had he been depressed?" I asked. "How long had he been taking antidepressants?"

She looked stunned. "I don't know. He was taking pills? How did you find that out?"

"I, uh, found them."

"He'd stopped confiding in me. He was very angry with me." She blew out another fierce stream of smoke. "The last time I spoke to him we argued. You can't imagine how much I wish I could take it back and do it over again." She froze. *"Mon Dieu.* I'm so sorry. Of course you can imagine. You must relive that accident every day of your life. What a stupid thing to say."

"It's okay." I picked up a dish and began washing it. "I've moved on."

She looked at me shrewdly. "That's a clean dish you're washing."

I set the dish on the counter and wiped my hands on the towel. "Okay, so I think about it." I folded the dish towel, carefully aligning the edges and laid it on the counter. "I'm not Mother Teresa, but what's the use? What's done is done. I can't think about 'what if.' That goes nowhere."

She sucked hard on the cigarette again and eyed me up and down. "Then you are a saint. He walked away without a scratch on that beautiful face. If it was me, I'd want . . . I don't know. I guess I'd want him to suffer, too."

She squashed her cigarette in a saucer and sat down at the kitchen table, tracing a finger over a series of indentations in the soft pine. Eli's math homework from about twenty years ago was memorialized when the numbers transferred through his paper to the table.

"It was an accident," I said softly. "And I think we ought to change the subject." I picked up the coffeepot. "Want some?"

She nodded as her mobile phone rang. "Hello . . . yes? Where? No, wait. Don't do anything. I'll be right over." She disconnected and sighed, reaching for the coffee cup. "That was Joe. We're still trying to figure out what to do about tonight. In spite of everything we still have one hundred and fifty people coming for a sit-down dinner and three hundred more for the opening-night performance of *A Midsummer Night's Dream.* I don't know how we're going to pull this off."

"You'll have to move the dinner to the inn," I said. "Bobby shut down the winery completely."

"It's fully booked."

"Then maybe we ought to think about canceling."

She drank some of her coffee and reached for the pack of cigarettes. "Too late for that. Everything's ordered . . . and paid for."

"You're saying you can't give people their money back?"

She busied herself lighting another cigarette. "Have you ever heard the expression 'robbing Peter to pay the piper?'"

"Sort of."

She took a drag on the cigarette. "I ordered some new equipment for the catering company. The company I bought it from went bankrupt right after I paid for it."

"Before you got the equipment?" What was it about my family and money? She and Leland weren't even blood relatives. "So how much money are you talking about?"

"Seventy thousand."

"You're out *seventy* thousand dollars?"

"Closer to seventy-five. I've got it under control, though," she said. "Don't worry. Everything will be fine." Her phone rang a second time and she glanced at it. "Joe. Again."

She had another monosyllabic conversation, then hung up and rubbed her eyes. "He had some of Hector's men haul the picnic tables from the orchards to use as buffet tables for tonight. But Hector needed the guys somewhere else so they left all of them sitting in the road over by the Ruins."

"The men?"

"The tables. What a mess. I'd better get over there and straighten things out."

"Leave them there," I said. "Have the dinner right there in the middle of the road. There won't be any cars coming through since everything is off limits. You could string lights in the trees and use hurricane lamps for the tables. It'll be like fairyland."

"That," my cousin said, "is a brilliant idea." She stood up and smiled tiredly. "I need to shower and change. Then let's get over there."

"You go ahead. I'll have to join you later. The destemmer's broken. Quinn needs eight hundred dollars to fix it. Today."

"And where are you going to get *that*? Money. It's always about money." She picked up the pack of cigarettes and concentrated on rubbing a thumb across the cellophane wrapping. "You know, *chérie*, no one knows what I just told you, about the money, I mean. Be an angel. Keep quiet about it, won't you?" She wasn't really asking and her thin-lipped smile was chilly. "Besides, I'm taking care of it."

I said uneasily, "Sure."

She set her coffee cup in the sink as she left. A few minutes later I heard the pipes knocking in the walls and the sound of running water. Had Fitz known about the money? Dominique never explained what they argued about during that last conversation. Eli said they had quarreled over the subject of Fitz retiring.

Now that he was dead she wouldn't have to explain the seventy-five thousand to him. Nor did she need to persuade him to retire.

Just what I needed. Another family member with a motive for murder.

The door to Leland's study creaked as I opened it. Someone had closed the curtains and the hot, dark room smelled vaguely mummified. The air-conditioning seemed even feebler in here than in the rest of the house. I flipped on the light switch and saw the stack of yellowed newspapers that had toppled over, covering one of the floor vents. Opening the curtains set off a tornado of dust motes and the gloomy shadows became—wherever I looked—stacks of magazines, books, and newspapers piled carelessly and untidily on all flat surfaces or sticking out of shelves on the floor-to-ceiling cherry bookcases.

When my parents were first married, my mother had redecorated the study and she'd gone a bit mad in her use of the Montgomery tartan. Our ancient tartan was a lovely subdued heathery green-and-blue plaid, but for some reason, she'd decided to use only the modern tartan, a bold red-and-green plaid on a lavender background. She'd put it on the sofa, the recliner, an ottoman, and even the curtains. It was a lot of tartan in one room, even one as high-ceilinged and imposing as this one. Now, though, it was only evident in the faded sunbleached curtains. Everything else was covered with papers and books. The only place to sit was Leland's desk chair.

I found his appointment book on top of a pile of books on the edge of the desk, opened to the date he died. I shuddered as I leafed through it. He'd never been much for keeping records. A few names—the Romeos, mostly—scribbled on some pages, but that was it. I closed the book and sat down in the chair, sneezing in another storm cloud of dust.

The edge of the hunter-green notebook-style checkbook we used for vineyard business stuck out from under a pile of unopened mail. "Final notice" was stamped in heavy black letters across an alarming number of envelopes. After my mother died Leland had moved the winery's records from her study to his, and her tidy files and meticulous bookkeeping had quickly disintegrated into chaos. I slid the checkbook out from under the bills. There were dozens of missing checks with nothing written against them in the ledger. Half a dozen unopened bank statements had been stuffed in the back of the checkbook.

No way to tell if we had eight hundred dollars in the account— or eight cents. I reached for the telephone—under a copy of the *Wine Spectator*—and set it on my lap. We did our banking where everyone in Atoka banked, at Blue Ridge Federal. The private phone number for Seth Hannah, who handled our account, was written in my mother's handwriting in the flyleaf of the address book, which I found in the top desk drawer. Seth's secretary put me through right away.

"Lucie honey, there's just over four hundred dollars in that account as of today," he said immediately. He sounded friendly, but not happy. "You're a bit late with your loan payments, as well."

We had a loan. Wonderful.

"I'll get it to you, Seth. I promise. But couldn't you advance us just a little more to get us through harvest?" I asked.

"I'd like to, darlin', but I'm afraid that dog just don't hunt anymore. I'll give you a little extra time to make your payment, though. That's as much as I can do." He paused. "I hear you're going to sell the place, so I reckon we can settle up then."

This probably wasn't the moment to tell Seth we weren't going to sell, so I didn't. Instead I thanked him sweetly for throwing us a lifeline, although in reality what I'd probably gotten was more rope to hang myself.

Then I called my bank in France. At least I could get the few thousand dollars of remaining insurance money transferred back to the States.

I knew the woman who answered the phone. Gisèle. She sounded flustered and asked me to wait *un petit instant*. After a few thousand *"instants"* Bertrand Thayer, the manager, got on the line.

He sounded confused. "Mademoiselle, we closed that account for you yesterday," he said. "Monsieur Broussard gave me your letter stating that you returned to the *États-Unis* and wanted him to withdraw the money to send to you. Usually we cannot close an account without the owner being present, but under the circumstances, we did you this favor. Your *ami* was very persuasive."

I was silent for a long time.

"Eh, *bien,*" he said at last. "The letter had your signature on it, even the *notaire,* so we assumed it was genuine."

"It probably was my signature," I said, "knowing Philippe."

"*Désolé,*" he said. "I'm terribly sorry. I don't know what to say. Unfortunately he asked for cash."

Cash. So like Philippe.

He'd cleaned me out.

CHAPTER 9

The money was gone. Philippe had helped himself because he needed it and that was reason enough, as far as he was concerned. No doubt he was gone, too. The note I'd left him said I wasn't sure when I'd be back from America and he probably took that as a golden opportunity to float, along with the other flotsam and jetsam with whom he kept company, to some friendly new port. Of course she would have money, and Philippe would charm his way into her bedroom, putting him on a fast-track to her wallet. He did some of his best work lying down.

The phone rang on Leland's desk. I grabbed it before it rang a second time and answered in French, without thinking.

"*Oui, bonjour,* yourself." It was Kit and she was mad. "Have you read the *Post* today?"

"No," I said. "It's been a bit busy here."

"Well, guess what? Someone gave them the full story on Fitz's death and obviously didn't put a gag order on them, either. Do you know what my boss said this morning? 'If it's news, it's news to us.' Did *you* talk to them?"

"He was my godfather, Kit."

Silence. Then she said, "I'm sorry, Luce."

"What did the article say?"

"That he was found floating in a tank of Merlot."

"Oh God."

"So was it Merlot?"

"Does it matter?"

"Whoever talked to the *Post,* it couldn't have been that wine-maker of yours," she said. "I couldn't get two words out of him."

"I think it might have made the rounds at the Goose Creek Inn last night." Mason said he'd heard from Elvis Harmon, who was dining with the Romeos. All that was lacking, probably, was the megaphone. "Some of the Romeos had dinner there."

"The *Romeos*? Aw, for crying out loud. Of course it was them. They can be a bunch of real old ladies sometimes, gossiping the way they do," she said. "No wonder the *Post* got the story. Joby Matsuda eats at the inn all the time with that exotic dancer he's been trying to get into bed with. He probably didn't even need to interview anyone, just opened his notebook and listened."

"The difference between the Romeos gossiping and you gossiping would be . . . what, again?"

She said a bit stiffly, "It's an open secret about Joby and that woman. The only one who doesn't know is his wife. And we're off topic."

"It was Merlot and it doesn't really matter."

"Meet me for lunch? We should talk."

"I can't," I said. "I've got an errand in Middleburg."

"I'm driving over there myself. The deli. Twelve-thirty."

"You're going to grill me for this story, aren't you?"

"Of course not."

"You lie."

"I'll buy."

"I'll come."

"Good. See you there."

On my way out of the room I stopped and removed the water-color of Hugh Montgomery's gravestone from its hook on the pan-eled wall. Unlike everything else in here, there was no dust on the picture or the frame. Someone had done just what I had done, and not long ago, either.

More than likely it was Fitz. He'd probably wondered—as I did—whether it was a random choice that she used that note card or whether the painting held some clue about the location of whatever the key unlocked. I turned the painting over. Fitz, or whoever it was, already would have found a note or anything else she'd left tucked between the frame and the canvas. I checked anyway.

Just her signature, written lightly in pencil, and the vineyard's twining vine logo, which she'd designed.

I replaced the painting and met Dominique in the foyer. Her phone was clamped to her ear and she was giving orders. She nodded when she saw me, pantomiming that I should meet her at the winery.

I mouthed "later" and went into the kitchen. Quinn showed up while I was getting ready to put a plastic platter of Thelma Johnson's buttermilk fried chicken into our old cooler.

"I don't suppose you've got that money for me yet?" he asked, leaning against the doorjamb, arms folded across his chest. He was staring at me in that predatory way of his. I felt like he was mentally undressing me.

The platter slipped in my hands and two pieces of chicken skidded off and landed on the floor. "Damn." I put the chicken back where it belonged. "I said I'd get it to you by the end of the day. Why? Is there a problem?"

"I need it sooner than that. Carlyle's won't fix the destemmer without cash up front." He walked into the kitchen and lifted the top off a casserole dish, peering at the contents.

"If you're hungry, there's more in the refrigerator. This is spoken for." I took the lid from him and re-covered the dish. "Since when does Carlyle's need cash before they fix something for us? We've been going to them for years."

He opened the refrigerator and looked inside, then closed the door. He turned around and looked at me blandly. "Since the last time they fixed something for you."

I fiddled with the latch on the cooler and hoped he couldn't see my face, which suddenly felt quite warm. "I'll talk to Lew. He always takes care of us. You must be dealing with someone new." Before he could answer, I said quickly, "You'll have your cash this afternoon. I'm on my way to the bank right now."

I heard the refrigerator door open one more time. Philippe had the same exasperating habit, like a six-pack of beer might have materialized while he wasn't looking. "Are you taking all that food with you to the bank?" he asked.

"Of course not." I snapped the cooler latch shut. "I'm taking it to the soup kitchen near Philomont. I've put some aside for the crew, but there's more than we could possibly eat here. I thought we should donate it to them."

"I'll take it for you," he said, closing the refrigerator a second time. His voice sounded gentler than it had a moment ago. "I've got to meet someone in Bluemont so I'll drop it off for you."

"Are you sure?"

He nodded. "The money," he said. "The sooner the better. You take care of that."

I left.

Dominique was right. It was all about money.

I drove to Middleburg, with no idea what to say to Seth. I parked in front of the ice cream parlor on Washington Street and walked the two blocks to Jay Street. Middleburg got its name as the midway point on an old stagecoach trading road that connected Alexandria and Winchester. George Washington's cousin sold the land for the town to Leven Powell, a Revolutionary War officer who laid out the streets in a neat grid pattern and named them for friends who were signers of the Constitution. If Powell came back for a visit today, he'd still know the place, except for the lone traffic light at the intersection of Washington and Madison.

I turned onto Jay Street. Mac Macdonald, who owned Macdonald's Fine Antiques on the corner of Jay and Washington, stood over a window box deadheading petunias. Mac was one of the Romeos, tall and skeletally thin, dressed characteristically in a bone-colored linen suit, pale blue silk tie, and matching pocket handkerchief. Leland said once that Mac's idea of casual dress meant he took off his tie clip. He was more stooped than he'd been two years ago and his white hair was a thinner monk's tonsure. He'd been at the funeral yesterday but we'd only spoken briefly.

He bussed me on the cheek. His cologne, something pleasantly old-fashioned, smelled like limes. "I heard the news," he said. "You must be pleased."

"You mean, about Fitz?" I asked stunned.

"Good Lord, of course not! I meant that the house passes to you."

"Oh. So you've been talking to Mason?"

"Actually, I went 'round the general store this morning."

He heard it from Thelma. If that woman had her ear any closer to the ground, she'd spit dirt when she talked. If she knew, the whole town knew.

"Eli says you're going to sell the place."

"He's been saying that." I kept my face expressionless, but I'm not a good liar. If Mac found out the truth, it was a sure bet the news would boomerang right back to Thelma.

"Lucie honey, let me be frank. I know we just buried Lee but I'd like to buy the contents of your parents' estate. I'll give you a good price, too."

I stared at Mac, not sure if I'd heard right. "You want to buy our furniture?"

"Yes, ma'am. Furniture, books, jewelry, the lot. I sold your mother some of her . . . better . . . pieces of furniture before you were born, so I know what they're worth. She did, too. She had a good eye for what was dross and what was the real thing. You have some very fine, very valuable items, my dear, including some interesting French pieces. They could fetch a nice sum for you." He folded his arms and rocked back and forth on his heels, studying me. His eyes were sparrow-bright and twinkling.

I said, truthfully, "I don't know what to say, Mac."

He stopped rocking. "I could come 'round this afternoon and we could talk, Lucie."

The answer to my prayers.

But to hand everything over to Mac? Just like that?

I'd read once that an original handwritten version of one of George Washington's undelivered speeches was found under a sofa in a cottage in some little hamlet in the middle of England. Later it had sold at an auction for a small fortune. Not that it was likely we had something lying around with that kind of provenance, but who knew? Leland, with his squirrely habits, my mother's missing diaries, and the lost diamond necklace . . . it seemed a bit dangerous to let Mac back his moving truck up to the front door and cart everything off lock, stock, and barrel.

"Mac," I said, "what if I sold you a few pieces now and we could talk about the rest later on?"

The eye-twinkling stopped. "Now, honey, if you're going to make me buy it piecemeal, I can't make you as good a deal as I can on the whole shebang. You got a few things there that ought to go straight to the dump. If I take them for you, it'll save you hauling fees and a lot of fuss and bother." He smiled benevolently, showing a lot of teeth, but there was something vaguely Big Bad Wolf about that smile.

"I guess I'll have to take my chances," I said, "but I am interested in selling a few things right now."

He did some lightning quick calculating. "Let's see. I'll take the tall case clock and the Duncan Phyfe rolltop desk in the parlor. Also the two Hepplewhite chairs and the Federal mirror in the upstairs hall."

I closed my eyes. He'd certainly cherry-picked the finest items, especially the clock. The house would be tomblike without ever hearing its gentle, comforting chime again.

"How much?" My voice wavered.

"Five thousand."

"No," I said. "They're worth far more than that."

He sighed noisily, to let me know he was not pleased at having to dicker. "Six thousand."

"Ten."

"Ten *thousand*? Good Lord, child! Absolutely not. Seventy five hundred."

"Ninety-five hundred."

"I'll give you nine thousand, but it's robbery. I won't make any money at that price." He sounded definite and a bit peeved. "I'm only doing this for your parents."

Mac was a good soul, but he was the kind of person who'd peel postage stamps off letters if they hadn't been canceled and reuse them. He wasn't going to lose money on this deal, in spite of the Sarah Bernhardt speech.

"I appreciate that."

He harrumphed again. "Why don't I stop by your house this afternoon and pick them up? Randy's going to be here from the Georgetown gallery, so I'll have the truck."

I shouldn't have been surprised that he wanted to move so quickly, but I was. Probably best to get it over with. "Sure. Fine. I've got to be over at the winery so maybe we could take care of the money right now. Then you could stop by any time you want. The door's unlocked."

Mac's face softened. "I haven't got nine thousand in cash, Lucie honey. I can give you a thousand, though, and the rest in a check. Will that fix you?"

I nodded.

I wandered around his gallery and stayed generally away from the mahogany partners' desk he used for his paperwork, while he scratched out a check and fetched the money. He put an arm around my shoulders and walked me to the door. "Call me when you're ready to talk."

"Okay." He handed me an envelope, which I shoved into my purse. "Thanks, Mac."

He kissed me again and this time it was gentle. "Thank you. And, by the way."

"Yes?"

"Randy will take your things directly to Georgetown. You won't be seeing them here."

I bit my lip and nodded. The silvery bell on his door tinkled merrily as it closed.

Enough money to solve all the immediate problems.

I was no longer broke, but I sure felt poor.

• • •

Kit was sitting on the battleship-gray wooden swing on the deli's front porch when I got there. Today she wore a shocking pink sleeveless shirtdress with a gold belt, gold stiletto mules, and more troweled-on makeup. She held up a white paper bag and waved it at me. "You're late. I ordered. A Reuben with the works for me and a vegetarian on a croissant for you. I also got us each an iced tea, even though what I could really use is a drink."

"Me, too."

She squinted at me. "You look like something they forgot to shoot. We don't have to stay here if you don't want to. We could go some place more private."

"Too late for that," I said. "Thelma must have had the bullhorn out this morning."

"I, er, heard about you and Eli throwing dice for the house. Wish I'd been there to see his face when he lost." She grinned. "Congratulations."

"Who told *you*?"

She jerked her thumb toward the door to the deli. "Hazel did, when she was making our sandwiches. She gave me your dill pickle since she remembered you hate them."

I sat down in the swing next to her and leaned my cane against the porch railing. She handed over my sandwich and the tea and for a split second, time rewound and we were a couple of kids whose feet didn't touch the ground yet, sitting here exactly like this, doing exactly what we were doing right now. For a flash of a moment I saw us as we had been, filtered through the refracted light that made the grass greener and the skies bluer. A time when life was simple and our problems inconsequential.

If education is what's left after you've forgotten everything you've learned, then memories—especially the good ones—are, as someone once said, a second chance at happiness. The swing creaked as it always did and the street noises of Middleburg faded to a peaceful thrumming of blurred summer sounds. We ate in silence.

"I stopped by the inn," Kit said after a while, "looking for your cousin."

"She's over at the Ruins trying to organize this dinner we're having tonight."

"The pig roast? You're going to go through with that?"

I bit into my croissant and nodded.

"She didn't waste any time." Kit stuck a straw in her iced tea and sucked on it. "Fitz isn't even dead twenty-four hours." She looked sideways at me. "You know Dominique's got a motive, Luce."

Had Kit already found out about the money? I said neutrally, "What makes you say that?"

"They had a huge argument the day before he died. She threatened to kill him." She drank more tea and fiddled with her straw. "I was at the inn having lunch when it happened. On my way to the ladies' room."

"They were arguing right there in the lobby?"

"More like in his office."

"His office is nowhere near the ladies' room."

"So sue me. I took a little stroll to walk off a piece of cheesecake."

"Oh, for God's sake. You snooped!"

"I guess that means you don't want me to tell you what she said." She glanced sideways again when I was silent and grinned. "I knew you'd want to know. She wants to take over running the inn by herself and he told her no way."

"I already heard that from Eli."

"Yeah, but did Eli tell you that she said Fitz couldn't stop her?"

"She threatened him?"

"It sounded like it to me. Too bad I never made it past French 1. She didn't count to ten or say anything about colors or the days of the week. What does 'John ate Mark' mean?"

"John ate . . . oh, Lord. *J'en ai marre.* It means 'I'm sick of it.'"

"Well, she said that a few dozen times." She lowered her voice. "Then *he* said something about having her green card yanked for what she'd done." She narrowed her eyes, which with all the mascara she was wearing made it look like her eyelids had temporarily fused together. "The next thing you know he's dead."

"Dominique did *not* kill Fitz," I said. "Whatever it sounded like. Besides, you heard Bobby. We were robbed. Fitz surprised that guy Zeus, or whoever it was, in the middle of taking the payroll money out of the safe in Quinn's lab."

"The cases of wine Fitz was supposed to pick up that night were in the villa," Kit said. "What was he doing in the barrel room?"

"I don't know. Maybe he saw a light or the door propped open and went to check it out."

"Maybe." She stood and collected our sandwich wrappers and iced tea cups. "You want dessert? I saw a few pieces of Hazel's homemade peach pie when I got our sandwiches. The peaches are from her orchard."

"No, thanks."

"A latte? With a shot of hazelnut or chocolate syrup in it?"

"Just coffee." I reached for my cane and started to stand up. "Black."

"Sit there. I got this." She opened the screen door to the deli. "Well, it was just a theory. That robbery sounds too pat to me."

The door banged shut. I leaned my head against the swing and pushed off the floor with my good foot. So maybe Fitz did know about the seventy-five thousand dollars. Dominique hadn't actually told me what the argument had been about.

Kit returned holding a tray with some whipped cream concoction in a soup-bowl-sized mug, my coffee, and a large slice of peach pie. "I brought two forks," she said.

"I couldn't."

"I can't finish this myself." She dug her fork into the pie. "What are you going to do after you sell the vineyard? Go back to France?"

"We're not selling."

She said through a mouthful of peaches and crust, "Eli change his mind?"

"Nope. But now that I own the house, I have two votes in the company and I vote not to sell."

THE MERLOT MURDERS 109

"What did Mr. Control-Freak say when you told him?"

"We didn't exactly have that talk yet," I said. "But what can he say?"

"Jesus, Luce. Plenty. I'd love to be a fly on the wall when you tell him. Eli doesn't lose an argument. You know that." She picked up her mug and stirred the slurry mixture of chocolate, whipped cream, and coffee. "So who's going to run the place?"

"I am. And Quinn. And Hector."

"Quinn," she said. "Somebody ought to send that man to charm school. He's a bit tough to take. I never understood how Leland could have thought he would replace Jacques."

"Eli said he was the low bidder for the job."

"I believe it." She paused. "Are you sure you're capable of taking on something like that? I mean, it's a hell of a job for a normal person and . . ." She broke off. "Oh God, I wish I hadn't said that. I'm really sorry."

"That last summer before the accident," I said, "before I was supposed to go to law school, I spent every day helping Jacques in the fields and in the winery. Remember?"

"Yes, but . . ."

"I'm not a neophyte. I've helped with harvest since I was old enough to hold a pair of pruning shears. I know what I'm doing. Give me a little credit, Kit. Eli's got a career and Mia's not interested in the winery. I am. I love it here. Why shouldn't I run my family's vineyard?"

"What happened to law school? And saving the planet? You could probably get your old job back or work for some other environmental group. You were good at that." She set the plate of peach pie in my lap and handed me the clean fork. "Finish this. You've gotten so skinny you'll blow away in the next strong wind."

"I want to continue what my mother started." I picked up the fork. "After the time I spent in France, I understand even more why it was important to her."

"Because the French drink a lot of wine?"

"Because the French know how to live." I chewed on a fresh

peach from Hazel's orchard and closed my eyes. "I mean, in France everyone slows down to . . . enjoy life. It's hard to explain. But taking time over a meal, shopping for the ingredients, preparing the food, choosing the wine . . . and then lingering to talk after it's finished. Or even sitting in a café with a coffee or a glass of wine. People enjoy that. Here they think you're loony. Or lazy. Everyone's in such a rush to grab something at some fast food place and keep on going like life's a big race and the first one to get to the finish line wins. In France you want to enjoy the journey." I opened my eyes and glanced at Kit. "You think I'm strange, don't you?"

She scraped the last of the whipped cream from her mug and licked the spoon. "I think you've changed."

I drank my coffee as a monarch butterfly landed on the railing close by. "I like the fact that wine is somehow connected to so many pleasurable things in life. It's got romance, history, mystery . . . what more could you ask?" The butterfly disappeared gracefully into the bushes below. "I like the fact that archaeologists found wine jugs in the tombs of the pharaohs and that Noah is supposed to have owned the first vineyard."

"That sounds more like the old you. An impossible romantic." She stood up and brushed crumbs off her dress. "Well, okay. Count on me for moral support. You're gonna need it if you take on your brother. He'll do anything to please the Queen Bee and I'm sure she's the reason he's so hot to sell the place. She wants him to build her Buckingham Palace."

"I heard."

She walked me to the Volvo and waited while I got in and rolled down the window. "Hey," she said, "with all that talk about lingering over a glass of wine, how about meeting for a drink down at the Goose Creek Bridge like the old days? I'll even bring the hooch."

"I'll come, but I'm bringing the wine. The stuff you used to bring either tasted like motor oil or grape soda pop."

"Fine," she said. "Be a wine snob. See you."

Some of the haze had evaporated for the first time since I'd come home and I could see the faint outline of the Blue Ridge as I drove back to Atoka. There were no glacier white peaks that awed like the Alps did, just a lovely blue line of gently folding hills older than time.

George III had once declared them the easternmost boundary of colonial settlement, since they were a naturally prohibitive barrier. What lay beyond them seemed uncertain and possibly dangerous.

Just like my future.

CHAPTER 10

When I arrived at Mosby's Ruins, Quinn Santori was helping Dominique set up for the dinner, along with Hector and the rest of the crew. The cast of *A Midsummer Night's Dream* was gone, but a few people were fiddling with scenery and lights and the air was heavy with the fragrant smoky scent of spit-roasted pig.

Quinn took the cash Mac had given me and stuffed it in his pocket without a word. It was hard to tell if he was surprised that I actually showed up with it, since he immediately turned his attention to two sweat-drenched Mexicans who were stoking the coals in the charcoal pit underneath the gently hissing, sizzling pig.

I joined Dominique, who was setting up buffet tables and covering another in aluminum foil to be used later as a carving station for the meat.

"Can I ask you something?" I said. We started laying ropes of ivy down the middle of the row of linen-covered picnic tables, twining them around the bases of the hurricane lamps she'd placed every few feet. "Did Fitz know about the problem with the equipment you ordered?"

"Are you asking if he knew about the money?" She nodded, smiling thinly, but I noticed she was strangling a piece of ivy. "He was as mad as a wet blanket."

"Was that what you argued about the day before he died?"

"No." One of the lamps teetered precariously as she jerked another piece of ivy and moved it into place. I caught the lamp before it tipped over. "*Merde*. We might not have enough ivy."

Ivy didn't require this much angst. Changing the subject had been deliberate.

"So what did you argue about? Did you know you were overheard fighting in his office?"

She looked at me like I'd betrayed her. "We were arguing—discussing—whether his forgetfulness was the beginning of Alzheimer's." She reached into the pocket of her paisley Capri pants and fished out a smashed pack of cigarettes. "Don't look so shocked. You weren't the only one he kept in the dark. He managed to pull the rug over everyone's eyes. Both his parents had it so he figured it was probably inevitable. His mother once attacked his father with a carving knife because she thought he was an intruder."

"Oh my God."

"It was an accident that I found out about his parents." She bent and cupped her hand around her cigarette as she lit it. "I bet that's why he was taking antidepressants."

"Eli said he was drinking too much."

"He was. I think it was all related." A cloud of smoke floated through her words.

"So what was he forgetting?"

"The usual. Names. Faces. Where he left his glasses or keys." She shrugged. "I did some reading about it and I talked to Dr. Greenwood. You know it's fatal, don't you?"

"No." I tied a small strand of ivy into a knot. "I didn't."

"Well, by that time, the person is delusional, like his mother was, or has hallucinations. It's a horrible, undignified death at the end. You lose control of . . . everything."

"Do you think he might have been delusional the other night at the winery? Thought someone was after him or something?"

"Dr. Greenwood—Ross—told me it's a gradual decline. I don't think he was at that stage yet." She sucked on her cigarette. "But what do I know?"

"Fitz thought Leland's death wasn't an accident."

She nodded and exhaled out of the corner of her mouth.

"Do you?" I asked.

"Bobby says it was. I believe Bobby."

"Did you tell Bobby any of this? About the Alzheimer's, I mean? I assume he questioned you."

My cousin looked at me assessingly, then let her cigarette drop to the ground. "Of course I told him. I am not stupid, *ma puce*. I have a motive for Fitz's murder, don't I? He left me the inn as his partner, but he wasn't ready to retire just yet. If he'd stayed on, with his condition deteriorating, who knows what might have happened? He might have wrecked everything he built. And the inn would be worth nothing. It's no secret I wanted him to retire." She ground out the butt under the toe of a sandal. "I didn't kill him."

We finished arranging the last table in silence. Then she said, "I'm going back to the inn to take care of a few things. I want you to go home and change. Eli threw a fit about wearing Elizabethan costumes, so I decided to forget the whole idea. Be back here at five-thirty. Wear something pretty."

"Of course."

"And, Lucie?"

"What?"

"If you loved Fitz, you will say nothing about this. Bobby will keep it confidential, of course. And no one else needs to know. So promise me, *chérie,* that you will not mention it to anyone."

Another request for my silence. Dominique had as many secrets as Eli did. I shrugged. "Sure."

By the time I got back to the house to shower and change, Randy had come and gone. The spaces where the furniture had been—particularly the clock—screamed mute reproach at what I'd done. Dust bunnies the size of small boulders rolled across the floor like tumbleweed in the prairie. Though it was cooler inside than outside, I was sweating as I walked from room to room. The house was eerily silent.

I was in the shower with cold water sluicing over me when I figured out what was wrong. I hadn't heard the asthmatic hum of the air conditioner as it cycled on and off. When Highland House was built, there had been no heat, electricity, or indoor plumbing. They'd been added over the years as they became commonplace in most homes, generally in the late 1800s. Leland was the one who put in the air-conditioning. Unlike the heat and the electricity, which were added externally, the ductwork had to be tunneled throughout the house, which meant tearing into the lathe and plaster walls and making a colossal mess. My mother said afterward that Leland had handed over our money to the P. T. Barnum of the cooling business who knew a sucker when he saw one and promptly went bankrupt partway through the job. Leland found a retired plumber with dubious credentials who finished the work for a cut-rate price and, as we discovered later, installed a system that was left over from another construction project. It was too small for our house but by the time we figured out why the upper floors were always a lot warmer than the downstairs, it was too late to do anything.

I wrapped a bath towel around myself and wandered through the bedrooms, placing my hand in front of the vents to feel whether any air, cool or otherwise, was blowing through them and maybe I was mistaken.

I wasn't.

We needed every penny of the money Mac had given me to get through harvest. I might even have to sell a few more pieces of furniture, though if I kept that up, I'd be sleeping on the floor before long. Fixing the air-conditioning was a luxury.

Anyway, it was nearly the end of August. From one day to the next, the light would change from the white-hot glare of summer to the slanting pale gold of autumn that would finish ripening the vines. The hammering heat would recede and the days would be pleasantly bearable for harvest.

I could sleep in the hammock on the veranda. Somewhere in the attic, there should be a few portable fans. I'd done without air-conditioning in France for two years and I could get along without it for a few more weeks.

• • •

The dinner at the Ruins went well, under the circumstances. Most of the guests were unfamiliar faces and there were a lot of D.C. and Maryland license plates in the parking lot, so at least there were some folks who weren't scared off by our macabre news. At dusk, we lit the candles in the hurricane lamps, which made a pretty necklace of yellow lights down the middle of the road, supplemented by the dancing orange flickering of the fireflies and the fairy lights in the nearby trees. Later still, Hector lit citronella torches, which glowed serenely in the still night air along the pathway leading to the amphitheater in front of Mosby's Ruins. The quiet clink of glasses and china and the indistinguishable murmuring of voices was peaceable and pleasant.

I glanced over at Eli, who had come straight from his office, shirtsleeves rolled up, as he helped Quinn open bottle after bottle of the Pinot Noir we were serving with the roast pork. Earlier he came to me and said quietly, "I've got Austin and Erica Kendall coming over to take a look at the house tomorrow. I'll fill you in after dinner."

Austin Kendall was another Romeo and the owner of the largest real estate agency in Loudoun and Fauquier Counties. His daughter Erica now ran the business, but Austin still got involved when listings were in the multimillions of dollars.

Eli had just upped the stakes, setting up that meeting, and we both knew it. He'd also caught me off-guard.

It was neither the time nor the place to discuss anything so I just said, "Yes, I think we should talk later."

After that, I stayed by the buffet table helping Dominique and her staff in an assembly-line preparation of dinner plates. Across from us, Joe Dawson and Greg Knight carved mounds of roast pork under the direction of one of the chefs from the Goose Creek Inn.

Mia, who was ferrying the heaping platters of meat to the buffet table, set one of them down in front of me and said quietly, "Greg and I stopped by the house on our way here. What happened to the clock? Is it being fixed or something?"

"Not exactly," I said.

"Then where is it?"

"It's a long story."

She stared hard at me. "Lucie, you didn't sell it, did you?" Her tone was somewhere between accusation and disbelief.

"I had no choice. We needed the money to fix the motor on the destemmer. Plus we've got to pay the workers for harvest."

"How could you? That clock has been in our family for over a hundred years!" Her voice rose sharply and a few dinner guests looked our way. She stormed on. "I would have begged or borrowed the money instead. I never would have sold it!"

It was completely out of character for Mia, the dreamy, artistic unmaterial girl, to get worked up over the loss of a piece of furniture, sentimental value notwithstanding. Mostly she fretted over more abstract matters like the hole in the ozone or space debris.

I said, stunned, "If you're so broken up about it, how come you're willing to sell the house and the vineyard? I didn't like it any more than you do."

"*Assez!*" Dominique shushed both of us. "People are watching. Back to work, please. Both of you."

Mia glared at me, then walked over to Greg, flipping her hair off her neck like the twitching tail of an angry cat. She'd been this edgy and irritable at Leland's wake, but since then things had been okay. Now it was back to fireworks between us. Not because of the clock, either.

I watched her touch Greg's elbow, then pull his head down so she could whisper in his ear. He listened briefly before turning away. I caught a glimpse of the expression on his face. He looked irritated.

I saw her face, too. She looked hurt.

Though I avoided making eye contact with him, I knew he watched my every move for the rest of the evening like I was an exotic bird in a cage. As the evening wore on, it was obvious I wasn't the only one who noticed. Mia, increasingly morose and unhappy, slammed a tray down in front of me, sending a spray of Pinot Noir sloshing from a glass and cascading in a graceful arc across my yellow sundress. I looked like I'd been shot.

"Oops." She smiled. "Sorry." She wasn't.

"It was an accident. Forget it." I poured sparkling water on a napkin and dabbed at my skirt.

Someone was at my elbow. Quinn handed me a salt shaker. "What was that all about?" He, too, had changed his clothes. Yet another Hawaiian shirt. This one was brown and green with dancing martini glasses, parrots, and tropical foliage.

"An accident," I repeated taking the salt and sprinkling it on the largest stain, which turned dull purple. "Thanks for the salt. The tray slipped out of her hands. Anyway, it's an old dress. It doesn't matter."

"If you say so." There was a nearly simultaneous scraping noise of many chairs being pushed back. "I'd better get going. Some of these old folks might need help navigating that path over to the Ruins. Don't want anybody losing their footing and suing. You coming?"

"I'll help clean up here first."

I began stacking plates when someone said behind me, "You look like you could use this." Joe Dawson held two glasses of Chardonnay. He smiled and handed one of them to me.

"I probably shouldn't until we finish cleaning up."

"Aw, go ahead." He clinked his glass against mine. An ex-baseball player in his days at the University of Virginia, he'd been good enough to be scouted by professionals until a broken hand during a beach week surfing accident ended his career. He was tall and rangy, dark-haired with flecks of gray, and good-looking in the kind of wholesome, ruddy-cheeked way that went over big with the group of jailbait girls he taught. From what Dominique said, they revered him like a minor god. He smiled and flashed boyish dimples. "It's good to have you home, sweetheart."

"It's good to be home."

He drank some wine, gesturing to the empty tables with their hurricane lanterns still gently flickering and the fairy lights in the trees above. "Place is beautiful, you know? I just can't imagine it without your family running things. I heard you're giving the listing to Austin and Erica. They'll do right by you."

"We're not giving the listing to anyone. The vineyard's not for sale."

His eyebrows went up. "Not according to your brother."

"He doesn't have the final word."

"So who's going to run the place? Not you, surely."

"Why not?"

He said, in a schoolteacher's patient voice, "Look, darlin', you of all people know what punishing physical work it is. Only people who don't have a clue what's involved think we live in a Dionysian paradise where we toddle around with a glass of champagne all day and life's a big party. And frankly, I'm not sure how to put this, but for someone who is . . . who doesn't . . ." He stopped talking and looked embarrassed.

"Use a cane?" I waved mine. "You mean, like Franklin Roosevelt shouldn't have been president because he was in a wheelchair?"

"Oh, come on, Lucie. You know I didn't mean that."

"You know, one thing I've learned about being handicapped is that people tend to marginalize you right off the bat. We're treated as a subclass of humanity because we're broken, somehow, or deformed. Do you know what it feels like not to be given the same chance as everyone else? For people to assume automatically that you're inferior?" It slipped out with more passion than I intended.

Even in the darkness, I saw him flush. He set down his glass and mine and pulled me to him, brushing my hair off my face and tucking a strand behind my ear. "I'm sorry, sweetheart. I really am. You know I'll help out around here like I always do. As long as I'm still in town."

I pulled away. "Are you going somewhere?"

"Didn't you know? I took a sabbatical from the academy. I'm off to Charlottesville in a couple of weeks. Finally gonna finish my dissertation. It only took me ten years."

"I hadn't heard. The sound of hundreds of teenage hearts breaking must have been deafening when you made that decision."

He grinned, but it was rueful. "Yeah, well, maybe. Unfortunately the one heart it didn't break belongs to your cousin. I think she's pretty exasperated with me. Maybe some time apart, you know? The other night she asked me in her own special way if I was ever going to put my head to the grindstone and get my doctorate. I figured it was about time."

"Good for you," I said. "And don't worry about Dominique. She'll come around. She's just overworked right now."

"I know. Fitz's death was a huge blow, too." He picked up his glass and finished his wine. "Plus she's nervous as all get out ever since she decided to apply for her U.S. citizenship. She's been reciting the Pledge of Allegiance in her sleep the past couple of nights." He sounded gloomy. "I hope she doesn't say 'I pledge ingredients to the flag' when she's in front of the judge."

A dark-haired waitress with her hair in a long braid came up to us. She held out a laundry bag and waved it at Joe. "We're clearing the dishes. Dominique wants you two to take care of the tablecloths."

"Whatever the boss wants." Joe took the bag.

"Come on," I said. "This won't take long. You can tell me about your dissertation."

"Nah, it'll put you to sleep."

"Is that a nice way of saying I wouldn't understand?"

He flushed. "Sorry. I guess it was. You really want to know?"

I nodded.

"The title is 'The Potential Economic and Social Implications of Thomas Jefferson's Efforts on Behalf of a Nascent Wine Industry in Virginia' but I might change it to what my students call it." He handed me the laundry bag. "'Grape Expectations.'"

I laughed and he added, "Hold this open. I'll clear off the tablecloths."

We moved systematically down the row of tables. "Can I ask you a favor?" he said a moment later as he balled up a tablecloth and pitched it at the open sack.

"Of course." His aim was slightly off or maybe I moved. I shifted quickly and caught the tablecloth before it hit the ground.

"Nice save. Look, when I was doing research on my dissertation,

Leland used to give me carte blanche to use his library. He really does have the best private collection of books around on that particular aspect of Jefferson's life. Do you think I could still come . . . ?"

"Sure, Joe," I said. "Help yourself to whatever you need. Although the place is a mess. I don't know how you can find anything. There are newspapers in there that quote what Noah said about the flood."

He grinned. "You want to get rid of them?" I nodded and he added, "Tell you what. I'll stop by and fill up the back of my truck in the next day or two. I pass the recycling center all the time."

"That would be great."

"No problemo." He chucked me under the chin. "Give me that sack. It weighs a ton."

We walked together toward a large white van with Goose Creek Catering stenciled on the sides in gold and green. Joe tossed the laundry bag inside.

"I guess I'd better find Eli," I said, "and get him to stop whatever it is he's got going on with Erica and Austin before they show up at the house tomorrow."

"Jeez, glad I'm going to miss that conversation. Might as well try to stop gravity while you're at it, changing Eli's mind. He's pretty determined to sell."

"Thank you so very much for that vote of confidence."

He looked down into my eyes. "I forgot. You may have the face of an angel," he mussed my hair, "but you've got the disposition of a mule. Family trait. Good luck, sweetheart."

I heard applause and cheering from the Ruins before I'd gone very far on the dirt path that led from the road to the amphitheater. Though it was lit by Hector's brightly burning citronella torches, it was hard to see the uneven ground in the shifting shadows. Getting caught in a crowd is one of the few things that still panics me. I moved to the edge of the path and missed seeing the large tree root.

As I tripped, I knocked into one of the torches. It went down with me and hit the ground as I did, sending sparks shooting like a miniature Catherine wheel.

"Holy Christ, you're on fire!" I sensed rather than saw Greg in the flickering firelight, materializing out of nowhere. He stripped off his shirt as he knelt next to me, beating the glowing orange cinders that winked like tiny fireflies on my dress and my flesh. "Give me that torch," he ordered. Dazed I watched him right it and fix it firmly into the ground again. "There's blood all over your dress."

I said shakily, "It's Pinot Noir."

"Christ," he said again. "You're lucky you didn't set the woods on fire. The drought's turned everything into a tinderbox. Are you okay, love?" He touched my hair. "You're hair's singed, too. Maybe we should get you to a doctor."

The last time he called me "love" was before the accident.

"I'm fine." The places where the embers burned my arms and legs throbbed. My dress had torn when I fell; the pinholes from the places the sparks had landed looked like an attack of moths. I winced as I tucked my misshapen leg under me so it was invisible. God help me, not a sprained ankle, too. "I lost my cane." My voice sounded far away.

"I'll find it in a second." He pulled me to him and cradled me in his arms. "You look like you're going to pass out. Let me call Ross Greenwood and get you over to see him."

"No, don't! I'm fine." I closed my eyes so I couldn't see the torchlight gilding his deeply tanned skin and dark hair, turning him into a godlike burnished statue, as perfect and beautiful as he'd always been. He was too close, this was too familiar.

His kiss was swift and fierce, tasting oddly of wine and fire, blurring my senses and eroding my resolve. He wore the same musky cologne, now mingled with the scent of something charred. I kissed him back. His hand closed around my throat as he pulled me deeper into him. His hands started to move as we stayed locked in that eternal kiss. Then I tasted salt, from tears. The beginning of redemption.

What I didn't know was whether it was his or mine.

CHAPTER 11

"Somebody lose this?"

Greg and I broke apart as swiftly and combustibly as we'd come together. I wiped my mouth with the back of my hand and tried to sit up, groaning as more pain shot through my ankle. Quinn Santori stood silhouetted against the torchlight, holding my cane like a javelin.

"Evenin', folks. Didn't mean to, ah, interrupt you." He held out the cane. "Lucie, this is yours, isn't it? You all right?"

"She fell," Greg sounded tense. "She tripped and took a torch down with her. I caught her as she fell."

"Holy shit." I couldn't see Quinn's face in the darkness, but he sounded genuinely disturbed.

"I'm fine." He handed me my cane and as I half-rose to take it, my ankle buckled. For the second time Greg caught me again. I noticed that he was still shirtless.

"Like hell you are," he said. "She's got burns on her arms and legs. Scorched hair, too. I managed to extinguish everything with my shirt but I think she ought to see Doc Greenwood."

"Who needs to see Doc Greenwood?" Eli, out of breath like he'd been running hard, showed up with Mia at his elbow. "Lucie!" he said. "What the hell happened?"

"I tripped over a tree root in the dark," I said. "Calm down. It's nothing serious."

Though I couldn't see Mia's face either, the anger in her voice was palpable. I wasn't the one she was worried about. "Greg! I've been looking *everywhere* for you. You're going to be late for work if we don't leave now. You heard Lucie, she's *fine*."

"I don't think Lucie can walk, Mia." Greg calmly pulled on his shirt. To me he said, "What'd you do, sprain your ankle?"

"I think it's just twisted. I'll put ice on it. Really, I'm okay."

"Will you *listen*? You'll never make it to the studio in time! You can't keep showing up late." Mia, agitated, now seemed near to tears. "We need to go!"

He stood up and folded his arms across his chest, fixing Mia in his stare. Then he said so softly that the hair on the back of my neck prickled, "I've got it under control, baby. I don't need you telling me what to do. Understand?"

I watched the flickering torchlight next to us lash tiger stripes across his face. His eyes glittered and the muscles in his neck were thick as ropes.

There was a long moment of silence before Mia stammered, "Of course. I'm sorry. I didn't mean it."

He smiled coldly. "I thought so."

There was a new flash of fire across from me and I jumped. Quinn had struck a match, lighting one of his ever-present cigars. "Well, if Lucie can't walk," he said laconically between puffs, ignoring the tension that hung in the air like fog, "I'll get the Gator and run her back to the house."

"If you can get her to the parking lot, I'll drive her home." Eli seemed relieved to change the subject. "She and I need to talk about something."

"I guess I'll take off, then," Greg said. To Mia he added in a curt voice, "Let's go."

After the others left, I was alone with my brother. "You mind telling me what that was all about?" He sounded mad.

I'd learned, over the years, to keep my cool when Eli lost his. It annoyed the hell out of him. "I was on my way over to the Ruins looking for you when I tripped over a tree root. Apparently Greg was walking down the path behind me so he caught me as I fell. And the torch, thank God."

"Well, let me tell you, from what I saw it looked like a replay of your X-rated sessions at the Ruins. What were you doing, half undressed like that?"

"We weren't doing anything. Mind your own business, Eli."

It was Quinn who carried me to the Gator, a low two-seater vehicle that looked like a cross between a golf cart and a tractor. We used it for getting around the vineyard and, with a wagon attached to the back, for hauling brush, lugs, and equipment. As he set me down on the cracked leather seat, my torn dress fell open revealing my bad leg. Though he acted like he hadn't noticed, I knew he'd seen how twisted and deformed it was. I held the fabric together as we jounced along the rutted path toward the winery parking lot. The glowing end of the cigar danced next to me in the darkness.

I suppose the main reason I hate being pitied—by Quinn or Eli or anybody—is because it's an emotion propelled by relief rather than empathy at someone else's plight and thank God it didn't happen to you. It's a cold cousin to sympathy.

When we got to the deserted parking lot where Eli waited in the Jaguar, Quinn said, "Stay right where you are. I'll get you."

"I can manage."

He slid out of his seat. "Stop being a martyr, will you, and stay put. I said I'll get you."

He deposited me in the passenger seat next to my brother. "See you tomorrow. 'Night, Eli."

Eli called Brandi on his phone as we drove back to the house. "No, honey . . . the second I get home . . . sweetheart, of course . . . absolutely . . . not staying one minute longer . . . okay, angel . . ." He blew kisses into the phone and snapped it shut. I glanced at him but he stared resolutely ahead at the well-known road. "You and I need to have a talk, Luce. Unfortunately it has to be tonight and, as you heard, I'm already overdue at home. Brandi likes me to massage her feet before she falls asleep. She's retaining fluid in her ankles. So let's get this over with as soon as we get back to the house."

"We don't have to talk tonight," I said, as the saccharin cloud enveloping him began to evaporate and he pulled into the driveway. "Call off Erica and Austin, Eli."

"That's not an option." His voice was frosty. "Do I need to carry you into the house?"

"No."

"It's like a damn oven in here, babe," he complained when we were inside. "How come you didn't leave the air on? Don't tell me you roasted like this in France for two years. And what happened to the clock?"

"The air-conditioning broke and we can't afford to fix it right now," I said. "And I sold the clock to Mac Macdonald."

"You did *what*? By whose authority . . . ?"

"Mine. I'm going out on the veranda. I'm sleeping in the hammock tonight."

"Erica will be here first thing in the morning."

"Call her off, Eli."

"I'm getting a glass of wine and we're going to settle this. You drinking something or not?" When I nodded he said, "Then go on out and I'll bring it. I assume you didn't sell the sideboard?" He sounded mildly sarcastic.

"Don't be an idiot. I loved that clock as much as you did. It broke my heart to sell it. I couldn't bear to even be around when Randy came and took everything away."

He had started toward the dining room, but stopped and turned back to me. "What 'everything'? What else is gone?"

"The Duncan Phyfe rolltop desk, the two Hepplewhite chairs, and the Federal mirror upstairs."

"Oh, God. Tell me you didn't. And I bet you probably gave them away. Brandi will be beside herself."

He left himself open to the obvious retort about this being none of Brandi's business, but all I said was, "I didn't give them away. I'll be outside."

He brought a bottle of Sancerre, two glasses, and a bucket of ice. "Don't sell anything else before we unload the place," he said, opening the wine. "It'll look too bare."

He handed me a glass and I took a long, deep drink. "I already told you, Eli. We're not selling."

He nearly spat out his wine. "Don't be an ass. We *have* to sell."

"No, we don't. I've got two votes. No."

"Goddamnit, Lucie! There's no money! We have no choice! Don't you get it?" He banged his glass down on a small mosaic table so hard that the stem broke in his hand. He grabbed the balloon part of the glass, which was still half full of wine, with his other hand and managed to keep it from spilling on the wooden floor.

"We have to bail out while we can. And you're not going to stop me, either. I'm not letting you ruin things for Mia and me," he shouted. "Aw, damnit, I'm dripping blood all over the place. Get me something for this, will you? The first-aid kit is in the kitchen. These trousers are 100 percent linen. Hugo Boss, so they weren't cheap, either. If I get any blood on them, they're ruined."

"God forbid." I leaned on my cane and pulled myself up. My ankle throbbed but I'd be damned if I'd say anything to him. I went inside, letting the screen door slam behind me. "And I know where the first-aid kit is."

He was leaning against one of the white portico columns, staring in the direction of the Blue Ridge when I returned with the first-aid kit. I could just make out the low dark silhouette of the mountains faintly illuminated by the light of a crescent moon.

"If you need the money so badly, why don't you sell the house in France?" I said.

He turned around. "I'll give you the house in France." He sounded tired. "Brandi doesn't want it. It's too . . . old. Just tell me you agree with me about selling the vineyard."

"Mom's heart is in that vineyard. And the land's been ours for centuries. I'm not giving it up." My voice rose.

"Look, babe, your last name isn't Mondavi or Gallo. What do you know about running a vineyard?"

"Plenty," I said. "More than you think. I worked with Jacques. I paid attention. I listened to him."

"You were a kid! It was a *game*!" he yelled. "Look, there's no point discussing this any further with you in your present state of mind. Tomorrow you'll see reason."

I moved over to the hammock and flopped into it. "I'm going to sleep. Good night, Eli." I closed my eyes and turned away from him. "I'm not changing my mind, so I mean it about calling off Erica."

I heard footsteps and the screen door opening. "We'll see about that. Good night, Lucie." The screen door banged shut.

A minute later I heard the engine of the Jag, then the sound of a motor being revved as he roared out of the driveway. I lay in the hammock and rocked back and forth with my good foot.

The noise, sounding like it came from somewhere near the greenhouse where my mother's rose garden had been, seemed amplified in the night stillness. I stopped rocking and lay rigid and motionless, waiting for the sound of footfalls coming closer. A cat yowled and another answered in the distance. I bolted up from the hammock and turned on the floodlights that shone out over the yard. In the unnaturally green grass, a ginger-and-white cat threaded its way through the brush and disappeared.

The bottle of Sancerre was still in the ice bucket where Eli left it. The ice had melted and the wine was warm. I poured what was left into my glass and drank it anyway. Then I sat down on the wicker love seat. The portable clock radio on the end table read ten past three.

I reached over and turned it on. Not too surprisingly, it was tuned to WLEE.

Greg was talking. I'd never heard him on the radio before. There was something different about his voice, which, in the night stillness, was as mellow and caressing as velvet. He was consoling some woman whose boyfriend had left her. They talked for a long time, their conversation floating over me and melting into the night.

I must have dozed off. All of a sudden he was saying, "You want to hear 'I Get Along Without You Very Well' by Billie Holiday? Sure thing, angel. For those of you who've just tuned in, this is Greg

Knight on WLEE in Leesburg and you're listening to *Knight Moves.*
I'll be with you till dawn."

The last thing I remember was Billie, all honey and gravel,
crooning about her man and Greg's voice wrapping itself around
me like smoke and seeping into my mind.

I slept.

CHAPTER 12

I woke, crumpled over on the wicker love seat. My empty wineglass was in my lap and the radio was still on, though now it was broadcasting the farm report. Quinn Santori was standing over me holding two mugs of coffee.

"You follow the farm report, do you?" He handed me one of the mugs.

"I've been known to." I set the wineglass on the coffee table. I was still in my dress from the night before.

"Rough night?" He stared at the wineglass.

An excessively cheery voice sang that we were listening to WLEE, "the number-one station for you and me." I turned it off. "I must have dozed off before I could get upstairs to change. Thanks for the coffee."

He sipped from his own mug and gestured generally at my hair and clothes. "No problem. I like a woman who doesn't care what she looks like when she wakes up in the morning. The natural look suits you."

He walked back into the house, letting the screen door bang shut.

I sat on the love seat and nursed my coffee. He'd been wearing the now-familiar combat fatigues, dirt-stained and wrinkled, yet another Hawaiian shirt—this one with dozens of monkeys eating bananas—and the customary clanking collection of heavy metal around his neck and wrists. His eyes were bloodshot and he hadn't shaved. Who was he to give fashion advice?

I set down the coffee mug and tried to pat down my hair, which was probably sticking up so I looked like Tintin. Finally I gave up and went inside. Quinn was pacing the floor, an ear attached once again to a mobile phone. I walked past the dining room and he motioned to me. He put a hand over the mouthpiece. "I need to talk to you."

"Fine, but I'd like to shower and change first."

"Make it fast, then."

I banged my cane on the floor more sharply than usual as I climbed the stairs.

I showered and changed into jeans and a yellow T-shirt, twisting my damp hair into a knot to keep it off my neck since it was going to be another scorcher. By the time I came back downstairs, I was sweating.

Quinn was still on the telephone and held up a finger, indicating that I should wait for him to finish his conversation. I pointed toward the kitchen and left.

Dominique had put some of the leftover food from last night's dinner in the refrigerator. I lifted lids to casserole dishes and foil wrapping on platters. Cold roast pork didn't appeal for breakfast, so I found a baguette in the bread box, sliced a piece lengthwise and put it in the toaster oven. Quinn joined me as I was spreading Dominique's homemade gooseberry jam on my toasted bread.

He opened the refrigerator and pulled out the platter of meat. "There's something I need to ask you." He set jars of mayonnaise, mustard, and ketchup on the counter. Then he took out a tomato, a small dish of leftover green beans and morels, another of fingerling potatoes, and the remnants of a platter of local cheeses. "Is there anymore of that bread?"

I passed the rest of the baguette over to him. "What?"

He sliced the entire piece in half, spread goat cheese thickly on it and began laying slices of meat on top. "Are you people putting the vineyard up for sale? Because if you are, I think I have a right to know." He dumped the morels, beans, and potatoes on top of the meat and arranged them with his fingers.

I sat down at the kitchen table. "Who said we were selling?"

"How dumb do I look?" He opened a drawer and pulled out a sharp knife. For someone who had only been here a day, he'd sure learned his way around the kitchen.

"We're not selling."

"You and Eli gonna work this thing out?" He sliced the tomato and laid it on top of the potatoes.

I finished chewing my baguette. "I said we're not selling. Okay?"

"That's not what it sounded like." He was busy completing his masterpiece with heavy doses of mayonnaise, mustard, and ketchup.

"That's not what *what* sounded like?" That noise in the garden. It had been a lot of noise for one cat, come to think of it. "Were you here last night?"

"I was in the area."

"You were eavesdropping!"

"Honey, they could hear you two hollering clear out to Up-perville. That was some fight you and Eli had." He came over to the table and set down a plate with his oversized sandwich on it. It drooped off the edges. "Is that homemade jam? What kind is it?"

"Gooseberry. It doesn't go well with ketchup," I said, coldly. "And my conversation with Eli was none of your business. Don't you have any respect for people's privacy?"

"If you want to fight in private, go inside and shut the door. You were outside, bellowing." He sat down across from me and picked up the jar of jam, staring at the label.

"The tenant cottage where you live is nowhere near this house."

He set the jar down. "I asked your father if it would be okay to use that abandoned summerhouse you've got if I repaired the places where the wood's rotted, and he said it was fine by him. I had no intention of listening in on you and Eli, but it happened I was there when you two started yelling like a couple of banshees."

"We were *not* yelling like banshees and if you had any decency, you would have said something so we would have known you were there."

"It didn't seem like a good idea," he snapped. "I'm a winemaker, not a social worker." He picked up his sandwich and studied it.

"Why are you here?"

"I'm hungry."

"That's not what I meant and you know it."

"I'm not a mind reader, either."

"The vineyard. *This* vineyard. Why did you leave California for Virginia?"

He bit into the sandwich and began chewing placidly, staring into my eyes. He swallowed and said, finally, "Why wouldn't I? I like the pioneering spirit you Virginia folks have got. I'd like to settle down here, maybe someday buy some land and run my own place. As for this place, it's a good vineyard. It has potential. You've got a lot of acreage you ought to be planting out. There's some new varietals I think we ought to be trying. I know your former vintner stuck with *vitis vinifera,* but those grapes aren't the be-all and end-all. I've sent off some soil samples to Virginia Tech and the results are pretty good."

"They are?"

He took another hearty bite. Ketchup dripped down his chin. He wiped it with the back of his hand. I got up and opened the pantry door and took out a bag of paper napkins. I slapped one down next to him. He looked at it, then went back to eating.

"Mmpfh," he said. "Thizis bery dub beat."

"You don't say."

He finished chewing and switched back to English. "I was thinking of planting a few acres of hybrids like Vidal, Seyval, or Chambourcin. Maybe even try Norton since it's a native Virginia grape. I'd like to do some experimenting with blending wines, too, not just the standard stuff you've been doing. Use a little creativity for a change."

Vitis vinifera are the grapes Noah planted after the Flood. These were the seeds found with the mummies of the pharaohs in the pyramids in Egypt, the noble grapes that make some of the world's most fabled wines like Cabernet Sauvignon, Pinot Noir, or Chardonnay—all of which we grew at the vineyard.

Maybe Jacques had been a bit of a purist, just keeping us in top-drawer French wines, but in his defense, Virginia's climate is a lot like Bordeaux where he came from and those were the vines he knew best. Still, Quinn was right. Maybe we should try something new.

I ignored the implied jab at Jacques's abilities as a winemaker and said neutrally, "Where were you thinking of doing this?"

"I'll show you," he said. "Come on."

"Aren't you going to finish your breakfast?"

"I'll take it with me." He held out half the sandwich. "Want a bite?"

"No, not really."

"You don't know what you're missing." He wrapped the napkin around it. "I brought the Gator over here. My car wouldn't start this morning. I'll get the field test stuff in the dining room and meet you outside in a minute."

He left and I cleaned up. Then I got two bottles of water from the refrigerator and retrieved Eli's old New York Mets cap from the floor of the front hall closet. The sun would boil us like lobsters out in the fields.

Quinn was waiting in the Gator with the motor running by the time I joined him. I set my cane on the wagon bed and climbed into the passenger seat. There was no sign of the sandwich, just a crumpled napkin shoved in the open glove compartment.

"When are you going to work things out with your brother and sister?" he asked, as he shifted into first gear and we motored down the driveway toward the winery.

"I own the house," I said. "As far as I'm concerned, there's nothing to work out."

"It didn't sound like that to me."

"We've been over this. Why don't you run the vineyard and let me handle my family, okay?"

As we pulled into the parking lot next to the winery, he said, "I heard you sold your clock and some other furniture to raise the cash for the destemmer motor."

"How I got the money is none of your business."

"Your brother and your father were a whole lot easier to deal with."

"I was just thinking the same thing about Jacques."

"You know, one of the reasons I came here is because this place is so underdeveloped and there's a lot I could do. No offense to your buddy Jacques, but he was resting on his laurels," he said. "I could put this winery on the map. I could produce some award-winning wines that would give the Californians a run for their money. I could get us noticed."

I, I, I. I like a man who's comfortable in his skin. Quinn seemed a bit oversized for his, like the Michelin Man untethered, to be precise. Could he really do all that? Or was he just blowing more hot air?

"Jacques was a very skilled enologist," I said.

"If you lived in the nineteenth century. Honey, this doesn't have to be a cottage industry."

"I'm not looking to mass-produce plonk in a six-pack with screw-top bottles, Quinn," I said. "*Vin de ramassage,* Jacques used to call it. Wine from the bottom of the barrel."

He put the Gator in gear and we roared out of the back of the parking lot, climbing onto the rougher terrain leading toward the vineyards. I held on to the edges of my seat with both hands.

"Look," he said, "let's get something straight. When your father hired me, he said he was a hands-off manager and he'd let me do the job the way I saw fit. If you're going to big-foot every decision I make, then we're not going to get along and I need to be looking for another job."

I hate ultimatums or being backed into a corner. My first instinct was to take him up on his offer to move on. Surely I could find someone equally qualified who would be more pleasant to work with. How hard could it be to find a winemaker who didn't have the personality of Dirty Harry and dress in Salvation Army couture?

Though, of course, it was possible he actually could deliver on those boasts. What if he were good enough to make us into a first-class vineyard, like he said? He was ambitious, like I was. Actually, he was pushy. But we both wanted the same thing.

Too bad Leland wasn't the best judge of character. Eli said he'd hired Quinn because he came cheap. But why would Quinn sell himself short if he thought he was so good? It was possible he'd left California, the Mecca of American wine making, to come to Virginia because the potential here appealed to his maverick side. But it was also possible he'd left for another reason and Leland hadn't bothered to inquire about it.

I couldn't afford to have Quinn walk out now, just before harvest. But I wasn't going to let him run the place as blindly as Leland intended, either.

"The difference between Leland and me," I said, "is that he wasn't interested in the vineyard. I am. Just like my mother was."

"Meaning?"

"My mother and Jacques worked together, as a team. He made the call about when to pick, when to blend, when to press . . . all those decisions. But he consulted with her on everything and she had her own opinions."

"I assume she knew something about what she was doing?"

"I'm not a novice," I said. "Give me some credit. I grew up here. Jacques taught me and I paid attention. The summer before I . . . before my accident, I worked here full time."

"A hobby," he said, "is not the same as a profession."

"It was my mother's life's work! My family's name is on every bottle of wine that leaves here. It is not a hobby. It is a *passion*! They're different."

He was silent, but he'd shifted the Gator back into first gear so now we'd slowed considerably as we approached the beginning of the Chardonnay block.

"Besides," I continued, as his silence grew into a substantial

void, "unlike Leland, I'd sell every piece of furniture we own to fi-
nance the expansion you're talking about."

That unstuck his tongue. Money. "Okay," he said. "I'll listen to
what you have to say, but I run the show. Completely. We'll see if it
works. If it does, I'll stay. If it doesn't, I'm gone at the end of harvest."

"Fine."

The end of harvest could be anywhere from six to eight weeks
away, depending on the ripening of the different varietals of grapes.
We'd know each other pretty well by then. There would be days
when we'd be working together practically around the clock.

He looked sideways at me. "I'm not kidding."

"Me, either."

He banked the Gator hard to the right and headed down an aisle
of Chardonnay. I held on to the edges of my seat again as we now
were driving along the contours of a steep slope. The vines were
planted in rows eight feet apart, just wide enough for the Gator or
our tractor to navigate. We puttered slowly down the aisle, examin-
ing the heavy clusters of translucent green-gold grapes.

I had forgotten how churchlike the vineyard was, silent but for
the cicadas' song, muted by the dense canopy of vines, and the sop-
orific buzzing of honeybees drunk on fermenting grapes. Every so
often a crow cawed, and I saw the shadow of its wingspan as it
wheeled and turned above us.

It was probably at least the tenth time someone had looked over
these vines since the last harvest. Pruning, spraying for pests, tending the trellises, overcropping if there were too many buds, and
general fretting over the state of the grapes and the date to harvest
were all reasons warranting a visit. Quinn shut off the motor,
climbed out of the Gator, and clipped a cluster of grapes with the
pruning shears. I joined him after retrieving my cane.

Grapes used in wine growing are smaller than table grapes and
densely packed together in bunches. They're also much sweeter because it's the sugar that makes the alcohol. Quinn ate a few from
the bunch he'd picked and gave me the rest. Although the drought
was devastating for crops, gardens, and livestock, it was a blessing

for a vineyard since the parched conditions meant the vines worked harder to find water, adding flavor and complexity found in the deeper mineral-rich soil. The longer they hung on the vine once the ripening process, or *véraison,* began, the richer and fuller the wine and the higher the alcohol content.

Unfortunately *véraison* didn't last forever. At temperatures over ninety-five degrees Fahrenheit, the grapes shut down and stopped ripening all together. Today it was well over one hundred. I looked at Quinn, who was frowning as he chewed. It would be his call when we harvested, a nerve-wracking decision somewhere between a crap shoot and a matter of scientific judgment.

"What do you think?" I asked.

"Let's test Brix."

He got the refractometer, a beaker, and a small piece of equipment that looked like a garlic press. Brix measured sugar content of the grapes, probably the most important factor in deciding when they were ready to pick. He crushed several grapes until a straw-colored liquid dripped into a beaker. Dozens of tiny black flies swarmed around us, coating the hood of the Gator like an ink spill. Yellow jackets, excited by the newly released sugar liquid, dive-bombed us and strafed the vines.

"These grapes have had plenty of hang time," Quinn said swatting a bee, as he swirled juice in the flask. "I don't think we ought to leave it any later than the day after tomorrow to harvest."

He poured a few drops onto the refractometer and he closed the top. Then he pointed it at the horizon and looked through the eyepiece.

"Read that," he said, handing it to me. I squinted toward the light.

"Twenty point eight. Or point six."

"That's what I got." He shook his head. "If this heat keeps up, it could go to twenty-two in the next day or so. It'll be too high for a Virginia Chardonnay. You don't have the sunshine California does. Out there we got too much sugar to deal with. I prefer a wine on the drier side like you get here."

"What if Bobby still has us shut out of the winery?" I swiped at more buzzing insects.

"I'm working on it." He pulled a pair of half-glasses from the pocket of his Hawaiian shirt and put them on. I watched while he did some calculations, then I got the two bottles of cold water I'd taken from the refrigerator. They were already tepid. I handed one to him and opened the other for myself.

"You got any idea where the root stock for these vines came from?" he asked. "And when they were put in?"

"I think these might have been put in when the vineyard was a few years old—but I'm not sure." I splashed water on the back of my neck and face. "Isn't that information in Jacques's files?"

"If it was, it isn't anymore. Somebody's been through them. They're—well, I guess you'd call it, incomplete."

He meant Leland. "My mother kept her own garden journals. Not just what was planted here, but also the flower and vegetable gardens, too. She was very meticulous. I'll have a look."

"That'd be good."

He stuffed his glasses back in his shirt pocket and squatted down, cutting another bunch of grapes from a different vine. "Damnit. Damn crows. And deer." There were empty spots on several vines along the row where the grapes had been stripped down to the stems.

"Why didn't you put out the owls?" I asked. My mother had a huge collection of owl statues she put along the fences that surrounded the vineyard. They frightened the birds off. Sort of."

"Statues? I didn't know about them. Where are they?"

"The smokehouse. I'm surprised Hector didn't remember."

"We'd taken to shooting them. The crows, I mean. Until recently." He didn't elaborate. He didn't have to. "Let's get some samples from other parts of the block. I'll do TA and pH back at the house to be sure, but I don't think it's going to change anything about when we pick."

TA is titratable acidity and is a measure of the total acid in the grape juice—pH is sort of related to titratable acidity and is the third important component for determining ripeness. If the pH is too high, the grapes could be overripe. The ideal time to harvest is when there's a good balance between the sweetness and the acidity in the wine, and that could change in the space of a day.

He started the Gator. "I had a call from Elvis Harmon. Seems our neighbor lost a calf," he said. "Got through a hole in the electric fence. I promised we'd keep an eye out for it."

"If it's been too long the foxes probably got it, poor thing."

"Or the coyotes."

"We don't have coyotes in Virginia."

"They're moving into the area. We've got coyotes, honey."

He clipped three more bunches of grapes from other vines in the Chardonnay block, then we headed out into an open field toward the larger of our two apple orchards. Quinn kicked the Gator into third gear and we roared bumpily across the hard-packed terrain.

He slowed down as we came to the orchard with its uneven rows of trees, as pleasantly untidy as the vines were orderly and well trained. Apple-picking time began in September and stretched into October, coinciding with the harvest of our reds. A few men from the vineyard crew were sent to the orchard to pick and the apples were made into sparkling cider.

My mother, like Jefferson, believed in experimenting in the garden, and the orchards had been no exception. We had at least a half dozen kinds of apples—the usual Jonathans, Winesaps, and Red Delicious, but also the more exotic Ginger Golds, Cox's Orange Pippin, and Jefferson's own favorite, the Esopus Spitzenburg, which despite its homely name, tasted sweetly and smelled of orange blossoms.

We passed the dry-stacked stone wall at the end of the orchard and drove down an allée of cherry trees my mother had planted as seedlings. My favorite time of year to come to this part of the vineyard was spring, when the sprays of pale pink blooms made it look as though the tree branches were covered in a lace curtain. Some years the blossoms didn't last long and on windy days there would be a pink blizzard that stripped the trees and left a carpet of petals on the ground.

"When did you start working here?" I asked Quinn.

He smiled. "In time to see these in bloom. They were real pretty. I like dogwoods."

"They're cherry trees. You're in George Washington's back-yard."

"I thought they were dogwoods."

"We've got dogwoods, too. There's a grove by the Merlot block. My French mother was very patriotic. It's our state tree."

"Ah," he said. "The Merlot block."

"That's where Leland . . . ?"

"Yup."

"I'd like to see it, please."

He swung around and we drove back in the direction we'd come from. The Merlot block was nearest to the road, not far from where Sycamore Lane split into a "Y" behind Quinn's and Hector's houses. We drove by the dairy barn and the dogwood grove without speaking, but I saw him studying the trees. After a moment he stopped at a post marked "A46, R4" and turned off the motor. All vineyards have a numbering system so it's possible to keep precise track of the location of a trellis needing repairs, a section of vines with yellowed leaves, or so we'd know where the workers had left off pruning for the day.

There was a small rosebush at the end of the row. It appeared re-cently planted, and it wasn't doing well in the heat. There were no blooms.

"Here?" I asked.

"Not right here. In the middle of the row." He climbed off the Gator and I followed. He wanted to walk, not drive.

Here the rows were about as long as football fields, with the vines planted about three feet apart. We got to the spot and Quinn knelt down, pointing to a section of trellis. "That's where the vine came down and we had to fix the wires and put in a new post."

I leaned on my cane and knelt next to him, touching two of the frayed red hay bailing ties on the bottom wire where the vines had broken away. You couldn't tell anything anymore, except for the newness of the post, which would weather after a couple of seasons. Then there'd be nothing left to physically mark the place where Leland had died.

"Who planted that rosebush?"

"Hector's wife."

"I'll have to thank her."

"That'd be nice. Hey, are you all right?"

I nodded.

"My old man took off and left my mother before I was born." He reached over and moved away the canopy of leaves to reveal clusters of Merlot grapes. We were weeks away from picking them, probably not until some time in early October. "I never knew him."

The sandy loam soil hadn't compacted yet into concrete where they'd fixed the post and trellis. I picked up a handful and let it run through my fingers. Leland had been around, but I hadn't really known my father, either.

"Eli said . . ." I paused.

"Yes?"

"He said there was a lot of blood. Where . . . ?"

He looked uneasy. "There was. I wasn't sure what to do about it, so I brought one of the coolers and poured water everywhere until it was gone. Kind of returning him to the land, if you know what I mean. It seemed okay, when I thought of it that way."

"Thank you. That was very thoughtful."

"You know what was strange?"

"What?"

"I found a bullet here when I did it. I thought it might have been . . . well, it was old. Really old. It must have been there for years."

"It could have been from the Civil War," I said. "We find things all the time. Bullets. Pottery. Even a belt buckle, once, from a Confederate soldier."

He was silent, then he stood and held out his hand to me. I took it and he pulled me up. "Are you okay?"

"I think so."

When we got back to the Gator, I poured the rest of my water bottle on Serafina's rosebush.

He started the motor. "You still want to see those new sites?"

"Yes," I said. "Let's go look at the future."

His mouth curved in a small smile, but he didn't say anything as he swung around and we drove away.

Highland House is set back more than a mile from Atoka Road, the main road, so much of our vineyard is actually in front of the house, though it's not evident because we've got so much land. My mother and Jacques had planted only twenty-five of our five hundred acres in vines, yielding about five thousand cases of wine a year. In California, twenty-five acres is nothing, but in Virginia it's a decent-sized vineyard.

"How many more acres were you thinking of planting?" I asked.

"Ultimately I was figuring on seventy-five. Fifteen thousand cases. I also think we don't have to plant only French grapes."

That would catapult us into the big leagues. It would also cost us a fortune. "You're very ambitious."

"We'd do it in stages."

"We'll have to." It takes at least three years before a vine will yield fruit that can be used for making wine, real quality grapes, meaning there are three years of up-front costs before there's a return on the investment.

Long ago my mother had cross-stitched a quote of Thomas Jefferson's she liked that she'd framed and hung in her office. It read, "Wine being among the earliest luxuries in which we indulge ourselves, it is desirable it should be made here and we have every soil, aspect, and climate of the best wine countries." Though Jefferson had tried for years to grow grapes at Monticello and encouraged a wine-making industry in Virginia, it had never happened during his lifetime. Now, sitting next to Quinn, I thought about the possibilities and promise of what could be, that here we *did* have the soil, aspect, and climate to plant vines that could yield world-class wines. Every reason to hope that we could do something extraordinary.

We had passed the last of the existing vineyards. I figured he was headed toward a series of old fields rimmed with more dry-stacked stone walls that checkerboarded the landscape. Beyond them, the terrain swept up to the highest point of our property. It was covered with trees and underbrush. If he wanted to use that hill, we'd have the additional expense of clearing it, but then slopes were the best place for siting vines.

He stopped by one of the stone walls and pointed to the hill. "Beginning over there," he said. "It's cooler and a different micro-climate from the rest of the vineyard so we could experiment. South-facing slope. Good drainage. It would be above any frost pockets and we'll take out any impediments to cold-air drainage."

I'd gotten out of the Gator when Quinn had been speaking and was about to head across the field.

"Umm."

"Hey," he said, "are you listening, or am I talking to the crows? Where are you going?"

I hadn't been to this part of the farm for years, quite deliberately. The vegetation had changed the topography of the landscape, so at first I hadn't been sure.

"Excuse me for a moment."

After a few tries I found the small flat cross made of gray field-stones next to the wall. It was nearly buried by tall grass and weeds that I pulled away with my metal cane, using it like a scythe. I'd made the cross years ago to mark the place where my mother had fallen after Orion, her horse, had thrown her. I knelt and was pulling weeds when I heard Quinn's footsteps behind me.

"I never saw that marker when I was here before."

"You wouldn't have. It was covered by brush."

He grunted. "You bury a dog here or something?"

I finished clearing away debris around the stones and wiped the dirt off my hands on my jeans. I leaned on my cane and pulled my-self up. "No."

"What's the cross for, Lucie?" he asked as we walked across the field to the Gator.

"My mother. Look, can we please get out of this heat?" I turned away from him.

"Sure," he said gently. "Let's go."

When we got back to the Gator he said, "We don't have to plant here."

I shook my head. "She'd like it if we did."

He chewed on a piece of wild chicory and said nothing.

"You know," I continued, "my mother thought only the French could make good wine. I wonder what she'd make of you being the vintner here."

He smiled that half-smile again. "Thomas Jefferson said every man has two countries. His own and France. I figure that makes me a little bit French. Besides, Jefferson's good friend was Filippo Mazzei. A good *paisano* from Tuscany, just like my phantom father. Jefferson gave Mazzei two thousand acres near Monticello to grow *vinifera* in Virginia and produce some good Italian wine in the New World. So if an Italian vintner was good enough for Jefferson, it ought to be good enough for you. And your mother. Okay?"

I stared at him with my mouth open, as though he'd just spoken to me in perfect Attic Greek. "Well," I said at last, "I guess so."

"Good."

We didn't speak on the trip back to the winery. Quinn began humming relentlessly, something tuneless and off-key and loud enough to be heard over the puttering Gator. Like white noise, I tried to let it block my thoughts, but without much success.

Producing wine is as emotional a task as it is technical. To drink a glass of a wine you have helped create is to remember the weather that year, the events that happened in the world, and, inevitably, the events in your own life. As a result, I could never drink one of our wines from the year my mother died, for it seemed I always tasted a sadness that had seeped into the finish.

I wondered if it would be the same with wine from this harvest, the year of Leland's death—whether Quinn would somehow unin-

tentionally infuse it with a sense of loss or whether he could over-
come that and instead we'd taste his hopes and the promise of the
future as he produced his first vintage in Virginia. I didn't say any of
this to him, because I didn't want to jinx things.

But after he dropped me off at the house no matter what I did
the sterile anonymity of Section A46, Row 4 stayed with me. I
thought about Quinn washing away all that blood and the hasty funeral my brother had organized.

Leland hadn't been out there in the vineyard alone. Someone—
someone I knew—had been there with him.

CHAPTER 13

The house at noontime was worse than a blast furnace, and the heat so oppressive it weighed me down like the gravity on Jupiter. I took another shower and dressed without drying off. It helped for ten minutes and then I was as enervated and listless as I'd been before.

I'd been putting off making a trip to the attic, which would be even more suffocating and airless than the rest of the house, to retrieve one of the old fans, but it was getting down to choosing between the lesser of two evils. I rummaged in the kitchen for a flashlight, betting the lights would be burned out in the attic. When I found one, the batteries were dead so I pawed through more junky drawers looking for fresh replacements. After half an hour I quit looking.

I could buy batteries at the general store, which would be quicker than a trip to Middleburg. Besides, Thelma had already squeezed every bit of news about our family out of everyone else in Atoka, so there wasn't much chance I'd get mugged for new gossip.

There was no one in the store when I walked in, even though three pickup trucks were out front, angled so they filled all the available pavement on either side of the gas pumps, the area Thelma liked to call "the parking lot." The sleigh bells attached to the front door jingled as I entered. The store smelled, as it always did, of fresh-brewed coffee and pine-scented sawdust. Abruptly, voices in the back room stopped talking and a moment later, Thelma scooted out front. She was small and compact, a woman of "a certain age" as the French say, or, as she put it, "I'm not as young as I look." She had the tornado energy of a twentysomething, but a lot of the old-timers said she was over seventy if she was a day. She was dressed completely in lime green from the bows in her bright orange hair to the killer pair of stiletto slingbacks. She wore the usual tonnage of makeup, though she'd gotten a bit whimsical drawing in her pencil-line eyebrows. I'd once heard her described as the Mata Hari of Atoka, with her va-va-voom style of dressing and her success at weaseling information out of her neighbors—but with the eyebrows she looked more like Spock from *Star Trek*.

"Lord love a duck," she said when she saw me. "I swear, that Marissa is some hussy! They've just let her out of prison for forgery and already she's trying to take away poor Katarina's husband. And he doesn't recognize her after all the plastic surgery she had after the fire so he believes every word she says. And her pregnant with twins by Diego, that gorgeous prison guard who's really Dr. Lance Tarantino!"

"*General Hospital*? *Days of Our Lives*?" I guessed.

"A new one. It's called *Tomorrow Ever After*. The characters are so *real*, Lucille, they're practically like family. I just *love* that show." She put her hands on her hips and studied me. "You know, child, you lost too much weight while you were over there in France. How much do you weigh now, anyway?"

"I don't actually know. I'm okay, though."

"Can't be more than a hundred and ten pounds soaking wet," she said. "You need to put some weight on, Lucille. I think there's one blueberry muffin left from this morning's delivery. Better'n those cross-ants you got in France, too. Hampton Weaver wanted it when he was here earlier, but Lordy, that man must be close to three hundred pounds and lookin' like a doublewide trailer, so I said, 'Hamp, you put that muffin back and you get yourself on a diet, you hear me?' So you take it, now, and you eat it. On me."

Stiletto heels clacking like castanets on the wooden floor, she crossed the room. The blueberry muffin sat, on its own, in the glass cabinet where she kept the fresh bakery items she ordered every day. She wrapped it in a piece of white paper and handed it to me. "Now eat that."

"Yes, ma'am."

She picked up a dish towel and polished imaginary fingerprints off the glass cabinet. "I heard that new winemaker of yours is over seeing Bobby Noland right now, trying to get him to speed up the investigation into poor ol' Fitz's death so you all can get back inside your winery."

I coughed on a piece of muffin. "Mmmm."

She eyed me. "So it's true, then?"

I swallowed. "I don't really know where he is right now. Where did you hear that?"

She stopped polishing and touched her hand to the back of her hair. "Why, from him. 'Course he didn't actually *say* that's where he was heading, but I know the receptionist over to the sheriff's office. He'd called there a little while ago."

"You still know everything about everybody, don't you, Thelma?"

"Oh, I keep my oar in, Lucille. It's what keeps me so young. People are so interesting, you know? And, of course, I just plumb love the socialism of my job."

"I can see that."

"He left here a few minutes ago," she continued. "Nice-looking young fellow, except I wish he'd take off that jewelry. Worries me when a man wears a necklace and bracelet. Didn't waste any time getting himself a girlfriend since he got here though, did he?"

"I beg your pardon?"

She smiled sweetly. "That dancer."

"What dancer?"

"The one takes most of her clothes off."

I stared at her. "Are we still talking about Quinn Santori? Our winemaker?"

"Who else?" She resumed polishing. "She works at Mom's Place."

"That night club on the way to Bluemont?" The joke about that particular strip joint was that all the men who went there told their wives or girlfriends they were going to "Mom's," which saved a lot of grief and questioning—until everyone wised up about their real whereabouts. "How did he meet her?"

"How do you *think*?"

"Oh." He'd said he was headed over to Bluemont the other day when he took all our leftover food to the soup kitchen. He was probably going over to Mom's for a little lunchtime . . . refreshment.

"She's right pretty." Thelma said. "'Course I've only seen her with her clothes on. She's about your age, Lucille. I think at her place of work she goes by 'Angel.' Just one name, like some of those rock stars. Her real name is Angela Stetson."

"Angela Stetson? I went to high school with her! She was really quiet. I don't think I ever heard her say two words."

Thelma arched her eyebrows, which was not a good idea since they disappeared under her orange fringe of curls. "Still waters, Lucille. Still waters." She looked sly. "So what do you think about that?"

I'd finished my muffin and crumpled the white paper in my hands. "I think it's his business who he sees. And hers. Do you have any batteries?"

"'Course I do. They're over in hardware. What size do you need?"

"For a flashlight. D, I think."

"Hardware" was all of half a row, just behind camping items, fishing lures, and ammunition. The other half of the row was seeds and greeting cards. You could get anything at Thelma's, if you didn't mind the lack of variety. We walked over to hardware.

"Here they are." She handed me a package of batteries. "As long as we're on the subject, what's all this I hear about you and Gregory Knight? Is he trying to start a fire with you again, Lucille? And him sleeping with your sister, too. That boy has no shame. A regular Casablanca, he is, a real two-timer."

Some government ought to hire this woman for serious under-cover work. Where had she heard *that*? "I don't know what you heard but there is absolutely nothing going on between Greg and me."

"Is that so? Well, let me tell you, my sources are the horse's mouths themselves. I spoke to Gregory when he was in here this morning after getting off work at the radio station. He went redder 'n a tomato when I asked him. If that isn't an admission of guilt, I don't know what is." She clacked over to the cash register leaving me to trail behind her while she rang up my sale in silence. Then she added her denouement. "I have it on good authority that last night he was seen in the throes of passion, kissing you for all the world to see."

"Oh gosh, Thelma, it's not what you're thinking."

"I knew it! You're redder 'n a tomato, too, Lucille. You stay away from that boy." She wagged a finger in my face. "He's too dang good-looking for his own health and he knows it. I don't like a person takes advantage of another. It isn't right."

"No, ma'am." I started to move away from the cash register. "Thanks for the batteries and the muffin."

"You're welcome."

"I know you're looking out for me and I appreciate it. Really."

"Well. 'Course I am." Her voice softened and she seemed some-what mollified. "But there is one more thing."

"Yes?"

She put her hands on her hips and thought for a moment. "There's something you need to know, child. I've been debating whether or not I ought to keep it a secret, but you know me. I be-lieve it's best if you just let it all hang out."

"I know that."

"You believe in the power of spirits, don't you, Lucille?"

"As in alcohol? You mean wine?"

"I do *not* mean alcohol. I mean *spirits*. You know, communicating with . . ." She paused and looked significantly at me. "The Great Beyond."

It wasn't too hard to see where she was going with this. Years ago Thelma used to see a psychic over in Delaplane who happened to correctly predict that she would soon meet a tall stranger who had just come into a large sum of money and would ask her to marry him. She met the guy, all right. It's possible he's still doing time at some correctional facility in North Carolina for armed robbery.

"I believe in life after death," I said carefully.

"Now, honey, I'm going to tell you something and I don't want you to be too upset."

"Okay."

She clasped her hands together and leaned toward me. "I can't be too specifical about details," she said, lowering her voice, "but I have it on good authority that your mother is absolutely committed, I mean *committed,* to your hanging on to the house and the vineyard." She straightened up and put her hands on her hips again. "What do you think?"

What horse's mouth told her that? "How do you know this?"

"Oh, the spirits often use me as their medium. I have excellent psychedelic powers. Your mother told me herself when she paid me a little visit."

"My *mother*? You're quite sure it was my mother you were talking to?"

"I am positive. Charlotte and I were very close, Lucille." I'd forgotten she used to call my mother Charlotte.

"I remember."

"Though I admit," she added, "that I was surprised when she called on me. It was the first time I'd heard from her. Since before, well, you know when."

"When did you two have this discussion?"

"Why, just this afternoon," she said. "I had my Ouija Board out because Muriel Sims wanted to talk to Henry. She likes to keep in touch pretty regular, you know, since he went over to the other side. And, plain as day after Henry left, there was Charlotte. I knew it was her because I didn't understand what she was saying at first. I think it was something French. Too bad I can't remember it now."

"And she told you she didn't want us to sell the vineyard?"

"Yes, indeedy." She frowned, pursing her lips. "You're sure you're okay, Lucille? It isn't too much of a shock? Maybe I shouldn't have told you."

"I'm glad you did."

She looked relieved. "Well, that's a big load off my mind. I might of figured. You know, you've got Charlotte's backbone, child. And you look just like her. She was a beauty, was Charlotte. Shame your daddy didn't . . ." She stopped and glanced down at her hands.

"Didn't what?"

She started fiddling with the lime green bows, spinning them around like tiny propellers. "Oh my, how I do run on!" She looked at her watch. "Time for my next show." She sidled toward the back of the room.

"Wait!"

She turned around.

"Do you think there's a chance you might be hearing from Leland on that Ouija Board?"

She looked surprised. "Now, Lucille, this isn't 'Dial-a-Spirit' I got going here. I cannot just summon people up willy-nilly. They choose their moments. And frankly, I don't figure Lee would come to me with whatever's on his mind, anyway. The man always did keep to himself. Folks don't change their stripes, just because they're dead. Tootle-oo, honey."

She was back at her soaps before I made it to the door. Whoever was trying to pressure Leland to sell the vineyard had been remarkably discreet if Thelma hadn't got wind of it. She would have either pumped me for more information or else spilled the beans about what she knew. Even the devil himself would have had a hard time keeping a secret from her. Someone had done a good job of covering his or her tracks.

When I got home, I put the batteries in the flashlight and went upstairs to the attic. Years ago Leland had a carpenter convert half the space into a bedroom for Eli. When I was small, it seemed a remote, distant kingdom, far from the rest of the house, a lighted outpost carved out of the cobweb-filled tomblike darkness. Eli hadn't liked the room much either, though he refused to admit he believed the stories about dead ancestors' bones rotting in its far recesses. When he was older, though, the bones stopped bothering him and he realized he could get away with anything in the privacy of his secluded eyrie. I never figured out how Mom didn't smell the cigarette smoke on him, but by then I'd begun filching unlabeled wine bottles from the barrel room to drink with Kit over at Goose Creek Bridge, so I didn't begrudge Eli's tobacco habit.

Opening the attic door was like opening the door to a blast furnace. I waited until some of the pent-up heat dissipated before going in. The windows in the gabled front of the house, opaque from years of accumulated dirt and sealed shut with grime, were completely inaccessible on account of an obstacle course of dusty boxes, old suitcases, broken toys, appliances, and other things too wearying to catalog. I tried not to breathe the suffocatingly stale air. Luckily I found the fan almost at once, wedged near the door between a suitcase and a box with "baby clothes" written on the side in my mother's handwriting.

It didn't seem likely that someone as fastidious as she had been would have left either a priceless diamond necklace or her diaries up here. No heat in the winter and no air-conditioning in the summer. I shone my flashlight around the room. And mice.

I left, closing the door firmly behind me. Maybe I could get one of the barn cats to move in for a while.

The rotting plastic handle on top of the fan disintegrated as I carried it down the stairs. I watched it crash down the last few steps, the metallic sound reverberating like dissonant cymbals in the empty house. Fortunately it still worked when I plugged it in to an outlet in Leland's bedroom. It sounded like an asthmatic on a bad day. I banged the top of the case, which only changed the noise to a new, more annoying whine.

The master bedroom, furnished with antique carved mahogany pieces from my mother's family in France, was as disordered as the rest of the house and smelled of the same vague decaying abandonment that pervaded the downstairs. For months after my mother died, Leland had kept her clothes, her lipstick, her hairbrush, and even some lingerie she'd washed and left to dry in the bathroom untouched. Finally Serafina, who used to clean for us, put away the lingerie and makeup and hung up the clothes. It wasn't healthy for Mr. Lee, she'd said, living and sleeping among the dead like that.

I didn't want a living shrine for Leland, either, but I couldn't bring myself to touch his heaps of clothes or his rumpled, stale-smelling bed linens just now. Maybe I could persuade Serafina to come back and help me sort though his things, like she'd done for my mother. It didn't seem right to displace Leland's personal effects just yet. It was too soon.

Frankly, the thought of trying to restore the house as it had been when my mother was alive seemed overly daunting on top of the more urgent problem of keeping the vineyard solvent. For hundreds of years my ancestors had managed to fuse the past with the present, burnishing memories that gave the house a patina of genteel nostalgia. As I looked around the bedroom, I couldn't summon any of the regenerative magic of my family. Today as I sweltered in the late August heat, the place felt like a mausoleum.

I sat on the edge of the bed and rifled through the pile of magazines and papers on Leland's marble-topped nightstand. It looked like he had taken to transacting some of his business from bed, instead of his office. The top piece of paper was a two-month-old bill from the company that made our labels. No doubt unpaid.

I pulled the wastebasket next to me and began tossing things. He'd obviously continued investing in what Eli called his "fly-by-night" scams. With money we didn't have. The first one involved a soon-to-be-created tax haven off the coast of Central America. Some guy who called himself Prince Larry was building a pontoon island called "Heaven." Reading between the lines, it would be a no-questions-asked place to park cash that couldn't show up on a tax return or a set of corporate books. That would be in addition to the research center devoted to the study of eternal youth. First, though, the prince needed a little seed money to get going and Leland was one of the lucky ones to appear on his radar.

Another brochure advertised lunar real estate. Eli hadn't been kidding. A group of Florida developers claiming to be affiliated with NASA were selling plots of land on the moon. They were currently seeking investors in the "preconstruction phase."

I tossed the prince and the lunar condos in the trash along with a few other gems, but kept a folder called "Blue Ridge Consortium." Inside was a single sheet of paper—a letter called "Preserving Our Heritage, Protecting Our Wilderness." It was addressed "Dear Heritage Friend." It, too, was an appeal for money.

"All donations to the Blue Ridge Consortium will allow us to continue buying land for the purpose of turning it into parkland. This land will never be developed," the letter stated. "It will be your legacy to your children and your children's children. We cannot allow the natural beauty of our region to be paved over to make way for shopping malls and condominium developments. Your generous donation will continue to preserve a region of great historic significance." It was signed by Nate Midas, who was appropriately named. He owned a media conglomerate and had a stable full of prize-winning horses over in Upperville.

The minimum donation was $10,000. Depending on the size of the contribution, the organizers wanted to express their thanks. An all-expense-paid weekend at the Greenbriar. Box seats at the Kentucky Derby. Four days and three nights in Vail during ski season. A week in Tortola at a private villa. It was a safe bet we weren't members of the consortium.

I could see through the paper that there was writing on the back so I turned it over. Doodling.

Mason's name, with an elaborately embellished box around it. Two phone numbers at the bottom—outside the box—neither of which I recognized.

I reached for the bedside phone and dialed the first number. After a few rings an answering machine kicked in.

"Hi, it's Sara. I'm not here. Leave a message and have an awesome day. Here's the beep." A singsongy girlish voice like a teenager. If she'd written the message, there would be little hearts instead of dots over the i's. I hung up.

The second number rang half a dozen times then someone answered.

"Gas-o-Rama, whacanidoforyou?" He sounded Hispanic.

"Uh, nothing. Sorry, wrong number." A gas station.

Whatever Leland had been up to before he died, he hadn't left any obvious clues about who wanted to buy the vineyard. I reached in the pocket of my jeans for the little key Fitz had given me. I'd been carrying it around like a talisman, trying it out on anything in the house with a lock on it. The mantel clock in the parlor. The elaborately carved chest with its mother-of-pearl inlay containing the Bessette family silver in the dining room. Even the old bread box.

It would be just like my mother to leave whatever the key opened here in this room and Leland to never find it. I walked over to her mirrored dressing table, pulling open the drawers. They were empty. The drawer and cabinet of her matching bedside table were also empty. Under the bed was a different story. Besides the now-familiar basketball-sized dust bunnies were more newspapers and magazines. I used my cane like a hook and pulled some of them out so I could see them. Old copies of the *Wine Spectator,* the *Post,* the *Tribune,* along with the Loudoun and Fauquier regional newspapers, plus a robust collection of hard-core porn magazines with busty nudes in naughty or teasing poses on the covers.

The magazines needed to return to utter darkness where they came from—or some gutter—but when I tried to shove them back under the bed, something blocked the way. I knelt down and pulled out a shallow box that probably once held a case of beer but now was filled with papers.

More bills, these from months ago. Also a copy of the *San Jose Mercury News* from last January. The lead article on the front page explained why Leland had kept the paper. Next to the headline SOUR GRAPES: WINEMAKER JAILED was a photo of Quinn Santori and two other men. The subheading read BIOTERRORISM SCARE REVEALED FRAUD.

The jailed winemaker was not Quinn but a man named Allen Cantor, who had been the senior winemaker at Le Coq Rouge

Winery in Calistoga, California. He'd been adulterating wine—with tap water, no less—and selling it under a different label to distributors in Eastern Europe and Russia. He'd gotten away with it for several years, making millions of dollars under the table, until someone analyzed a bottle of Chardonnay at a competition. The Homeland Security people got involved, suspecting possible bioterrorism and instead they uncovered fraud and embezzlement. Assistant winemaker Paolo Santori had not been charged, but the owner, Tavis Hennessey, fired him anyway.

Cantor's personal financial records showed a man who was heavily in debt and on the verge of declaring bankruptcy. Authorities suspected he'd merely moved money to an offshore bank and were pursuing the matter. A photograph taken in the wine cellar of Le Coq Rouge showed Tavis Hennessey, Allen Cantor, and Paolo Santori in happier times with their arms around one another's shoulders. The last sentence quoted Hennessey who said he expected to close the winery.

Though he had a ponytail back then and he wasn't wearing a Hawaiian shirt, it was clearly Quinn. I called directory assistance and got the phone number for Le Coq Rouge. An automated voice announced, not surprisingly, that the number was no longer in service. There was no forwarding number.

How long had Leland known about this? Had Quinn given him the article himself, been up front about his past? Had Leland decided to hire him, anyway? Someone with this kind of dicey background wouldn't bother Leland in the least. Hell, people like that were his business partners. They probably got along like a house on fire.

It was also possible Leland hadn't known anything about this. Maybe Quinn caught a lucky break when his new employer skipped the background check in a rush to find a winemaker after Jacques's sudden departure. Obviously, though, Leland found out somehow about what happened in California.

Then what? Had Leland threatened to expose him? Dismiss him? In that case, Leland's death had been convenient, even helpful, for

Quinn. Not to mention he'd freely admitted going back to the Merlot block and cleaning up all traces of what had happened, even down
to looking for the bullet that had killed Leland. Out in the vineyard
this morning he'd tried to bully me, saying he was going to run
things his way, listening to my opinion but doing what he pleased.
With Leland out of the picture, Quinn probably figured now he had
carte blanche, with no one to stop him from doing just that.

Which meant he, too, had a motive for murder.

CHAPTER 14

The phone rang while I was still holding the newspaper.

It was Dominique and she sounded elated. "You'll never guess what Quinn has done."

"I can't imagine."

"He went by the sheriff's office this morning. They're taking down that yellow tape. Can you get over here? We're moving the buffet and the wine-tasting back to the villa. Isn't that great?"

"He's full of surprises, isn't he?" So Thelma had been right about his whereabouts. "Give me twenty minutes."

I drove to the winery after I'd changed into an off-the-shoulder white knit top and a long gauzy gypsy-like skirt. What would I say when I saw him? "So, how's the wine market in Eastern Europe? Do they drink a lot of lite wine over there? I'd like to hang around if you do any blending."

But I would keep my mouth shut and play it cool. Besides, maybe he and Leland had already worked out a deal about his past. All I'd do is get him stirred up if I confronted him without knowing the facts. Then he'd threaten to quit. Again. If he walked out on us just as harvest started, I might as well hand the keys over to Eli.

Dominique was in the courtyard, conferring with two waitresses. Unlike the house, the winery still looked like somebody cared for it. The halved oak wine barrels my mother had set out as planters along the loggia's curved perimeter were filled with lacy red geraniums and trailing variegated ivy, which overflowed the containers and spilled onto the ground. Her collection of vintage wine-making equipment placed between the planters was clean and still looked in working order. The one exception was the Civil War cannon, now strictly decorative, which reportedly had been used at the battle at Goose Creek Bridge when Confederates delayed Union forces, allowing Lee's Army to march north to Gettysburg.

Dominique turned at the sound of my footsteps and the tap of my cane on the gravel. "You're just in time."

"The place looks lovely. The flowers are gorgeous."

"You can thank Serafina. Leland let her do whatever she wanted after Jacques left. He didn't really care much."

We walked to the far edge of the courtyard where the terrain fell away, giving a clear vista of grape-laden vines aligned like soldiers in precise rows. Beyond them a sweep of interwoven low green hills and a darker ridge of conifers and deciduous trees stretched nearly to the edge of a horizon neatly bisected by the powdery blue flatline of the mountains and the milky light of a late-afternoon sky.

"Do you think Quinn will take care of things the way Jacques did?"

She shrugged with Gallic expressiveness. "Bah. Who knows? He doesn't talk much, that one."

"What do you think of him?"

She shrugged again. "I don't know. There's something about him. He seems sort of crispy all the time."

She meant *crispé*. Tense. Fidgety. She reached in the front pocket of her mini-skirt and fished out a crumpled pack of cigarettes with a book of matches stuffed inside the cellophane wrapping.

"I heard you finally told Eli you didn't want to sell the vineyard." She lit a cigarette and blew out the match, which she dropped on the ground, grinding it under her sandal. "That was some argument you had."

"You know about it, too? Was somebody recording us or something?"

"The Romeos were talking about it this morning when they came by the inn for breakfast. You and Eli didn't exactly discuss things between closed walls, from what I heard. By now they probably know all the way to Paris."

I'm sure she meant Paris, Virginia, the last town in the stretch of what was called the Mosby Heritage area. Paris got its name from Paris, France, as a tribute to George Washington's good friend, the Marquis de Lafayette, because it was his hometown.

"Which Romeos?"

"Austin, Mason, Doc Harmon . . . I forget who else was there."

"Oh Lord. I bet Eli told Erica who told Austin, who told the rest of the Romeos," I said. "They probably know about it all the way to Richmond. What else did you hear?"

She took a drag on her cigarette. "Brandi's upset, too, and spent the day in bed. Eli won't be coming by tonight. He said to tell you he probably won't be coming by the vineyard for harvest. Or any more festival events, for that matter. He's got some deadline at work."

"That's an excuse. He's playing hardball. He really wants to sell."

"*She* really wants to sell," Dominique said. "They need the money."

"I thought her family had money."

She rolled her eyes. "Her father's an actor and her mother is a dancer. Brandi says they travel all the time because of their work. I think they travel to avoid paying their bills." She looked at me significantly. "Brandi thought *Eli* had money. And of course she was impressed that he has relatives who are counts and countesses in France. Eli made it sound like she was going to be 'Madame la Marquise' when she married him. I think she wasn't too happy when she found out the family ties were so remote it's like saying we're all related to Adam and Eve."

"Do you think she loves him?"

She chose her words carefully through a cloud of exhaled smoke. "I think she likes the way he treats her. Like she is some kind of goddess."

"He carries it a bit far, don't you think?"

She stared at the lighted end of her cigarette. "Well, that depends. He didn't used to act like this before Gregory moved back to Atoka."

"What do you mean?"

"You of all people," she said, "ought to know exactly what I mean."

I looked across at the mountains, already growing paler in the silky light. "She said nothing happened that night."

"Well, what *would* she say? That she seduced him and cheated on Eli? Especially after Gregory dropped her like a dead balloon."

"So what's going on now?"

She dropped her cigarette and ground the butt under her foot. "I heard a rumor about the two of you the other night. Is it true?"

"He made a pass at me. I lost my head. It was stupid," I said. "Besides, there's Mia. Do you think there's something new going on between Greg and Brandi?"

"I think he makes Brandi nervous now that he's back here," she said, bending down and picking up the cigarette butt. "If those old rumors are true and I were Brandi, I'd want the rug swept under the carpet, too. Wouldn't you?"

"I suppose I would."

She glanced at her watch. "We'd better get moving. Be an angel. Can you go down to the barrel room and make sure there are enough wineglasses? I asked one of the men to set them out, but I'm not sure he understood where he was supposed to put them. Quinn said he'd be tasting Chardonnay and Merlot in the barrel room and in the villa it will be the new Cab and Sauvignon Blanc."

I hadn't been in the barrel room since I'd returned home. I expected the sudden drop in temperature—nearly forty degrees colder than it was in the courtyard—but I still shivered. It was an enormous space, the length of an Olympic-sized swimming pool, with thirty foot ceilings, fieldstone walls, and four deep interconnected bays where oak barrels were kept in cool darkness. It smelled of the familiar tangy odor of fermentation, an acrid scent like vinegar but infinitely more potent and complex.

Near where I stood by the roll-up hangar door were pallets stacked with cases of wine being held back until they had been in bottles long enough. The wine that was ready to be sold was on another section of pallets. Along the right wall were the numbered stainless-steel fermenting tanks, some with wax-crayon writing on the front panel indicating the variety and how many hundred gallons were in the tank, but most with the hatch door popped open ready for harvest. In the middle of the room and along the other long wall were rows of oak barrels on metal stands. Quinn's glassed-in lab was at the back of the room.

I didn't see him when I walked in, but I heard voices. He must have heard the metal door as it shut because a moment later he stepped out from behind a row of barrels.

"Hi. Looking for something?" Somewhere, surely, there was a world shortage of Hawaiian shirts because it seemed most of them hung in his closet. This one was gray with pink flamingoes.

I smiled brightly. "Yes, actually I am. The wineglasses for tonight's tasting. Dominique asked me to make sure they were set out where they're supposed to be."

He must have wondered what was going on with the toothpaste-ad smile because he looked puzzled, then turned and spoke to someone obscured by the wine casks. I didn't catch what he said but a willowy blonde stepped out from behind the barrels. "Hello, Lucie. I was just starting to do that. Long time no see."

"Hello, Angela."

Angela Stetson looked nothing like she had in high school. Like Kit, she'd switched hair color from brunette to blonde. Unlike Kit, she didn't look as though she'd dumped a bottle of peroxide on her head. Instead her long, straight hair, which she wore in a high ponytail, was honey-colored and sunstreaked and it flattered her immensely. Her close-fitting cream-colored halter dress showed off tanned, well-defined arms; her legs, revealed through an off-center slit in the dress, were long and lithe.

Quinn was watching me watching her. "You two know each other?"

Angela nodded. "We went to high school together."

"Really?" He was still looking at me. "That's great because Angie's agreed to help out for harvest this year when she's not at her other job. We're going to need all the help we can get."

"Oh," I said. "Wow."

"I've got to take care of something over at the villa. You guys can handle this."

"Sure," Angela said, sounding perky.

He laid a hand on her back and looked into her eyes. "Thanks, baby. I'll be back."

After he left, Angela studied her manicure. I walked over to a long table covered with a white tablecloth. Hector's man had neatly stacked the boxes of glasses next to the table, but hadn't set any of them out.

"Well," Angela said, "long time no see, hunh, Lucie?"

"I've been away."

"I know. France."

"Maybe we could get started with the glasses?"

"You got a problem with me being here or something?"

"No." I set a box on the table. "I have a lot on my mind, that's all. Thanks for helping."

Her eyes, which were expertly made up with smoky blue eyeshadow and blue eyeliner, narrowed. Before she'd looked innocent. Suddenly she looked tough. "I'm only doing this for Quinn."

"How did you meet him?" I asked, pulling glasses out of the box.

"He showed up at Mom's Place one night." She sounded tough, too. "We've been seeing each other for a few months."

"Weren't you and Billy King . . . I mean, I thought you . . ."

"Eloped? Yeah, we did. I got tired of being his punching bag when he came home drunk." She placed glasses on the table with aggressive precision. "When Raven—that's my kid—was born, I threw him out. Then I needed a job so Vinnie hired me. It beats working checkout at Safeway for eight bucks an hour getting varicose veins."

"Vinnie?"

"Carbone. From high school, remember? He owns the place."

I did. A nerdy, overweight guy with acne and greasy hair. "The guy who set fire to the chemistry lab with his model rocket fuel?"

"I forgot about that. Good ole Vin."

"So what's it like working there?"

She tossed her head and her ponytail swung jauntily. "Come around and see for yourself."

I shoved an empty box under the table harder than I needed to. It bounced against a table leg and hit my shin. "I think we're about done."

She continued as though I hadn't said anything. "You'd be surprised who you'd run into, you know?" She gestured at my cane. "Including the asshole who did this to you."

"Pardon?"

"You heard me." She picked up a wineglass and ran a thumb along the stem. "He comes by a lot before he goes to work. He's got a thing for Sienna. He's always trying to pay her for a private dance."

"Who's Sienna?"

"A friend of your sister's." She leaned over to get her purse. I could see a generous amount of cleavage down the front of her dress. "The guy's bad news. Mia ought to stay away from him. He's just using her like he uses everyone else. See you around, Lucie."

As she passed by, I smelled her perfume. I didn't recognize it though I did detect something floral mingled with the earthier scents of incense and musk. It was as provocative as everything else about her. It didn't take a genius to figure out what attracted Quinn.

After she was gone I straightened a row of glasses that didn't need straightening, then reached for my cane. Men paid to see Angela Stetson dance with no clothes on. Why did that bother me? I was halfway back to the villa when I finally admitted to myself that I knew perfectly well why.

For the rest of my life, I would try to hide my body—at least, my bad leg—because I was ashamed and embarrassed to let anyone see it.

I was jealous.

• • •

Joe Dawson, dressed in khaki shorts, docksiders, and a navy polo shirt, stood by the mosaic-tiled bar opening bottles of Cabernet Sauvignon. At the far end of the room and on the terrace Dominique's staff set up the pre-theater buffet dinner. "Hey, sweetheart. You working here selling or helping out in the barrel room with the tasting?"

"Probably the barrel room." I said as he kissed me on the cheek. "What's left to do?"

"Get out the dump buckets and the bread baskets. Dominique left a couple of baguettes that need cutting up."

I got the small buckets we used for guests who wanted to pour out the remnants of a wine they either didn't want to finish or didn't care for and set them on the bar. The multicolored baskets made for us by an artisan in North Carolina were under the counter.

"I heard you talked to Eli," Joe said.

I set one of the baguettes on a bread board and began slicing it. "I was going to hire a Stearman from the Flying Circus down in Bealeton to pull one of those signs behind it in case anyone missed the details of what we said, but I guess I don't need to."

He grinned, showing the boyish dimples, but his eyes were grave. "You know how word gets around."

"Who told you?"

"Seth Hannah. At the town council meeting this afternoon." He set down the corkscrew and picked up a sponge, wiping an imaginary spill on the counter. "I thought you might appreciate a little head's up, Lucie. Seth's thinking about calling your loan. You're into him for a lot of money. Over one hundred and fifty thousand dollars. Leland put up the house as collateral."

The knife slipped. I missed the baguette, nicking the knuckle of my index finger instead. "Damnit!"

A red stain spread across the white bread. "Give me that." He threw the sponge in the sink and took the knife from me. "The napkins are under the bar. You're getting blood all over the place."

I knotted a paper napkin around my finger and watched the blood seep through almost immediately. "I will pay him back. Completely. All I need is a little more time . . . he owes me that, at least. For Leland's sake."

Joe looked at me the way you look at a child when you finally have to explain the truth about Santa Claus. "Naw, sweetheart, that's not gonna work anymore. In his lifetime Leland cadged money from just about every member of the Romeos and never paid most of 'em back. I swear to God there were some folks so mad at him they wouldn't spit if he was on fire after he stiffed them. Seth held out longer than most, kept giving him extensions. Now he wants his money. All of it. The bank's money, I mean."

"You think we should sell the place, don't you?" I said bitterly. "Just like Eli."

"I'm wondering what choice you have, under the circumstances."

"There are other things I can sell first. Like some of the furniture. I already sold a few things to Mac Macdonald."

"That's like owning a car but selling the engine," he said. "Though I suppose if you're bound and determined, you could sell the Jefferson letter. It won't fetch much because it's torn where it's been folded and the contents are pretty tame. You'd get something, though. I can help you find a buyer, if you want."

"What Jefferson letter?"

He looked surprised. "The one Thomas Jefferson wrote to the Countess de Tessé. That relative of your mother's. He was helping her acquire American plants for her house near Versailles. The letter asked whether she received a shipment he'd sent. Nothing to set the world on fire, but still. Didn't you know about this?"

"Nope. Not a word. What makes you so sure Leland didn't sell the letter already?"

"It's in his study in one of those hollow books where you hide things. *Crime and Punishment*. I saw it the other day when I borrowed a couple of books," he said. "Besides, Leland thought anything that belonged to Jefferson was sacred. No offense, but he would have sold one of his kids before he sold anything Jefferson owned."

"Family didn't mean much to Leland." I removed the napkin and examined my finger intently. "I guess no one knew that better than his children." I looked up at him. "But, yes, I'd love some help finding a buyer. Maybe someone in that Blue Ridge Consortium."

"Uh." His eyes crinkled and he looked puzzled. For the first time I noticed deep marionette lines on either side of his mouth that belied the boyish features. "Why do you mention them?"

I shrugged and turned on the faucet under the bar, running my finger under cold water. "I found a letter from Nate Midas with Leland's papers. He was asking for money. I don't know why Leland got one of those solicitations, under the circumstances. But a ten-thousand-dollar donation? I guess you need real money to be part of that group. If they're interested in preserving historic sites, maybe one of them would be interested in a historic letter."

He lined up corks from the bottles he'd opened like a kid playing with soldiers. "I was thinking more of contacting the folks at Monticello. Or Sotheby's." He swiped at all of the corks with the side of his fist dumping them into the palm of his other hand. "I'd better clean this up and see what Dominique needs. And you'd better get over to the barrel room."

"Sure."

He walked through the arched doorway that led to the wine library and the offices. I left for the barrel room in the dreamlike twilight. It was too early for the fireflies but the crickets were singing in full voice. Somewhere beyond the courtyard two bullfrogs called back and forth to each other.

Had Joe clammed up when I mentioned the Blue Ridge Consortium or was I imagining it? If the group bought land to turn it into parkland—preserving the wild and historic places in the region—was it possible the person who approached Leland about selling was representing the consortium? Fitz said whoever it was had offered a lowball price and Leland refused to sell. Had the buyer been one of the people Leland stiffed for money?

Maybe this was about revenge.

During the past two years when I'd worked at the Perfume Museum in Grasse, I'd honed my sense of smell, learning to distinguish a number of essences without knowing beforehand what they were, a useful talent in wine making as well. Perfume has three notes—top, middle, and bass—which refer to their volatility, or the speed with which they diffuse into the air. When a bottle of perfume is opened, the first fleeting scents are the top or headnotes, which disappear almost instantly. Next are the middle notes, which are the heart of a perfume, until finally what lingers are the forceful bass notes. My life seemed as layered and complex as the most exotic scent right now.

The bass note, or what stayed with me, was the need to hang on to the vineyard, whatever it took to do it. The middle notes, or the heart notes, were pretty clear, too. I had to find out what really happened to Leland—and Fitz. What eluded me were the top notes, the headnotes. There were too many of them and they were too ephemeral—the unknown person who wanted to buy the vineyard and whether Eli was involved in that, Fitz's murder, Dominique's money woes, and now the news that Quinn might have been involved in embezzlement and fraud before he came to us.

What I needed to do, before I could understand the headnotes, was to stay with the heart. I needed to probe it and understand its essence, which somehow seemed to have its origin in Leland's death.

CHAPTER 15

When I arrived in the barrel room, Quinn was already talking to a small group of people, including a heavyset woman wearing enough bracelets to rival the percussion section of a small orchestra and a broad-brimmed hat that threw everyone around her into shadow. She was visiting from England.

"No, ma'am," he was saying. "In the United States we name our wines by varietal, not region. It's different than Europe. A wine in this country can be labeled with a particular varietal designation—like Cabernet Sauvignon or Pinot Noir, for example—as long as seventy-five percent of the wine is made from that grape."

"Give me a good Bordeaux any day," she said. "I'm a bit of a purist."

"Actually," Quinn said politely, "most of the great Bordeaux are blends of more than one kind of grape. It gives the wines more structure and complexity."

"You don't say."

The barrel room, dramatically illuminated by electrified candles in wrought iron wall sconces and recessed can lights glittering like tiny stars, was becoming more crowded. Someone had placed the hurricane lamps we'd used at the outdoor dinner on the tables where Angela and I had arranged the wineglasses. The flickering light from the real candlelight made the huge room seem warmer and more intimate. I preferred it like this, moody and romantic, rather than the heavy industrial lighting we needed for working purposes.

Quinn introduced me as one of the owners but it was clear he was in charge. He stood behind a large old barrel on which my mother had stenciled the vineyard's twining vine logo and used the top as a table for his notes and bottles of wine as everyone gathered around him. On the wall behind him hung another one of her cross-stitched prints, our logo and a quote from Plato—"No thing more excellent nor more valuable than wine was ever granted mankind by God."

I stared at the print and thought of her as Quinn began talking, raising his voice so he could be heard over the hum of the fans and the gentle gurgling of the glycol-and-water solution circulating in-side the refrigeration jackets on the stainless-steel containers. For someone who'd only been here a few months, he'd done his home-work about our history.

"We'll start with our newest Chardonnay," he said, moving to the tables behind and filling rows of glasses about a quarter full. "We just released it, so congratulations, everyone. You're the first to try it. It's been aged in French oak for about seven months, then bottle-aged for another year. My predecessor, Jacques Gilbert, used French-oak barrels exclusively, which are sweeter than American oak. We're going to be mixing things up from now on and this year's harvest will be aged in barrels purchased from a Missouri cooper. Come back in two years and see if you can tell the difference."

I leaned over and said in his ear, "I didn't know that."

"That French oak is sweeter than American oak?"

"That you were switching to American oak."

He smiled for the benefit of the crowd and murmured to me, "You do now. Let's get these glasses filled, shall we?" He raised his voice and added, "We're also planning to keep some Chardonnay exclusively in stainless steel. We'll get a brighter fruit that way."

Another news flash. Jacques would have had a coronary.

I helped him pour wine in silence, then we passed glasses through the crowd. "We always start tastings with the lightest wines," he said. "This particular Chardonnay comes from some of our oldest vines. The older the vine the more complex the wine." He raised his glass. "To your health, everyone."

There was a murmured response and quiet clinking of glasses. Quinn turned to me. "A good harvest."

"A very good harvest."

We drank in silence. The wine reminded me of Jacques. Elegant and smoky like the French oak he loved. Okay, some sweetness. What would Quinn's American-oaked wine taste like? Big and brassy? Definitely no sweetness.

"So how old are the vines this wine comes from?" the English woman asked.

Quinn raised an eyebrow at me. "Uh, probably . . . eighteen to twenty years old. Or thereabouts."

I nodded. "Probably."

He leaned over. "I asked you for that information the other day. And where you bought the root stock."

"You'll get it," I said. "As for information, in the future I wouldn't mind getting briefed about your plans in private before everyone else in the world hears about them."

"We have a deal," he said in a low voice. "My running the place includes not questioning my every decision—or when I reveal it."

I set my glass down a bit sharply on the barrel. "What's next?"

"Merlot. We're doing a vertical tasting."

As opposed to a horizontal tasting, which features the same wines from a region or varietal—such as Virginia Cabernet Sauvignons from the same year—a vertical tasting featured the same wine from the same winery, but grown in consecutive years. It was an ideal way to educate people because it became immediately apparent how the weather affected the way the same vines could produce such different wines from one year to the next.

Quinn was good at leading the group through our last five Merlots, four in bottles that Jacques had blended with a small amount of Cabernet Sauvignon. The fifth and most recent harvest was still in barrels, where we always kept it for at least twenty months.

"This wine will probably be in barrels for a total of sixteen, maybe eighteen months," Quinn was saying. "I'll siphon some from one of the barrels with this hose we call a 'wine thief' and you can see how it's developing."

I chewed my lip and watched him work. Was he putting his own stamp so definitively on our wines, changing absolutely everything that Jacques had done, because of his ego? Or because it was a smart decision? He was moving a lot more aggressively than I'd realized.

After the last person had left, either to buy wine at the villa or head over to the performance at the Ruins, it was just the two of us cleaning up.

Finally he said, "I've been around enough women in my life to recognize the silent treatment when I'm getting it. You're mad because I'm not coloring inside the lines the way you think I ought to be. I told you I'm not going to be put on a leash and you agreed."

"I didn't think that meant changing absolutely everything we ever did." I set an empty wineglass box on one of the tables and glared at him. "People buy our wines because of our reputation. Because of the reputation Jacques established for us. What do you think you're doing, anyway?"

"Me? What about you? Your grip on this place is getting more tenuous every day, from what I hear. You sold your soul to the company store, Lucie. Or Leland did. Now you have to pay back what you owe and you can't."

"Do not underestimate me," I said. "I can and I will."

"That remains to be seen," he snapped. "I think we're done here." He strode around the room and began turning off banks of lights.

"What are you doing?"

"Closing up. Then, if it's any of your business, I'm going to watch Angie. She's doing something new for her last show. I'd like to see her."

How many different ways were there to take off your clothes? Somehow I figured Vinnie ran a cut-rate operation that didn't include extras like costumes and accessories. "I'll finish here," I said. "You can go."

"I can handle it." He walked over and stood in front of me, staring at me with those dark, intimidating eyes I'd noticed the first time I saw him—when he told me Fitz was dead.

I said sharply, "You don't need to be so defensive. I'd like some time alone here. Please leave."

"Suit yourself." He let the door bang shut, on purpose, when he left.

Maybe I was mistaken about him. I had thought he was extremely ambitious, just like me, and that we could be a good team professionally, even if personally we were about as compatible as bulls and china shops. But maybe "extreme ambition" was a polite way of papering over ruthlessness and greed.

The article in the *Mercury News* said the police never found any of the money Allen Cantor had embezzled from Le Coq Rouge and that he'd probably parked it in some offshore account. What if he'd paid off his assistant winemaker as well, and bought his silence? The day Quinn took me out in the fields he said he might like to buy land in Virginia, own his own vineyard someday.

Maybe he already had the money to do it. He obviously knew how dire our financial situation was. Maybe he'd been the one to make that fire sale offer and that's why no one knew about it.

Because it had been an inside bid.

I drove too fast on the short trip back to the house, pushing the Volvo harder than it deserved. It responded like the workhorse it had always been, immune to my irritable mood. As soon as I was in the house I went straight to Leland's office and found the copy of *Crime and Punishment* on his bookshelf. The Jefferson letter was, as Joe warned, not in good condition. I put it back on the shelf as the small clock on the fireplace mantel struck ten. On my way out of the room I stopped in front of my mother's painting of Hugh Montgomery's grave.

There was something about it that eluded me. The clue to the necklace's hiding place was either in the painting, or possibly at the cemetery itself. It wasn't a random choice that she'd left the key and written the lines from *Richard II* in that note card. Somewhere there was a locked chest and somehow—if I believed what she'd written—it was tied up in her life and honor.

It was late, but I was in no mood to sleep. Instead I went to Leland's once well-stocked wine cellar, now nearly empty. I picked out one of the few remaining bottles, a Pomerol, and brought it outside to the veranda. While it breathed, I lit every candle and torch until it looked like the entire place was bathed in liquid gold.

Then I switched on the radio. WLEE. He was playing Coltrane. It matched my mood and perfectly plumbed the depths of my solitude and mined the ache in my heart. Why had I let him kiss me again? What was it that made me seek out the good-looking untamable bad boys like Greg and Philippe? Both were as seductive and dangerous as heroin and probably more addictive. Fatal charm. Devastating looks. James Dean bad-boy charisma. Any idiot knew how it was going to end. I always lost my heart to someone who didn't have one.

I always ended up alone.

Fortunately no one was around when I woke up the next morning, cradling yet another empty wineglass in my lap, still dressed from the night before. The farm report was on the radio. Someone was talking about the drought and the toll it was taking on livestock all over the state. We were in for some relief though, the announcer said. After one hundred and thirty-three dry days, there was rain on the way.

Not today, though. I walked to the edge of the veranda and looked out at the horizon. The sun was already punishing, a sharp-edged disk in a white-hot sky. The outline of the Blue Ridge was as soft and faint as a whisper.

I ate breakfast, showered, and changed into a black tank top and jeans. Then I did something I'd been avoiding ever since I came home. I went to my mother's study. The tight feeling in the back of my throat from the early days after her death was no longer there when I opened the door, but I did stand in the doorway for a while before I walked into the room. It had the museumlike quality of a shrine, preserved almost exactly as she'd kept it. The decaying odors that pervaded the rest of the house seemed not to have seeped into this space. Instead the chemical smells of paint and varnish hung in the air.

I opened the windows to air out the room. Mia must have been using it as her studio. A sheet draped over my mother's easel hid the outlines of a large canvas and on a table next to it were brushes, paints, and a much-used artist's palette, where my mother always kept them. I lifted the sheet. A partially finished painting of four women drinking wine at an outdoor café. There was a lightness that was almost ethereal about the scene—the colors, the expressions on the faces, the filtered sunlight and soft shadows on hair and clothing. Had I not known better, it could have been my mother's artwork—but it was my sister's.

I lowered the sheet and walked over to an antique trestle table where the phonograph sat. It looked like Mia had been listening to Mom's old vinyl records. An early Jacques Brel—*"Ballades & Mots d'Amour"*—was still on the turntable. The album jacket lay next to it. I switched on the machine and the needle dropped into place.

"Ne Me Quitte Pas." One of his signature songs. "If You Go Away" it was called in English. It had been a huge hit here, too. Everyone had covered it, from Frank Sinatra to Dusty Springfield, but no one sang it like the man who wrote it. I listened to that cigarette-raspy voice lamenting heartache and loneliness. Then I went over to the bookcase and got my mother's copy of *The Complete Works of Shakespeare.*

She had bookmarked the page from *Richard II* with a pressed red rose. The edge of a petal crumbled when I touched it. I closed the book. Brel's voice soared and he sang about sailing on the sun and riding on the rain. If I had been hoping for a clue to the location of the "jewel in a ten-times-barr'd-up chest," I found none.

The shelf below held her gardening journals, a neat row of green leather-bound volumes with gilt-edged pages and the title stamped in gold on the spine. I pulled out the first one and opened it.

She'd written in French and, as I expected, there were detailed lists of everything she had planted. Even better, the book was filled with sketches, ideas for gardens she'd tried and discarded, as well as the final outcome. What I did not expect was that she also had written about her life, her marriage, her children. How odd that neither Fitz—nor I—had guessed that she would have chosen to weave together the history of her family and her gardens—her two passions—and that these were the diaries we'd been searching for.

If I destroyed them as he'd wanted I'd lose any chance of recreating her plans. Who would care if I kept the books now? The meticulous accounting of plants, seeds, fertilizer, even the weather, probably wouldn't interest Eli or Mia. I'd been the only one who liked helping in the garden. Eli used to pretend not to know the difference between a plant and a weed and Mia somehow successfully made a case for being allergic to dirt.

I brought them all over to her desk and stacked them in a pile. Then I went through them in order. Each volume spanned two years and on the back flap my mother had listed important events and a page number, like an index. I read about people and places I had long forgotten. A picture may be worth a thousand words, but a thousand words—especially when infused with emotion and warmth and the richness of well-observed detail—can bring back powerful memories.

What was surprising was that she'd stopped writing for one two-year cycle—or else that volume was missing. I did some figuring, trying to recall what happened twenty years ago.

From what she'd written in the previous volume it was obvious these were the years when the first vines had been planted, when Jacques and Hector had come to work for us. I had been eight years old, Eli was ten, and Mia wasn't on the scene yet—though my mother would have been pregnant with her. It had been a busy, productive period. Odd that she would not have wanted to document it, unless the two births—Mia's and the vineyard—kept her too busy to write.

Brel was singing, *"Je Ne Sais Pas"*—"I Don't Know." It sounded jazzy and upbeat despite the words, another forlorn French song about lost love, except for the refrain.

I know I love you still.

If my mother and Fitz had an affair as I long suspected, had anything come of it? A daughter? I thought about that joyous picture I'd found in Fitz's bedroom of him, my mother, and Mia. Even if Fitz were Mia's biological father, I knew I would love my mother still. Would Mia?

Everyone involved was dead, except my sister. If it were true, what would this do to her?

Maybe there was no necklace belonging to Marie Antoinette in whatever Fitz's key unlocked. Maybe it was, as Shakespeare wrote, the key to my mother's honor and her life. Maybe she'd hidden the missing diary to protect her daughter—and Fitz. That's why he wanted the diaries burned. He guessed the truth . . . or he knew it.

I returned the books to the shelf and switched off the record player, slipping the record into the dust jacket. Mia's sketchbook, which lay underneath, was open to a rough sketch of a design for the festival poster.

Her cheerful ideas, including the one we'd used with our twining vine logo and the dancing instruments, were all there. I smiled as I turned the pages. A few blank pages, then more drawings, pencil sketches, quite different from her other work. I stopped smiling. She hadn't been listening to Brel when she drew these. More like Wagner or Shostakovich. They were dark and macabre, the work of a tormented soul. Skeleton heads piled on top of each other in a room filled with wine casks. Another called *Requiem* of a face like Munch's *Scream* standing over rows of coffins at the cemetery. The giant sycamore tree at the fork in the road, distorted so it looked like a crucifix dripping in blood. On the last page a robed figure with a hidden face held a sword at the throat of a woman kneeling before him. Her hair was filled with snakes, like Medusa, and her hands were clasped in prayer.

Her face was mine.

CHAPTER 16

I slammed the book shut and flung it across the room.

The image was so lifelike, so true, that I wondered if she'd used a photo or if she'd been able to draw my face that perfectly from memory. The sketchbook had landed behind my mother's desk. I retrieved it and opened it again to that last drawing.

If it weren't so hideous—and it weren't me—I could admire it for her talent as an artist.

Now what? Ask her about it? Pretend I hadn't seen it? Were there more sketchbooks, more tortured drawings? Whose faces had she drawn in those? Fitz's? Leland's? More drawings of death and killing?

I left the book where I found it, then got the keys to the Volvo. I didn't know where I was going until I stopped at the cemetery. My old refuge.

For a long time after my mother died, I used to talk to her headstone, telling her about my day, my problems, my life. Since my accident, we hadn't spoken much.

Today I had questions for both her and Leland. Was Fitz Mia's father? If he was, had Leland known about it? It was an open secret that he had a roving eye, so by then did he care if she'd strayed? Maybe he'd sown a few oats of his own and I had other half brothers and half sisters out there somewhere who didn't know about me, either.

By the time my mother died, the state of my parents' marriage—if the truth must be told—was like the Easter eggs we used to make as kids where we'd first prick pinholes in both ends and blow the raw contents into a bowl. We'd paint the shells with my mother's paints or dye them pastel colors, then decorate them. They were always beautiful on the outside like small jewels, but so fragile—because they were hollow.

I left my parents' graves and went to sit by Hugh Montgomery's sun-warmed headstone. Hugh was buried on the crest of a hill at the highest part of the cemetery from where there was a magnificent panoramic view of the Blue Ridge. I watched stray clouds make harlequin patterns of sun and shadow on the mountains, then closed my eyes.

It had been hard enough maintaining the flimsy bonds that held Eli, Mia, and me together these last few years. Like the tilt-a-whirl ride at an amusement park, we stayed pinned in place as we spun around faster and faster, as long as there was some inner pull that kept us from flying off in different directions. Now that both my parents were dead, the inner pull—the centripetal force—was the vineyard.

I didn't hear the gate open and close, but I felt a presence in front of me that suddenly blocked the light against my eyelids. I opened them, shielding my eyes.

"Can I join you?" Greg sat down next to me.

"You just did."

"I was on my way over to the Ruins," he said. "I'm emceeing that jazz concert you're having tomorrow night. I thought I'd check out the sound system." He broke off a few stems of wild chicory from a clump next to us and handed me the pale blue flowers. "Peace offering? You're mad about the other night, aren't you?"

Wild chicory only opens briefly, in the morning. I loved the flowers, but it was a hit and run affair since they were gone almost as soon as they bloomed. Just like him.

"Those flowers belong to my Great-Great-Great-Uncle Hugh. Family lore has it that they were his favorite because they were exactly the color of his wife's eyes."

He set the flowers down near where he'd picked them and leaned against the gravestone. Our arms were touching. I shifted so they weren't. "I'm sorry if I upset you the other night. I don't know what came over me."

"Nothing came over you. It never does."

"Look, Lucie, I know this is awkward because of Mia. I swear to God, she reminded me so much of you."

Not if he'd seen that drawing, she wouldn't. Still, he was a cad playing us off against each other. "How could you do this to her? And me? What do you want, anyway?"

He flushed underneath his sun-god tan. "I know what I did after you got hurt was unforgivable. But give me another chance. I promise it will be different this time."

After I got hurt. That was one way of putting it. "You didn't answer my question."

"Come on, honey. Your sister's the one who came on to me. What was I supposed to do? I mean, look at her. She's gorgeous."

He'd said those exact words to me once before. The night of the accident, when he was driving too fast in the rain down Atoka Road. We'd been talking—no, arguing—about Brandi when he took that last corner and lost control of the car.

"Yeah," I said, bitterly. "She is. Don't worry, I remember how it goes. You can't help yourself."

"What are you talking about?" His pupils were two pinpricks in eyes the color of cold sapphires.

"Who's Sienna? Is she the new one?"

"What?" He looked stunned, then he laughed. "Oh my God. You think . . . it's not what you're thinking, Lucie." He seemed to relax visibly. "You must be talking about Rusty's daughter. Her name is Sara Rust. She's the daughter of my old man's business partner at the garage." He picked up a stone that was lying on the ground near the headstone. He tossed it in the air and caught it. "How'd you hear about the 'Sienna' name-thing?"

Greg's father, Jimmy Knight, and John "Rusty" Rust had owned Knight & Rust Auto Body in Aldie. After Jimmy died of lung cancer Rusty sold the business to an auto repair chain, then retired. Greg almost never talked about his family. I always thought it was because he was vaguely ashamed that his father came home at night with dirt under his fingernails and grease on his clothes.

"From Angela Stetson. She works with her at Vinnie Carbone's club," I said.

"I never understood how a guy who looked like a ferret in high school ended up getting himself a gig like that. The guy used to be a twerp. No girl would date him unless they got paid to."

"The story I heard is that you're at the twerp's place all the time."

"Look," he said. "Sara is like a kid sister to me. She got herself in a bit of a jam so I gave her some money." He didn't look at me while he spoke, just kept concentrating on tossing and catching that rock.

"I don't . . ." I said, then stopped. The girlish—almost child-ish—voice on the answering machine. "Hi, it's Sara! I'm not here. Leave a message and have an awesome day. Here's the beep."

It had to be the same girl. Sara Rust—Sienna—was the one whose phone number I'd found in Leland's folder. Though why he would be interested in a young girl who was an exotic dancer at Mom's Place was a mystery. The obvious reasons didn't add up. He didn't like them that young.

"You don't what?" Greg asked.

"I don't believe anything you say anymore. I want you to leave."

"Say you forgive me."

"No."

"Say it." He reached over and pulled me to him, just like the other night. "You know you want to," he murmured, pulling the clip out of my hair and easing me down so I was lying on my back. He pulled away the straps of my tank top and my bra as his mouth came down on mine then traveled down to the space between my breasts.

He shifted and moved on top of me, sliding his hand down to the top button of my jeans. I put my hand on his and pushed it away.

"No," I said. "I can't do this."

He sounded drowsily surprised. "Come on, Lucie. Just like old times." He grabbed my hand and pinned it behind my head. "You know you want to."

"Get off me," I said. He pulled back so he was straddling me now, sitting on his haunches. He caught my other hand and held them together. I wriggled against him and he tightened his grip. "What are you doing?"

"Having fun."

"Get off me, Greg. I mean it. You're hurting me."

Unexpectedly he let go of my hands and stood up. "Have it your way."

I sat up and fixed my bra and tank top without looking at him. Then I found my hair clip and twisted my hair back into a knot. He stood there, watching. I half-expected him to extend a hand and help me up but he did nothing. I leaned on my cane and pulled myself up so I was facing him.

"Don't ever do that again," I said. "It was a mistake."

"It was no mistake." He pulled me roughly to him and kissed me, a hard fierce kiss that was brutal, not tender. "We'll finish this another time."

He walked down the hill to the steal-me red Mustang convertible Mia had driven the other night. He'd left the top down on a perfect summer day. I watched as he angrily sped off, never turning his head to glance my way as his car churned up a cloud of boiling dust.

I put the back of my hand to my mouth. My lips felt bruised, but at least they weren't bloody. We'd done that before.

There was something different about this time. The passion I remembered from our marathon sessions at the Ruins two years ago was gone. Instead it seemed efficient and almost mechanical, like he was taking care of business.

Before I left I apologized to Hugh for cavorting on his tombstone. Then I said good-bye to Leland and my mother.

Why did all the secrets, all my unanswered questions, keep bringing me back to this cemetery? I stared at Hugh's grave for a long time.

The answer, I was sure, lay somehow with him.

CHAPTER 17

I heard piano music through the open windows as I pulled up in front of the house. Grieg's Piano Concerto in A Minor. That would be Eli playing my great-grandmother's concert grand Bösendorfer in the sunroom. If he was playing Grieg, he was upset.

Though I tried to close the front door quietly the music stopped at once and he appeared in the parlor doorway, dressed in pressed white shorts and a cerise-colored Lacoste shirt, carrying his Filofax. "I've been waiting for you." He glanced at his watch. "I've been here for thirty-nine minutes."

"I was out."

"We need to talk." He crossed the foyer and stood in front of me. "I'm sure, now that you've had time to think, you'll agree it's a good idea . . . what's that stuff on your arm?" He ran a finger from my left shoulder down to somewhere near my elbow. "It's *dirt.*"

"So?"

"Where were you that you're covered with dirt?" He walked over to the demilune table and set down the Filofax, pulling a snow-white handkerchief out of the pocket of his shorts. Carefully he wiped his hand.

"I am not covered with dirt. I was at the cemetery and I sat down for a while."

"What were you doing at the cemetery?"

"Thinking." I twisted my arm so I could see what he was talking about and rubbed at the brown smudge. "What were you saying?"

"For the last time, I'm *giving* you the house in France. A gift. But the quid pro quo is that we have to sell the vineyard and this place."

"Eli, we've already discussed this. No."

"I went to see Seth Hannah." He folded his arms and glared at me. "Seth Hannah."

I knew where this conversation was going so I just nodded.

"We're behind on our loan payments," he said. "Leland's loan payments. Seth told me he let you off the hook for this month because he thought he was going to get the whole caboodle repaid when we sold. Now he's upset because you told him we were selling and we're not."

"I never said we were selling."

"You mean you told him we weren't?"

"I really didn't say one way or the other," I replied. "I guess he assumed we were."

"Damnit, Lucie, he thinks you lied to him!" he shouted. "He's talking about calling the loan. He wants the money we owe him. He wants it now!"

"Who said he isn't going to get his money? We'll repay him."

"Oh, sure. Maybe we could rob a bank or something. Some other bank besides his, that is. You are out of your mind." The phone rang and he strode across the room and grabbed the receiver. "Hello? Yeah, sure. She's right here." He held it out to me like it was contaminated. "It's for you."

"Who is it?" He rolled his eyes and said nothing. I took the phone. "Hello?"

"What's up with Mr. Congeniality?" Kit said. "I think I just got frostbite."

"Fine, thank you," I said. "How did those tests go with your mother?"

"Can't talk while he's there? Figures. How about meeting me later at the Goose Creek Bridge? Nine o'clock. You can fill me in."

"Sounds good."

"I've got a bottle of something new I can bring. Have you ever tried Mexican wine?"

"Uh, no. Why don't you let me take care of that?"

"Sure. I'll save it for another time, then. See you." She hung up.

"Take care of what?" Eli asked. "If you were talking about her mother, then I'm Frank Lloyd Wright. You're seeing her, aren't you?" He rocked back and forth on his heels.

"She's a friend."

"She's a *reporter*. Do you think she has to spend even a nanosecond figuring out whether her job or your friendship comes first? For the chance to get a story on the front page of the *Washington Tribune* that woman would do anything. All that crap she hands out about being honest in her reporting. You know what this is about. It's *personal*. She's trying to get back at me because I broke up with her and she's using you to do it."

"Who gives you advice inside that head of yours besides the Easter Bunny and Tinkerbell? You think she still carries a torch for you? Get over it, Eli."

He shook his head. "You are so naïve. And you are meeting her again. Aren't you?"

"So what?"

"Let me guess." He smirked. "An alumni reunion of the Goose Creek Bridge Chapter of Juvenile Boozers Anonymous. See? I knew it!"

"We were not boozers. And how did you know about that?"

"Kit told me when we were, ah, seeing each other. I don't know how you pulled it off."

"We didn't pull it off completely. Dominique told me once that Jacques knew. She said he watered the wine before I took it."

He laughed, but there wasn't any mirth in it. "Good old Jacques. Not much got by him. At least it didn't if it involved me."

"What does that mean?"

"I caught hell for everything. But you—jeez—you could have tap-danced on top of the fermenting barrels and he would have thought it was cute."

"I hung around while he worked. Unlike you." I paused, then said, "There's something I've been wanting to ask you."

"Is it about money?"

"No. Something else. Do you remember Mom's gardening journals?"

"Vaguely. Why?"

"Fitz told me before he died that Mom kept diaries. Personal diaries. I said he was mistaken until I looked through her gardening journals. She didn't just keep lists about her plants and the gardens. She wrote about us, too. And some other things."

He bent and brushed imaginary lint off his shorts. When he straightened up his eyes were bland. "You mean her gardening journals were also her diaries?"

I nodded.

"Why are you telling me this?"

"Fitz wanted to burn them. He wouldn't say why and he got mad when I asked him. I think it was to protect her. There was something between him and Mom, wasn't there?"

A muscle twitched in his jaw and he looked beyond me, his mouth compressed into a tight line. "Yeah," he said finally. "There was."

"You know that for a fact?"

"I got up for a glass of water one night as he was sneaking out of her bedroom. He never saw me."

"You never told me."

"What in the hell was I gonna say?"

"The journal from the year Mia was born is missing. All the others are in the bookcase in Mom's study."

"Are you sure it's missing?" He sounded calm, but he folded his arms and began drumming his fingers on his forearms like he was playing Grieg again. "Maybe she didn't keep a diary for a while."

"Maybe. But I doubt it."

He stopped playing and steepled his fingers. It looked like he was praying. "Let's not borrow trouble, shall we? We've got enough problems without wondering about things we . . ."

"I know. I know."

He glanced at his watch. "Good Lord. I'm six minutes late to give Brandi her vitamins. I've got to go."

"Can't she take them herself?"

"She likes me to give them to her," he said, picking up the Filofax as he fished in his pocket and pulled out his keys. "Look, I want you to destroy those damn diaries just like Fitz said. Have a bonfire or something. And we still haven't finished our conversation about this mess you've created by refusing to sell. I don't want to play hardball, Lucie, but there are ways of forcing you to do it."

"Like what?" Someone tried to force Leland to sell and he was dead.

"I'm talking to Mason," he said. "Getting some legal advice."

"You're going to sue me?"

"I don't know. I just said I'm looking into it. And while we're on the subject of family relations, I'm really worried about Brandi and the baby. She's not sleeping well or eating right. It's not good for the baby's health." He paused and added, "Her problems started just after you came back."

"Meaning what? My being home is the reason Brandi isn't eating or sleeping? Are you serious?"

He looked pained. "Lucie, I've already told you how much this baby means to us. Brandi knows you don't like her and it bothers her. She shouldn't be upset. If you take the place in Grasse it works out well for everyone, you included. See what I'm saying?"

Love may be blind but in my brother's case it was deaf, dumb, and arrogant. I leaned on my cane. "I'm sorry she's not feeling well. During a pregnancy hormonal changes can make someone very emotional and that's normal. If she's not eating or sleeping, maybe you ought to take her to her obstetrician for a checkup."

"This isn't some hormonal thing." He glared at me. "It's real."

"Then you'd definitely better see the doctor."

"I'm warning you, Lucie. If anything goes wrong . . ." He turned on his heel and left, slamming the front door.

After he drove off I climbed the stairs even more slowly than usual and took a long shower and brushed my teeth good and hard. I was clean, except for the taste of bile that stayed in my mouth no matter what I did.

CHAPTER 18

The stone bridge at Goose Creek was built as a turnpike bridge in 1802 during the presidency of Thomas Jefferson. One of the last four-arch bridges in Virginia, it was also the longest one remaining from that era, measuring two-hundred feet in length. It was the site of a Civil War battle, a choke point for the Confederate Army, which, under Jeb Stuart, tried to delay Union troops in order to give Robert E. Lee more time to continue his advance toward Pennsylvania. Ten days later, the two armies met at Gettysburg.

In the late 1950s the highway department abandoned the bridge and redirected Route 50, Mosby's Highway, to its present-day location, so it was now looked after by the local garden club. It was a pleasant site for a picnic, with no traces of the bloody battle that took so many lives.

Kit's car was already there when I pulled into the gravel road near the path to the bridge. She came over as I parked the Volvo, dressed in a form-fitting pair of jeans and a low-cut halter top. The cloyingly sweet scent of honeysuckle hung in the humid air.

She shone a flashlight near my feet. "You going to be all right? I wasn't thinking when I suggested we meet here. It might be tough for you to walk to the bridge. The ground's pretty uneven and it's hard to see, even with the flashlight. We could just stay here if you want."

I probably wasn't ever going to take up mountain climbing or rappelling, but I had no intention of being sidelined by something as unadventurous as walking a few hundred feet on rough terrain in the dark. Defeat, as they say, is for losers.

"I'll be fine," I said. "If you carry the basket with the wine and the glasses in it and let me lean on your arm, I should be okay."

"Uh, sure." She walked very slowly and kept up a relentlessly encouraging monologue about our progress.

"Will you cut it out?" I said, finally. "We're not climbing the Matterhorn."

"Sorry," she said. "Did I sound patronizing?"

"You sounded like Annie Sullivan and I'm Helen Keller. I can manage just fine."

"In that case," she said, "shake a leg."

We sat on the edge of the bridge. "I can't hear the creek," I said. "It's strange not to hear any water."

"Been like that for most of the summer. I can't remember the last time we had rain. You want to open the wine?"

Kit held the flashlight while I extracted the cork from the bottle and filled our glasses.

"Mud in your eye." She set the flashlight between us so the light shone upward like a giant pillar candle. "Hey, this is premium stuff."

"It ought to be. It's ten-year-old Cab."

"Are we celebrating something?"

"Friendship," I said. "We're celebrating friendship."

We clinked glasses. "You want to talk about what's bothering you?"

"Not right now."

Fireflies winked and the cicadas sang as we drank in silence. Moths zoomed around the beam of white light. After a while Kit said, "I thought you ought to know. I've started seeing Bobby Noland."

"Are you kidding? Since when?"

"Yesterday. We got together because he was going to talk to me about Fitz. Started out all business then next thing I know, we're making out in the backseat of his cruiser. Those Crown Vics have no springs, I swear to God. I've got bruises in the weirdest places. It's not what you're thinking," she added. "He was off-duty."

"Did he tell you anything about Fitz before you got personal with him?"

She looked into her wineglass. "Apparently your cousin doesn't have an alibi for the time of his death."

"Dominique? She spent the night at Joe Dawson's."

"'Fraid not, Luce. She didn't show up until late. Really late." She drank her wine.

"She didn't do it, Kit. Maybe she did want to take over the inn, but she didn't kill Fitz to make it happen."

"Then who did?" She leaned forward so the flashlight's beam glanced off the angles and planes of her face, turning her eyes into hollow black pools like the empty holes of a mask.

I ran a finger down the stem of my wineglass and thought about what Eli had said, about where her loyalties really belonged.

"I thought you said we were celebrating friendship," she said. "So are we or aren't we?"

"Of course we are."

"Then maybe you could start trusting me again." She picked up the bottle and topped off our glasses. "Everybody needs a friend, Luce. You more than anybody right now."

"You mean with my family imploding?" I closed my eyes and drank. "God, it's hot, isn't it? I feel like I'm suffocating it's so humid. Nothing makes any sense since I came home."

"So tell me about it. It'll help."

I swung my feet around so they were dangling over the creek-side of the bridge and stared into the murky darkness. "Eli thinks you're going to splash some lurid story about us all over the front page of the *Trib*."

"Eli's an asshole," she said, "whose emotional sensibilities seem to have atrophied since he married the Queen Bee. He's become so materialistic he thinks the world is full of people just like him."

I smiled. "Point taken."

"Say hallelujah. Now tell me what's bugging you," she said gently.

I drank more wine while she watched me. "Fitz said before he died that someone tried to buy the vineyard and Leland wouldn't sell," I said finally. "He didn't know who it was."

"Ask Erica Kendall. She might have heard something."

"I'd rather not."

"Why?"

"Because Fitz thinks . . . thought . . . Leland's death wasn't an accident. He thought whoever was trying to get him to sell might have had something to do with it."

"Go on."

"He also said Eli stood to gain from Leland's death since now there were no obstacles to selling."

"Are you saying that Eli was involved in the death of his own *father*? And Fitz?" She whistled. "Jeez, Luce, you know I think Eli's turned into something you'd scrape off the bottom of your shoe, but I just can't see it. He's a henpecked wimp ever since he married Brandi. Not a murderer."

"I don't think Eli killed Leland. I never did. I don't think he killed Fitz, either. But with Leland out of the way, he had an easy way to solve his money problems."

An owl hooted nearby and we both jumped. I grabbed the edge of the parapet as Kit's fingers dug into my shoulder. "Watch it! You almost fell off!" Her voice was sharp. "Aw, damn. I spilled wine on my jeans."

"Sorry. There's a napkin in the basket. I wrapped the wineglasses in it." I swung my legs back around and faced her again.

"Okay, so someone murders Leland because they know Eli is cash-strapped and he'll jump at the chance to sell the vineyard." She rooted in the basket for the napkin, then began dabbing at a spot on her jeans. "What's so special about your land that someone would kill for it?"

"I don't know. Other than the fact that it's nearly five hundred acres." I reached for the bottle and poured the last of the wine. "Have you ever heard of the Blue Ridge Consortium?"

"Sure. Bunch of superrich environmental do-gooders. What about them?" She crumpled the napkin and threw it back in the basket.

"Do you know who belongs to it?"

Kit shrugged. "Most of the people you'd expect. A lot of the horse-farm owners. Some of the Romeos. Except Austin Kendall, obviously."

"Why 'obviously'?"

"The consortium wants to keep the region unspoiled, just the way it is. No housing developments, no shopping malls, not even a bus shelter. Austin thinks the go-go growth and all the construction in the high-tech Dulles Airport corridor is the best thing that happened since Leven Powell founded Middleburg. So there's a small difference of opinion." She drank her wine. "Why are you asking about them?"

"Leland had a letter from Nate Midas among his papers. Asking for a ten-thousand-dollar donation. I was wondering if they were the ones who tried to buy the place or . . ." I stopped.

"Or what?"

"Or someone else did." It sounded lame.

"I'm waiting."

"Or maybe Quinn did."

She chuckled. "You're joking, right? No offense, but the guy dresses like he buys his clothes at a flea market. Where would he get money to buy the vineyard?"

I had the copy of the *Mercury News* in my satchel. She took it and leaned toward the beam of the flashlight.

When she finished she looked thoughtful. "It's definitely Quinn in that photo, even with the different first name. So where'd he get the money from? You think Cantor paid him off to buy his silence? There really is money somewhere and maybe Cantor's not as broke as he seems?"

"The other day Quinn told me he'd like to buy land here and have his own vineyard some day. I didn't give it another thought until I saw this." I took the newspaper from her and stared at

Quinn grinning broadly like he didn't have a care in the world. "Maybe he meant our vineyard. Maybe he's the one who talked to Leland."

"Have you thought about tracking down his ex-employer?"

"I called. The place must have closed down. And there's no forwarding number."

"A friend of mine works for the *San Francisco Chronicle*. He might know someone at the *Merc*. I'll ask," she said. "Wonder why he changed his name? 'Paolo' sounds more exotic than 'Quinn,' don't you think?"

"His name could be Dom Perignon, for all I care. I'm getting rid of him as soon as harvest is over. I don't know why Leland ever hired him. It was a mistake."

"Well, it probably makes sense to wait until harvest is finished. No point shooting yourself in the foot." She froze. "Oh God. I didn't mean that."

"I know what you meant. Forget it." I finished my wine. "We ought to get going. You're being eaten alive by mosquitoes."

"And you're not?"

"One of us wore bug spray," I said. "And one of us wore perfume."

She stood up and waved her empty glass back and forth like a semaphore. "That was fabulous wine. As for the perfume, I've got a date with Bobby. Wonder if he likes his women lumpy. I'm a mass of welts."

"I guess you'll find out. Where's he taking you?" I leaned on my cane and pulled myself up.

"A romantic evening at the American Legion Hall in Philomont. Darts and a few beers with the guys. It's a cop hangout." She picked up the glasses and the empty bottle and put them in the basket. "You know Bobby. He never was a roses and poetry kind of guy."

I held her arm again as we walked back to our cars.

"Be careful," she said as I opened the door to the Volvo and got in. "Just, you know, keep an eye out. I'm worried about you."

"I'll be fine. I can take care of myself." I started the Volvo, which sounded more anemic than usual, and backed it out of the gravel road. Kit turned in the opposite direction when we got to Mosby's Highway. She tooted her horn and I watched the Jeep's taillights disappear in my rearview mirror, which is how I saw the black SUV come out of nowhere and move up right behind me.

Whoever it was, he was practically crawling up my bumper. I sped up and so did he. The turn for Atoka Road was coming up and I signaled. He'd probably blow past me as I turned, maybe stick his middle finger out the window. My bad luck to be sharing the road with some jerk with a road rage problem. Suddenly he moved up so he was right beside me. He wasn't going to let me make my turn. If I slowed down, so did he. No way could I outrace him in the Volvo. We roared past Atoka Road side by side. I glanced over to see if I recognized him but the windows were tinted and it was nighttime. I couldn't see anything.

I floored the gas pedal, which must have caught him off-guard because, astonishingly, I pulled ahead of him. Seconds later I heard the angry revving of his engine. He moved in tight behind me again, rather than beside me. The SUV's enormous grille filled my entire rearview mirror. The first jolt when he rammed me nearly caused me to lose control of the car. The second time he hit me I managed to cling to the steering wheel as he kept up his relentless pounding. The Volvo shuddered but held together and I thanked God for small favors—that I was in this car rather than the Mini I drove in France.

In the distance, a pair of headlights raked the road and another vehicle swung slowly onto the highway. At this speed, I would rear-end the slower-moving car in seconds. I swerved and one of the tires hit the soft shoulder. Though I knew better, I pumped the brakes. The car rolled and kept rolling. My head hit the steering wheel.

When the cartwheels stopped I was upside down, strapped in by my seat belt. Another set of brakes squealed, then headlights flashed outside my window. Two car doors slammed, then a man yelled, "Hey! Hey there!"

I was alone in a field late at night with whoever had tried to run me off the road. If he meant to kill me, there would be no one to stop him and no witnesses.

A flashlight beam skipped across the field. "Hey," the voice said again, "you all right in there?" He shone the flashlight directly in my face, blinding me.

"My head hurts." My voice sounded weak and far away. I closed my eyes. The light hurt.

"Why, it's a woman, Hollis," said a female voice. "I thought it was kids. She sounds kinda woozy."

"Well, she damn near killed us," Hollis said. "So she's lucky if a bad headache is the only thing she's got." He said, presumably to me, "Don't you know drag racing's against the law around here? You and your friend musta been doing close to a hunnerd. We all coulda been killed. You're mighty lucky to be alive, sweetheart."

It was the driver of the car I nearly hit. My pursuer, whoever he was, was gone. Unless he was somewhere nearby in the darkness.

"Not me. Someone else. Someone was chasing me," I mumbled.

"Hollis," said the female voice, "she's still got her seat belt on. Help her out of there. She ought to see a doctor. She sounds delirious."

"I am serious," I said. Or maybe I said "delirious." My head felt like someone was jackhammering from the inside, trying to get out.

"I can't get to you," Hollis said. "Can you undo that seat belt yourself?"

"I think so."

Luckily the car was so old everything worked manually. He reached in and rolled down my window. "Good thing you're small," he said. "Door's jammed. You'll have to come out through the window." He put his arms around me. "I'll pull you. On three."

He counted and pulled. My bad leg got caught on the steering wheel and I cried out.

"Take it easy, Hollis." The woman sounded anxious. "You're hurting her."

"Are you doing this or am I doing this?" Hollis said to the woman. To me he said, "Come on, we just about got you free."

I got my foot loose and he pulled me out. Then he sat me on the ground and played the flashlight over me. The backwash of light made shimmering halos around his face and the face of the woman standing next to him. Both were white-haired. I knew them.

They knew me, too.

"Well, I'll be," the woman said. "You're the Montgomery girl, aren't you? The older one. Linda."

"Lucie." The jackhammers wouldn't quit.

"That's right," she said. "Lucie. Thelma was just telling me about you. I'm Ellie Maddox. Maybe you remember me? I used to work the checkout at Red's Hardware in The Plains. I knew your folks real good, they were in all the time. And this here's my husband, Hollis. Are you all right, honey? Maybe we ought to take you to Loudoun General."

I shook my head and was immediately sorry I did. My brain felt like it had come loose from its moorings. I put both hands on the ground to stop the dizziness. "No hospital. I want to go home."

"Well, you ain't going anywhere in that car." Hollis shone the flashlight on the Volvo. "That's Lee's car, isn't it? Hell, those Volvos are built like tanks. You're lucky, young lady, that you weren't in one of them convertibles the kids are driving nowadays. You do somersaults in a car with no roof over your head and we wouldn't be here havin' this conversation."

"Hollis," Ellie admonished. "Look at her. She doesn't care about that stuff right now. The child looks like she's about to keel over. Let's get her home."

"Fine," he said, "but she's gonna care tomorrow when she doesn't have any vehicle." To me he added, "If you want, I'll call Knight's in the morning and have your car towed for you."

"Call who tonight?" Their halos were growing fuzzier. I could hardly make out the features on their faces anymore.

"*Knight*'s. The garage over to Aldie. I'll call them in the *morning!*" He raised his voice like he was talking to someone who didn't understand English.

"Oh," I said faintly. "Good."

"Used to be Knight & Rust Auto Body. You remember, don't

you?" he said. "I still call it that 'cept now it's Gas-o-Rama or some fool name, but they still got a halfway decent mechanic. Not as good as old Jimmy Knight, but then nobody's as good as Jimmy, God rest his soul. Not even Rusty was that good. There wasn't nothing he couldn't fix if your car was acting up. Did great body work, too. He coulda fixed this car so it would look newer than the day you bought it."

"Hollis," Ellie warned. "There you go, running your mouth again. She's gonna faint or something. Let's get her out of here."

Ellie was still fussing about the hospital, but when Hollis fished my cane out of the Volvo, I managed to walk reasonably steadily to their car, leaning on his arm. They agreed, reluctantly, to take me home.

As soon as they drove away I locked the front door. The lock groaned when I turned the key, nearly frozen from lack of use. I slid the deadbolt into place with some effort, then went into Leland's study and knelt by his gun locker. His old .22-caliber handgun was where he'd always kept it and so was the ammunition. I loaded the gun and—with excruciating slowness—climbed the stairs to my bedroom. No more sleeping on the veranda.

I lay in bed, exhausted and aching, the thrumming noise of the old fan blowing barely cooled air over me acting like white noise, blocking out all thoughts.

Except one.

Someone tried to kill me tonight out on Mosby's Highway.

CHAPTER 19

It was still dark when my alarm went off. I turned on the light and saw the gun. It took a moment before I remembered why I'd put it there and still longer before I remembered that the reason the alarm had gone off so early was because today was harvest. I sat up, moving like an arthritic marionette. The first thing I did was unload the bullets, putting them and the gun in the drawer of my nightstand. My head throbbed from the effort.

I took a shower that turned my skin the color of cooked lobster. It helped the stiffness but I needed drugs. I had forgotten about the bottle of postaccident painkillers that was still in the medicine cabinet. Past its sell-by date, but they'd still be potent. My hand hovered between that bottle and the ibuprofen next to it.

It had been pure hell weaning myself from the pain-free bliss of those drugs. Right now it would be so easy to start again.

I picked up the ibuprofen and took two with a glass of water. Then I shook out a half dozen bullet-shaped capsules and shoved them in my jeans pocket. I flushed the pain pills down the toilet.

Surprisingly after two cups of coffee and a toasted baguette, the ibuprofen kicked in and I felt somewhat human. Eli's bicycle was in the carriage house, but I wasn't sure I could navigate the pedals with my bad foot and my aching joints. There was nothing else with wheels or a motor that was going to get me to the winery. The darkness was slowly fading and the air was cool and still. I decided to walk.

Quinn was kneeling by a small pump on the crush pad, fiddling with a hose clamp when I finally got there. He wore jeans and a T-shirt and a goofy-looking straw hat instead of the customary fatigues and Hawaiian print.

He looked surprised to see me. "I didn't hear your car."

"I walked. The Volvo's in the shop."

"You should have called. Someone would have run you over."

I knew what he meant, but it still sounded strange. "It's okay. Have we got enough help?"

"Ten guys from the camp. We should be good."

"Angela coming, too?"

"Yeah. Why?"

"Just wondering."

"Check those hoses, will you, and make sure the clamps are fitted securely? I'm going out to the field to get the first lot of lugs."

"Sure."

Whatever he had or hadn't done in California, right now I needed him. Before he took off in the Gator our eyes met. What happened from now on depended on his judgment and intuition and how much we didn't screw up what the grapes had already done for us. We are, essentially, farmers, tied to the whims of nature however much we try to control our destiny and the fruits of our harvest. Despite his arrogant cockiness, I could tell he was wrestling with the nerve-wracking second-guessing that happens when there are no sure bets. By the end of the morning we'd have a pretty good idea whether he was right . . . or wrong.

He left for the fields, the flatbed trailer fishtailing in the red clay dust as he sped away. I walked over to the pump and slowly bent down to check the clamps on the hoses as he'd asked.

In the distance, the putt-putting of the Gator sounded like bees at their hive. Hector was probably riding on the trailer as it moved up and down the rows, jumping off to pick up the lugs where the men had left them under the cooler shade of the vines. Occasionally the workers called out to each other in Spanish. Though a me-

211 THE MERLOT MURDERS

chanical harvester—which looked like an alien space creature on stilts—could bring in the grapes faster and cheaper, we still picked by hand as they'd been doing since the time of the Romans. Most vineyards, the good ones, at least, did it the same way.

By the time Quinn arrived back at the crush pad with a full load of lugs, the rest of the crew was waiting. Someone turned up the volume on a boombox. One by one the men stripped off their shirts, laughing and singing with the pulsating Spanish beat. Quinn jumped off the Gator and started handing the lugs piled with translucent green-gold grapes to workers who set them on the scales. After they were weighed someone tipped the contents into the destemmer, then hurled the empty container onto a growing mountain of yellow plastic bins on the ground nearby.

Quinn joined me, eating grapes he'd picked from a bunch off one of the lugs. "Here, try these. They're good. Nearly everything's ripe." He leaned close to my ear so I could hear him over the racket of the destemmer as it spat barky stems into a barrel.

Even at this early stage it was possible to tell what the final product would be. I ate the grapes he'd handed me. He was right. They were good.

"All right, *hijos,* let's move everything into the press," he shouted. To me he said, "Grab the end of the hose and make sure it's aimed properly into that press."

The heavy-duty hose swayed like a snake being charmed as he flipped the switch on the pump. I held on though the jolting reactivated every ache and pain the ibuprofen had quelled. I gritted my teeth and watched the sludgy mass of grapes work its way from the destemmer toward the press. It would take a couple of trips from the field before the press, a large stainless-steel tank with an enormous drum, was filled. But after so much rushing to get the grapes in before the heat became oppressive, at this stage we had to slow things down. The process of gently squeezing the grapes to release the juice would take an hour or two, depending on how much Quinn wanted to extract. Pressing too hard would make the liquid harsh and bitter so it was his judgment call when to stop.

The hose continued to thrash about in my hands as the last of the grapes moved into the press. "I'm going back to the field," Quinn said to me. "What's wrong? You got a toothache or something? Why are you making that face?"

"I think I pulled a muscle last night. You go on back to the field."

He shrugged and left as a voice behind me said, "Here. I got that." Joe Dawson took the hose out of my hands. "You don't look too good, sweetheart."

I took two more ibuprofen out of my pocket. "I'm okay. Pulled muscle. Thanks for the help." I took the pills with a cup of tepid water from one of the nearby coolers we left out for the crew.

I knew Angela Stetson had arrived as soon as the catcalls and wolf whistles began. Dressed in bottom-skimming blue jean cutoffs, she also wore a deep V-neck hot pink halter top with "Babe" written in silver sequins and stiltlike hot-pink sandals.

"Jesus, Mary, and Joseph. Who in the world is that?" Joe asked.

"Your eyes look like they're bugging out of your head," I said. "It's Angela Stetson. Quinn's girlfriend. I thought you knew her."

"What'd she do? Have a whole body transplant? Didn't she go to school with you? I don't remember her looking like that."

"She took a lot of vitamins. Reel your tongue back in and keep an eye on things, will you? I need to talk to her."

Angela appeared to be reveling in the attention she was getting as the men continued to grin and wink at her. She'd come a long way from her Marian-the-librarian persona of our high school days.

"Okay, *hijos*," Hector said. "Everyone back to work. Leave the lady alone."

"Can I talk to you?" I asked her. "Somewhere out of this heat?"

We walked together to the open hangar door to the barrel room.

Though it was only 9 A.M., the sun was already boiling. The air smelled of sweet wine mixed with the faintly unpleasant tinge of carbon dioxide as the grapes began fermenting. Black flies edged the outlines of the hangar door and yellow jackets swarmed anywhere we'd spilled the sweet, sticky grape juice. Quinn had turned the fans on earlier to clear out the CO_2, but overnight it would

THE MERLOT MURDERS 213

build up in the airtight room to levels that could kill a person. We stepped inside. It was marginally cooler.

"I've never done this before." Angela was chewing gum. "I think I'm overdressed."

"Actually, you're dressed too nicely. Those clothes are going to be filthy when you're done."

"I thought they stomped grapes in the nude."

"Uh, some French vineyards still do it that way, but not us. It's pretty boring but we use a nine-iron from Leland's set of golf clubs and Eli's old baseball bat."

"That's kind of special." She arched an eyebrow. She'd worn full makeup, too. "Well, no big deal. I'm, like, totally washable. What did you want to ask me?"

"I was wondering if you knew whether Sara Rust is working at Mom's Place tonight?"

"Nope. Not tonight or any other night. She quit yesterday. Gave Vinnie her notice and said she's leaving town."

"Why? Did something happen?"

"What do I look like, her mother? How should I know? We don't talk a lot." She blew a bubble and popped it. "But I heard from one of the other girls that she had enough and she wanted out."

"Vinnie too hard on her?"

"Vinnie's a pussycat. Nah, it was something else. Someone's, like, stalking her. Some old guy was creeping her out, so she's splitting. At least that's what Desiree said."

I thought of my pursuer last night in the black SUV. Whoever he was, he didn't seem like an "old guy." The car, the speed. Someone young. "Did she know who it was?"

"Nope." She narrowed her eyes. "Why are you asking so many questions? What's it to you?"

"Lucie!" Joe's voice cut through a lull as someone turned the pump off. He was waving a mobile phone. "Dominique says she needs you right now down at the gazebo. Something about harvest lunch."

"Tell her I'll be right there." I turned to Angela. "Sorry. I better go. Thanks for the information."

"Yeah, sure." She was looking past me to where Quinn had just pulled up on the crush pad. He jumped out of the Gator and she ran to him, hanging her arms around his neck and swinging on him. He grinned foolishly down at her and put his silly hat on her head. They were like a couple of love-struck teenagers.

I left without looking back.

Dominique seemed tense and unhappy when I found her standing in the gazebo in front of a Limoges vase of pink and white roses.

"Can you take over today and run harvest lunch for me?" she asked.

"Sure. Why? Are you okay?"

She set down the pair of gardening clippers she'd been using to even the lengths of the roses. "Bobby called. He wants to see me." She began haphazardly sticking roses in the vase.

"Give me those. I'll do that." I took the clippers. "Well, go talk to him then. How bad can it be?"

Her cigarettes were next to the vase. She picked up the packet and extracted one. "I don't have an alibi for the time of Fitz's death. I was alone at the inn when he was killed."

"You didn't do it, Dominique. There must have been someone who saw you. Do you remember what time you got to Joe's?"

"Sure I remember. Two o'clock. I was listening to Gregory's radio program in the car. He was talking to someone who wanted to know if she should leave her husband after twenty-four years of marriage because she fell in love with her UPS guy." She lit her cigarette.

"Oh, yuck. Don't tell me what he told her." I finished with the vase. "Bobby can check on that. He should be able to ask Greg. They must keep some kind of log or record of callers."

"Maybe." She dumped the barely smoked cigarette into a Styrofoam cup of water. "Can you believe he told me if I don't show up on my own he will send someone for me with the cuff links?"

"I can't believe he'd do something like that."

"I'd better go." She gave me the list of lunch guests and left, still looking grim.

After I finished at the gazebo I borrowed Hector's blue pickup and drove back to the house to change. Leland's folder with the information on the Blue Ridge Consortium was still on his bedside table next to the phone. I sat on the bed and called Sara Rust's number.

Her answering machine kicked in again and this time I left a message. "Hello, Sara, this is Lucie Montgomery. I'm a friend of Angela Stetson's and I was wondering if I could talk to you. Angela said you're leaving town and . . ."

"Hello? Who is this?" Monitoring her calls.

"My name is Lucie Montgomery and I . . ."

"Mia's sister. Yeah, I know. Is she okay?"

"Yes," I said, surprised. "She's fine. I was wondering if we might meet?"

"Why?"

Angela was right about her being scared. "I think we have something in common. We ought to talk."

"I'm sure we don't, but if you want talk it'll cost you." I heard a click, like a cigarette lighter, then an expelled breath. "Fifteen minutes. A hundred bucks."

"A hundred . . . ? Oh, come on!"

"Good-bye."

"Wait! Okay. A hundred dollars."

"A hundred and fifty."

"You just said one hundred!"

"Those were old prices, from a minute ago. Yes or no?"

"Yeah, sure," I said. "But since I'm paying for this, we'll meet when it's convenient for me. Three o'clock. And I'll pay you *after* we talk."

"What do I care? Fifteen minutes, as long as it's before six and you come to me." She gave me directions to an address in Aldie, then disconnected.

I changed into a white eyelet skirt and white sleeveless blouse and drove back to the vineyard.

Harvest lunch was a tradition established by my mother and Fitz. Jacques continued it after her death, though he abandoned the practice of having guests each day during harvest since we were generally running flat out and couldn't spare the time or the manpower to take guests around the vineyard. More important, my mother wasn't there to hostess the event, which included chaperoning the guests to make sure no one got too near the equipment or decided to take one of the bung hole covers out of an oak barrel "just to see" what was inside. The one time that happened, we didn't discover it for months and ended up with a couple hundred bucks worth of red wine vinegar instead of a few thousand dollars of Pinot Noir.

Today the guests included a California congressman and his staff, three D.C. restaurant owners, a wine-tasting club called *Les Amis du Vin* from Charlottesville, and an event planner from a public relations firm who was looking for a place to host a dinner party for a group of international clients.

Whether it was because I was distracted or due to the constant needling from the California congressman—an unctuous white-haired man in a sharp suit who called me "little lady"—the lunch wasn't one of our better ones. But Dominique, as usual, had outdone herself with the menu, having gone to the farmers' market in Frogtown that morning making sure nearly all the produce had been in someone's garden only a few hours earlier.

After the tour, we ate in the gazebo. It faced my mother's wild-flower garden, a rioting mass of cosmos, coreopsis, black-eyed Susans, and a spectacular assortment of daylilies, whose colors ranged from sherbet pinks, yellows, and peaches to deeper oranges, golds, and plums.

The congressman, who sat next to me, represented a concrete district in Los Angeles not far from Hollywood. He kept haranguing me about the superiority of California wines. "You know, little lady, I had dinner at the White House the other night and what do you think they served as wines? Every course?"

"I'm sure you're going to tell me they were California wines."

"You bet, honey. They know their wines at the White House. Only the best."

"Actually," I said, "the first wines served at the White House were recommended by a Virginian. Thomas Jefferson stocked the wine cellar for George Washington and then for John Adams. And, of course, during his own presidency."

He'd been chewing on a piece of grilled lamb with a fresh berry sauce. "The wines weren't *from* Virginia, were they?" He grinned broadly so I saw the berry seed in his dentures.

"Give us time." I stared at the berry seed. "Our winemaker came from Napa to work here in Virginia. Our climate is a lot like France and we do a lot of experimenting. I'm sure you know that a number of top restaurants in your district already serve Virginia wines." I mentioned a couple of names.

"Good Lord." He seemed visibly peeved, but not enough to refuse my offer of a refill. He also didn't call me "little lady" or "honey" anymore. When he left, he bought a few bottles of Cabernet and Chardonnay, though he did wink at me and ask for the special "congressional discount."

I gave it to him. "That's in return for your promise to take one of these bottles along as a gift the next time you dine at the White House." I didn't wink back.

Dominique's staff cleaned up while I sold more wine to *Les Amis du Vin* and spoke with the restaurant owners, two of whom wanted to come back and do a comprehensive tasting before choosing the wines for their wine lists. The publicist said her people would speak with my people to make arrangements for their "event."

"I'll let them know," I said. Simpler than explaining that I was "my people."

After the last guest left, I got in Hector's pickup and headed for Aldie. The Scottish poet Robert Burns once described my ancestors as "a martial race, bold, soldier featured and undismayed." The Montgomerys were one of Scotland's oldest clans, warriors who came originally from Normandy—we were feared and respected.

The symbol on our crest was a woman holding an anchor in one hand and a savage's head in the other. Above it was our motto: *Gardez bien.*

Watch well. Watch out for us.

Driving down Mosby's Highway, I glanced constantly in my rearview mirror, in case someone was following me again.

This time I would be ready.

CHAPTER 20

———— ⊂≈≈⊃ ————

Sara Rust lived in an old stone cottage on Mosby's Highway, not far from the famous mill that had given its name to the village of Aldie during the Civil War, when the Gray Ghost and a handful of his Rangers routed two hundred Union soldiers who'd been out looking for him.

I parked on the dirt and gravel driveway and climbed the stairs to the front porch, leaning on the railing, which creaked and swayed under my weight. A couple of cardboard liquor boxes full of newspapers and what looked like heaps of old magazines and papers were scattered haphazardly across the porch. She was cleaning out the place and, by the looks of it, doing it in a hurry. I rang the doorbell but nothing chimed. After a moment, I opened the sagging screen door and used the tarnished door knocker.

The door opened a few inches. Sara Rust had chained her front door shut. The door closed again and I heard metal scraping metal as she released it.

"I'm Lucie," I said, as she let me into a dingy stone living room. The embedded, stale odor of wood smoke and dampness hung in the air. The only light came from two small windows.

"I know who you are. Did you bring the money?" She had thick Titian-colored hair, which fell in massed curls around her shoulders, alabaster skin, and hazel-green eyes. She seemed familiar enough that I recognized her in the way you recognize people you don't really know when you live in a small community. It must have been at least five or six years since I'd last seen her, though. Now she was tall and reed-slender, with that same suggestive sexuality about her that I saw in Angela. I wouldn't have called her beautiful, but there was something about her that would make a man take a second look. Barefoot and dressed in a pair of raggedy jeans with holes in the knees and a sports bra that belonged at the gym, she looked her age until I saw her eyes. Someone had already knocked the sense of wonder out of her.

She also appeared to be scared and dead tired.

"We agreed I'd pay you after we talk."

"I haven't got long. I'm leaving in a few hours." The room was nearly empty except for a floor lamp with a torn lampshade, a dirty beanbag chair pulled next to the fireplace, and two wooden crates full of file folders. The words "Knight & Rust Auto Body" were stenciled in black on the sides of the crate. The air-conditioning was on and the thermostat had been set to "arctic." I shivered.

Maybe a moving company had already come and taken away her furniture. Or maybe I was looking at the place fully furnished.

"I'd offer you a seat, but . . ." She gestured vaguely at the beanbag.

"I'm fine." I leaned on my cane.

"What do you want?"

"Angela told me you quit your job because someone was stalking you."

She walked over to one of the deep-silled windows and picked up a pack of cigarettes balanced against an overflowing ashtray. "You don't beat around the bush, do you?" She smacked the small box and extracted a cigarette, lighting it with the fluid movements of a well-practiced habit.

"You're the one in a hurry."

Through a blast of smoke she said, "It's true. What's it to you?"

"Who was it?"

She was standing almost in profile, caught in a shaft of midafternoon sunlight streaming in through the window. It cast her face in shadow and edged her silhouette—especially that russet hair—so she appeared to be backlit like some heavenly apparition. Another deep pull on the cigarette. "I don't know."

"Then how did you know it was an old man?"

"Because he left a calling card." She crossed the room to the fireplace mantel and picked up a pair of eyeglasses. She came over to where I stood and held them out. "Know what these are? Old people's glasses. You know, when you get old and you can't read small print anymore? He left them when he tossed my house."

I looked at the half-glasses and felt guilty relief. They weren't Leland's. He'd worn bifocals. "Some old man robbed you? What did he take?"

Sara shrugged. "Nothing. At least, I don't think anything is missing. He just trashed the place. I mean, he trashed everything."

"That's bizarre."

"He had a good time in my underwear drawer, let me tell you." She stubbed out the cigarette in the too-full ashtray. "Some people are sick."

"Did you report it to the police?"

She kept stubbing out the cigarette. "Nope."

"Why not?"

"I occasionally have, uh, friends over after work. I had a guest that night. We shared a couple of joints and I didn't want the cops around. Obviously I got on the wrong side of some jerk."

"And you're running away because . . ." I paused, trying to figure out how to say it. "Someone broke into your house and didn't take anything?"

"Oh, *please*. Whoever it was tried to burn this house down." She lit another cigarette. "With me in it."

"Oh my God." *Not* Leland. "What happened? When was this?"

"Two nights ago."

Definitely not Leland. "You stopped him?"

"My friend smelled gasoline. It was three in the morning. We weren't sleeping, thank God. He went outside. Next thing, I heard him shouting, then a car engine started and someone took off."

"He didn't go after him?"

"Not in his birthday suit he didn't. His wife might have been a little upset if he got picked up for indecent exposure." She inhaled deeply. "By then whoever it was probably was halfway to Philomont. Or wherever."

"Do you mind if I have a look around your yard?"

"Knock yourself out. You won't find anything. I hosed everything down the next morning." Sara flicked an ash into the fireplace. "I still don't know why you're asking all this."

Neither did I. Except there was some connection between us. I couldn't figure out what it was. "I found your name and phone number in a file that belonged to my father, Leland Montgomery. Did you ever talk to him? Did he ever come to see you at work?"

She snorted. "There were loads of guys who came to see me at work. You lose track, you know? And, to be honest, when I'm up on that stage dancing, I never focus on the faces. I wear contacts and I take them out when I dance so everyone is a blur. That way I never know who is out there. It's better that way."

That explained her tough as nails machismo. "What about the other entertaining you do? They're not faceless," I said. "Are they?"

"No." She flushed. "But it's over now. I'm out of here. I'm getting so lost in New York no one will ever find me."

"What about Greg Knight?"

"What about him?"

"He was hanging around you a lot at Mom's."

She stared pointedly at my cane. "Don't tell me you're still carrying a torch for him. He made you the way you are now."

My turn to flush. The way I was now. Just what, exactly, was that? "Don't be ridiculous."

"So what do you want to know about him?"

"Were you sleeping with him?"

Her laugh made me think of long shards of broken glass. She squashed her cigarette in the ashtray and mashed it down hard.

"Then why was he hanging around you?" I persisted.

"Our fathers were business partners," she said. "He was looking for a few things that belonged to his old man. Thought I might have them. Rusty took all the stuff from the garage after Jimmy died."

"What things?"

She shrugged. "I dunno. Papers. Records." She gestured to the crates. "He came over once and looked through these."

"Did he find what he wanted?"

"I guess. I don't know," she said again. "He was here by himself. It would have been simpler if he took the crates like I told him to. Save me getting rid of them."

"How long ago did he look through the papers?" I asked.

She looked at the ceiling and frowned. "Two months ago. Maybe a little less."

"Did he give you money to help you get out of town?"

"What of it?"

So maybe Greg had been telling the truth. Sara was like a kid sister to him and he was helping her out of a jam.

"So where's yours?" she added. "The *money*."

I took it out of my purse and handed it to her. "Can I keep those glasses?"

"I don't want them." She stuffed the bills inside her sports bra. "You still haven't said why you're asking me all this. You think the old guy might have been your father? Is that it?"

"No!" I said sharply. "These aren't his glasses."

"Your fifteen minutes are up." She shrugged then. "Time to go."

She held the door as I left and slammed it behind me. I heard the chain slide back in place before I got to the first step.

Most of the grass in her backyard was dead and the garden beds were bare spots and weeds. I walked slowly around the perimeter of the house and saw nothing. The same in the garage, except for two foul-smelling trash bins with flies buzzing around them. I turned my face away as I lifted the lids and then looked inside quickly.

Garbage.

I glanced at the house and saw a curtain move in a window. Sara Rust, spying on me. Unless it was someone else.

I had assumed she was home alone. Maybe I assumed wrong and she was still entertaining.

I had to return Hector's pickup, so I drove directly to the winery after leaving Aldie. The crush pad had been cleaned and someone had closed the hangar doors to the barrel room. I let myself in through the steel-plated side door. The exhaust fans made their usual heavy thrumming sound as they moved the cooling air around, clearing out the buildup of carbon dioxide. A grapevine thermometer on the wall near the door read sixty-seven degrees. The room needed to be between fifty-five and sixty-five. Jacques had drummed it into me the first time I left the door ajar when I was about six years old that air and heat are the two greatest destroyers of wine.

I moved into the room and saw Quinn through the glass laboratory window. He poured something from a beaker into a row of test tubes, then looked up briefly and nodded at me before returning to his work. Joe and Hector were over by the row of stainless-steel tanks, on their knees straightening out hoses. I joined them, holding up the keys to Hector's pickup.

"Your truck is in the parking lot. Thanks for the loan."

"No problem." Hector smiled, showing even white teeth against caffe latte skin, but he looked tired as he pocketed the keys.

"Where's the Volvo?" Joe asked.

"Garage."

"What happened?"

"It wouldn't start this morning."

"Tough break." He leaned a ladder against the tank.

"I'll do that, Joe," Hector said as Joe put a foot on the bottom rung. "You take care of the hoses. You do a good job getting the seals tight. This tank and number five need to be racked into number seven."

"I'll get the clamps," I said as Joe fitted the hoses between the smaller three-hundred-fifty-gallon tank, which had the ladder against it, and number seven, one of the large thousand-gallon tanks. I handed him the clamps and he fixed them so there was an airtight seal around the outlets.

Hector climbed the ladder as nimbly as a monkey and popped open the cover so the tank wouldn't collapse as it emptied. We'd only forgotten to do that once and ended up with something that looked like a crumpled oversized soda can.

Joe turned on the pump. "How was harvest lunch?" he asked above the noise of gurgling wine moving through the hoses from the smaller to the larger tank.

"Okay. One of the guests was a congressman who brought his staff."

"Great!"

"He was from California."

"Oh. Hard sell, hunh?" He tapped his finger against the gauge on the side of the tank. "I think after we rack this and number five over and sugar them, Quinn wants to move everything into barrels. What's left in the other tanks stays in stainless steel."

The pump sounded like it was beginning to suck air. Joe switched it off, unclamping the hose and unlocking the large port-holelike panel on the front of the tank. "Hit that switch, will you?"

He opened the man-sized porthole door and disappeared inside the tank from the waist up, taking the hose with him. I switched on the pump again and heard him vacuuming the remaining wine out of the dish at the bottom. A minute later his voice reverberated eerily against the stainless steel. "Okay!"

I flipped the switch and he popped back out of the tank, like a life-sized jack-in-the-box. "Let's get the other one. Number five."

Hector moved the ladder and popped the top of the second tank. "Stop flirting with Lucie, Joe, and get the sugar and the yeast."

Joe winked at me and left.

"You doing all right, Lucita?" Hector climbed down the ladder and reclamped the hose to the second tank. "Okay, you can turn the pump on."

I obeyed. "I'm doing fine."

"How come you didn't tell Joe the truth about your car?" He saw the look on my face and added, "You're lucky to be alive, you know?"

"How did you find out? Please don't say it was Thelma. I won't be able to go by the general store for a year."

He grinned and shook his head. "Hollis Maddox dropped by. He said to tell you the Volvo's at the Gas-o-Rama and the mechanic wants you to call him so he can tell you how much it's gonna cost." The pump was sucking air again so Hector switched it off. "You didn't answer my question."

"I think someone tried to run me off the road last night."

He vacuumed the rest of the wine from the dish. "I bet it was those kids. They get *borracho*—drunk—then they drag race along that flat stretch of Mosby's Highway. Didn't used to be like that when everyone knew everyone else around here. Now we got all those new subdivisions over in Leesburg and Sterling and parents too busy making money to spend time with their kids. So they get up to no good."

"I don't know who it was. It was just one car." But it wasn't drunk teenagers, either.

Joe returned with a fifty-pound bag of sugar slung over one shoulder and a large bucket of yeast. "Am I interrupting something?"

"Not at all," I said quickly, as Quinn joined us carrying a tape measure, calculator, and a clipboard.

"Private conversation?" He pulled a wax crayon from behind his ear.

"Nope." Hector said, glancing at me.

"Then let's get the show on the road," Quinn said.

I watched while Joe sugared the wine and Hector dumped the yeast into a bucket of distilled water. It hissed as it heated up, bubbling and foaming like witch's brew. He poured it into the tank as I stirred the mix with a large paddle.

When we were finished Quinn and Hector set up more hoses

for siphoning the wine into barrels. Almost as soon as we filled the casks and closed them, the wine began bubbling in the see-through air locks. The noise level in the room grew exponentially louder. Fermenting wine sounds like a roaring river.

"You all right, Lucie?" Hector joined Joe and me as we moved down the row, checking the air locks to make sure the seals were tight.

"I think it's the CO_2," I said. "It's making me dizzy."

Quinn came up behind us. "We're about done here. If you're feeling light-headed, maybe you should take off. I don't want you passing out and I don't need you anymore."

He moved on before I could reply. "Come on, chiquita," Hector said. "Let's get you out of here."

He spoke to Quinn in Spanish, "I'll take her home. Then I'll be back."

"Don't bother. You've done enough. Joe and I can take care of what's left." He, too, spoke Spanish and I'd noticed it was their preferred language of communication.

When we got to the parking lot Hector said, "How you gonna get around without a car, Lucita? Sounds like the Volvo will be in the shop for a few days."

"Rent something, I guess."

"You know," he said, "you could borrow the truck if you want. Bonita left her car here when she went back to Colly-fornia. Her last year studying enology at U.C., Davis. I can use her Corvette. Needs driving, anyway."

"That would be great, Hector. Thanks."

"Only thing is, you gotta drop me back at the cottage." He threw me the keys. "I need a ride."

Hector and Serafina lived in one of the two remaining tenant cottages on our property—Quinn had the other one. They were located off the main road on a small dirt spur, near where the road split at the sycamore tree.

"So Bonita's doing well at school?" I asked.

"Top of her class." He smiled broadly. "She's gonna be a first-class winemaker. You wait and see."

"She had a good example." I shifted the truck into first gear. "Maybe she could work here after she graduates. I don't know how long Quinn will be around. We'll need a first-class winemaker."

"You got one. Queen's a good man." It sounded like a reprimand.

"What makes you so sure?"

"I'm a good judge of what's in here." He laid a hand over his heart. "He knows what he's doing with the grapes, too. I know you miss Jeck, but you would be *loca en la cabeza* to let Queen go. I don't know why you don't like him."

"I don't like him because he swaggers around here like he owns the place and I'm in the way." I swerved a bit too sharply, overcorrecting to avoid a pothole. "He was fired from the last place he worked. Did you know that?"

"He was not fired. He left." Hector put a hand on the dashboard. "They drive like this in France?"

"Like what? And the winemaker is in *jail*. The vineyard had to close. Those aren't sterling references."

We pulled up in front of the red-brick cottage, which sat serenely in a clearing in the middle of the woods. A fresh coat of paint on the wraparound porch and masses of late summer impatiens, geraniums, and petunias blooming in garden beds and cascading from window boxes made it look like something out of a fairy tale. Pink, white, and lilac Rose of Sharon bushes lined both sides of a fieldstone walk.

I turned off the engine motor.

"You know, this is a great country you got here, Lucita. I'm proud my kids are citizens. Because in *los Estados Unidos* you believe someone is innocent until they are proven guilty."

"Do you really think someone as sharp as Quinn could be completely in the dark about what his boss was doing?" I folded my arms across my chest and stared through the windshield, unwilling to meet his eyes. "That's a bit of a stretch, Hector."

"I think when you respect someone, or love them, it can make you blind sometimes. Your mama was like that. She didn't see any of your papa's . . . ways. Some of the things he did that maybe he shouldn't oughta. I think it was like that with Queen. He respected that winemaker, that Cantor." He reached over and put his hand under my chin, turning me so I faced him. "Sometimes it's not about the *cabeza,* chiquita. Sometimes it's the *corazón. Entiendes?*"

I chewed my lip and nodded. He got out of the car and I started the engine. I saw him waving at me through the rearview mirror. He cupped his hands around his mouth and shouted, "Don't drive too fast!"

I waved a hand out the window. He was still standing there as I rounded a corner and could no longer see him.

The answering machine was beeping when I walked through the front door. Two messages. Kit, asking me to call her as soon as I could and Hollis Maddox giving me the phone number of the Gas-o-Rama, in case I didn't have it.

A stair tread creaked behind me as I copied down the number. Mia, tanned and gorgeous, dressed in a white mini-skirt and a cropped black sweater. She stood at the top of the stairs carrying a bright red canvas suitcase in one hand. In the other, she held Leland's revolver.

It was pointed at me.

CHAPTER 21

"Oh God. Please, Mia," I whispered. "Don't."

"Who's there?" Her voice sounded unnaturally high-pitched. I saw the flash of light and heard the bullet whiz past me. A vase filled with drooping flowers left from Leland's funeral shattered as she screamed. I knelt and covered my face with my hands against an explosion of water, porcelain, roses, gladiolus, and dagger ferns.

"Oh my God! Lucie! What are *you* doing here?" I didn't hear her come down the stairs since my ears were still ringing but suddenly her arms were around me and she was crying. "I didn't think it was you."

She helped me up, our arms around each other. "Where's the gun?" I asked. "Please, honey. We need to put it somewhere safe."

She had left it on the bottom step, next to her suitcase. I unloaded the remaining bullets. "You got this out of my nightstand," I said. "Why?"

"I was leaving you something." She spoke through hiccupy breaths, her tears making canyonlike tracks in what looked like an excessive amount of face makeup. "I could have killed you. Oh my God. I could have killed you."

"You didn't. No one got hurt. I want you to go outside on the veranda, okay? I'm going to put this gun away like I should have done this morning, then I'm going to get you something to drink. I think I saw a box of chamomile tea in the pantry. Go on, now."

"I'll clean up this mess."

"Leave it."

"No. I'll take care of it. It looks . . . awful."

She must have worked quickly because she was swinging absently in the glider, twisting a strand of hair around and around one finger, when I came outside carrying the russet-and-gold autumn leaf Rosenthal teapot that had been our mother's favorite. "Everything else is on a tray in the kitchen," I said. "Do you think you could carry it out here for me? The tea needs to steep for a while."

When she returned with the tray she said, "Mom used to make this for me when I got nightmares. Tisane, she called it. I haven't had it for years."

"I'm afraid the tea is old." I handed her a cup. "The box says chamomile but it smells like straw."

"Doesn't matter." She kicked off her sandals and tucked one foot under her. With the other, she pushed herself back and forth on the glider again. Someone might have taken her for about fourteen or fifteen just then. I couldn't reconcile this sweet-looking girl with the person who drew those violent pictures, including that brutal one of me. She leaned forward and took the cup and saucer I gave her.

"What were you doing with the gun?" I asked. "Why did you get it out of my nightstand?"

"What were *you* doing with it?" She sipped her tea.

"I asked first. I'm older."

Her smile was wan. "I was leaving you something. Mom's diary. The one missing from her bookshelf. I didn't expect to find the gun. Then I heard a noise downstairs."

"Go on."

I looked at my sister's lovely profile. Where her tears had left streaks, the bare skin around her eye was dark. She wasn't wearing makeup. It was some of the camouflage cosmetic war paint that I'd used to hide bruises on my face after the accident. "Who hit you, Mimi?" I asked quietly.

She turned toward me and her eyes were brimming with tears again. "Greg. I thought he was coming back for me."

"Come here." I held my arms out. She set down her teacup noisily on the glass coffee table, then came around to the wicker love seat and into my embrace. I stroked her hair and waited until she stopped crying. "Why did he do it?"

She wiped more tears and revealed more bare skin. It was a hell of a shiner. "He said it was an accident. He said he was sorry. But he got mad at me for something I did and, oh my God, Lucie, I've never seen him like that." Her voice shook. "Afterward he tried to make it up to me. He wanted to make love but I wouldn't let him touch me . . . he got so mad."

"Shhh. It's all right." I closed my eyes and rocked her. "He can't hurt you anymore. Don't you worry."

"I'm scared of him. I'm leaving," she said. "I'm going to New York."

I said surprised, "With Sara Rust?"

"How did you know?"

"I talked to her today. I know you're friends and that's where she's going, too. Does she know about this?" I pointed to the bruise.

"No!" She sat up, panicky. "Don't tell her, either! I don't think anyone knows about him—or this—except me. And now you."

"Knows what about him?"

She reached for her teacup and stared into it. "Wonder if you can really tell your fortune with tea leaves?" After a moment she said in a more composed voice, "I needed to finish registering for my fall classes at school. I didn't think he would mind if I used his computer. Lucie, he goes to those Internet chat rooms where you set up meetings with a stranger." She shuddered. "He said it's not breaking the law if both parties are consenting adults. I think he's sick."

I thought so, too. "You know he's been hanging around Sara at work," I said. "He told me he gave her money because she was in a jam."

"He must be lying or she knows about the sex stuff and she's blackmailing him. Greg never gave anyone a dime unless he had to."

Sara had been pretty quick to ask for the hundred and fifty dollars before I even got two words out of my mouth. A real hustler, that one. When I'd looked into her eyes earlier today it was like looking at two dead planets. Not the most wholesome friend Mia could have.

"I always wondered why Uncle Mason helped him out," Mia was saying.

"What?"

"Uncle Mason and Aunt Linda paid Greg's tuition at UNC. The full ride."

"I didn't know that. Why?"

"I don't know. They're rich. It was probably Aunt Linda's idea. She's always taking care of lost causes, the real no-hopers, helping out behind the scenes. Besides I think it bothered her that she and Uncle Mason didn't have kids. I think there were a lot of medical bills after Greg's dad died."

"Look," I said. "Go to New York for a few days, then come home, okay? Your classes will be starting soon. You need to pack and get down to Harrisonburg. James Madison University is a long way from where Greg is and, anyway, I'll take care of him. He'll never go within miles of you as long as he lives. Just promise me you'll come back."

She played again with that strand of hair, absently braiding and unbraiding it. "I never registered for my classes, Luce. I missed the deadline. Technically I'm not enrolled in school this semester."

"I can call someone . . ."

"I've been thinking about it for a while," she continued as though I hadn't spoken. "College is so hard, you know? Maybe I should just go to art school. I think I could get into a place like the Corcoran. It probably doesn't sound too modest, but I think I'm pretty good."

"You're very good," I said. "I saw the oil painting you started on Mom's easel. And your sketchbook."

She smiled. "What did you think?"

Maybe she was thinking about another sketchbook. She seemed genuinely interested to know how much I liked her work.

"That was a perfect likeness of me," I said carefully. "I always wondered what I'd look like with snakes in my hair."

She laughed. "Oh God, that's right. I forgot about those drawings. I had some horrible English class in allegory and mythology last semester that I absolutely hated. So I did those sketches for my final project. Got me out of taking the exam. My professor thought it showed what she called 'remarkable creativity, effectively demonstrating mastery of the material.' I got the highest grade in the class. I used a family picture of you that I had on the bulletin board over my desk."

"Who was the guy in the robe?"

"The Grim Reaper," she said. "Death. I was going to give it Eli's face from that same photo, but it kinda weirded me out. So I left him faceless." She stood up. "Sara's coming for me soon. I need to fix my makeup. I'll take the tea tray in."

I set the empty cups and the teapot on the tray. "How did you know I was looking for that journal of Mom's?"

"Brandi told me." She saw the surprised look on my face. "Eli told Brandi. You did talk about it with Eli, Lucie. I know you did." She bent over and picked up the tray and said without looking at me, "You two talked about Mom and Fitz."

"Brandi told you that?"

She straightened up. Her eyes had that same brightness as the day I saw her at the funeral home. "It's okay, Luce. I know people have affairs and I know what happened."

"You read all the diaries?"

"I had to use a dictionary, but yeah, I did. Really improved my French." Her smile was heartbreaking. "After Mom died and you and Eli left, I was alone with Pop . . . when he bothered to come home. He used to look at me in the oddest way, like I was some kind of alien. Once when he was drunk he let something slip about Mom and Fitz. I didn't hear him right and when I asked him to repeat it, he got mad and hollered at me. He never brought it up again and I was too scared to ask."

"Did the diary say anything . . . I mean, did she write about what happened?"

She stood in a shaft of strong sunlight, as fragile and beautiful as a porcelain angel. Except for the bruise.

"She was lonely, Luce. Who could blame her?" she said. "She loved Fitz, but she never stopped loving Pop. They were still sleeping together, right up until the time she died. She slept with Fitz, too, but . . . jeez, I mean . . . I'm Leland Montgomery's daughter, same as you are, if that's what you're getting at. She never wrote that I wasn't."

"He wasn't around when I was born," she continued. "Kind of a metaphor for my whole life." She smiled another poignant smile. "He left Mom for some big hunting trip in Montana when she was about eight months pregnant. I thought that was pretty callous. Of course she didn't criticize him. She never did." She paused, then added, "Did you know I was born in the backseat of Fitz's car?"

"Are you serious?"

"I swear to God. Apparently Mom called Uncle Mason when she went into labor but he never showed up. So she panicked and got Fitz to leave the inn and come get her in the middle of somebody's wedding reception."

"What happened to Mason?"

"He'd hit a deer. Speeding on Bull Run Mountain Road trying to get to the house. He practically totaled his car. Mom had no idea and he had no way of telling her." She shrugged. "Makes you glad there's cell phones now, hunh?"

"Yes. I suppose it does."

I was still on the veranda when she came back, makeup reapplied, looking calmer and more collected. "Sara's here. I've got to go." She touched a finger lightly near her eye, but this time she didn't wince. "Don't say anything to anyone. Promise?"

"It's pretty hard to miss."

"I walked into a door. Clumsy me."

"He shouldn't get away with it."

"Promise me, Lucie. I'm begging you. Please?"

I nodded, feeling sick.

She blew me a kiss. "I'll call you from New York."

The screen door slammed and a moment later I heard a car engine. Inside the house the phone rang. After a few rings the machine kicked in. With a small shock I heard Leland's voice. We had never changed the recording.

"You've reached the Montgomerys. Leave a message."

By the time I got inside the caller hung up. I hit the play button. A familiar Hispanic accent. "This is José at the Gas-o-Rama. We got your Volvo here and I need your approval and a credit card before I can fix your car. It's gonna be 'bout six hundred fifty dollars. Please call me soon as you get this message." He rattled off a number that I recognized as the one I'd called the other day.

The earlier messages from Kit and Hollis Maddox were still on the machine. I hit delete and dialed Kit's number.

"You sound terrible," she said. "Like you lost your last friend."

"What's wrong? Your message said it was urgent."

"Are you all right?"

"I'm not sure. It's a long story."

"Wanna tell me?"

"Not right now."

"How about later? I need to talk to you, anyway. Meet me after I leave work, say eight-fifteen? The home helper can't stay with my mom too late, so it's got to be quick. I know you've got that jazz concert tonight, but maybe you could slope off for a half hour."

"We could meet at the villa. Eight-fifteen's fine."

"See you."

She hung up and I glanced at my watch. Six-thirty.

I got the keys to Hector's truck and drove over to the winery. As I pulled into the parking lot, Mason Jones was climbing out of his silver Mercedes.

"Well, hey there, Lucie!" He came over and helped me climb down from the cab. "What're you doing driving that thing? It doesn't have any shocks left. I thought you were Hector, the way you tore in here. You're lucky you still have the teeth in your head, rattling around like that."

"Hector let me borrow his truck. The Volvo's in the shop."

"What's wrong with the Volvo? Don't tell me it finally gave up the ghost after all these years?" He sounded concerned.

"It's still got a heartbeat. Though it's going to cost me six hundred and fifty dollars to revive it."

He reached inside the breast pocket of his white linen suit and pulled out two tickets to the jazz concert. "That must be why you're looking so perturbed. You need a little help, sugar? I could give you a loan to tide you over."

"I've got it covered. Thanks, anyway."

He tucked my arm through one of his. "You going over to the concert? I'll walk you there. I'm surprised there aren't more folks showing up for this." He waved his tickets. "Parking lot's pretty empty."

"That's because the concert doesn't start for another hour. You're very early."

"Lordy. Guess I should have looked at these, shouldn't I? I must be getting old. I'd better call Linda and tell her she doesn't need to rush." He patted his breast pocket. "Left my mobile in my car, too. Old *and* forgetful. I'd better go get it."

The sun, blisteringly pitiless earlier in the day, was setting in the west, coloring the horizon rim pale red. "Can I ask you something first?"

"Shoot."

"Did you know that someone tried to buy the vineyard from Leland before he died?"

Mason tucked the tickets back in his jacket pocket and pressed his lips together, his expression slightly forbidding like I'd blundered into something the grown-ups were trying to keep hidden from the children. "I did. How'd you find out? We went to great lengths to keep that quiet."

"Fitz told me. Who was it? I'd like to know."

"Why, the consortium, of course."

"The Blue Ridge Consortium?"

"Yes, ma'am."

He reached into the pocket of his trousers, pulling out a folded nail file. I watched him unfold it, then gently pick at an imaginary piece of dirt under an immaculately manicured fingernail. Over the years I'd seen him do that dozens of times. A lawyer's delaying tactic. It gave him time to think.

"I'm going to tell you something." He leaned closer so I smelled his cologne. For a man who could afford anything, he still wore the same inexpensive scent that he'd always worn. "I didn't want you to know this, either. But, yes, we did offer to buy the place from Lee. Everyone figured out he was cash-strapped. Hell, you could have guessed even if he said nothing from the way he burned through money on those bogus investments of his. The consortium just wanted him to know his friends would help him out if he felt he needed to sell."

"Was someone else trying to buy the vineyard?"

"Besides us?" He shrugged. "Not that I know of. Your daddy had his pride, Lucie. It was just a quiet little talk among friends."

"Eli says we can't afford to keep the place."

"Well, can you?" he asked gently. When I didn't answer right away he added, "Look, sugar, I'm going to tell you the same thing I told your daddy and your brother when he talked to me the other day. If you decide to sell, come to me. I'll put together a deal so's the house and the land won't get split up. I'll take care of you. You'll get a fair price."

I leaned over and kissed his cheek. "You better call Aunt Linda. I'll meet you later at the concert."

"I won't be a minute. We can still walk over together."

I did not want to see Greg right now, especially with Mason by my side. I would keep my promise to Mia—for the time being—but my fury at what he'd done to her would almost certainly bleed through anything I said and Mason would start probing. The next time I spoke to Greg I wanted to be alone.

"Actually, I've got some winery business to take care of." I smiled. "You go ahead. I'll be there soon."

I waited until he left, then walked down to the barrel room. The shiny new heavy-duty lock was in the hasp.

I unlocked it, propping the door ajar with a brick. I hit the lights and held my breath. The grapevine thermometer now read sixty degrees. The carbon dioxide had built to toxic levels so I kept holding my breath as I swiftly crossed the room and flipped the switches on the fans. In another few minutes when the CO_2 cleared out, I could close the door again.

We had no money and no resources. How much longer could I keep the vineyard going on fumes? Leland's friends—out of pity— had tried to help him out, save him from further embarrassment and the crushing debt he'd left us.

I walked into Quinn's lab and leaned against the counter staring through the glass window at the rows and rows of casks. My mother's lifetime work. Something bulky dug into my hip. The reading glasses Sara Rust had given me were in the deep pocket of my skirt. I took them out and set them on the counter, just as the lights went out.

The light switch was next to the laboratory door. I groped until I found it, then flipped it on and off. Power failures were nothing new, the consequence of winter ice or summer thunderstorms, so we had a backup generator that would kick in momentarily.

I stood in the bleak silence of total darkness and waited for the small exploding sound of the generator, followed by the flash of lights, the whirring of fans, and the burbling sound of water moving through the space between the tank jackets as the refrigeration system kicked in again.

The silence lengthened and my heart started to pound.

I felt my way toward the outside door. In the complete, unnatural silence I heard the scraping sound of my brick being moved and the door closing. A second later someone put the lock into the hasp and snapped it shut.

If I didn't get out of here soon, the CO_2 would build up again and it would kill me.

CHAPTER 22

———— ∞∞∞ ————

Carbon dioxide works fast.

Like Fitz, I could die of asphyxiation. The fermenting wine bubbling merrily around me was filling the enormous room with lethal quantities of toxic gas. While Fitz's death had been instant—with only pure CO_2 in the tank—mine would be slow as the gas gradually sucked all the breathable oxygen out of the air. With no power and no fans there was no fresh supply of oxygen.

I had no idea how much time I had. More than a few minutes. Less than a few hours.

Though I knew my way around the barrel room, I had the temporary disadvantage of no night vision. If I made the trip across the room to the steel door—which I already knew was locked—I'd use up oxygen and time. I looked around for other ways to escape, but it isn't called a "cave" for nothing. My pulse was racing like a rabbit's and my heart thudded in my chest. I tried to slow my breathing.

Wine ages and ferments best in a cool, dark place. But for some reason our architect had mistakenly put in three slatlike casement windows located near the ceiling behind the stainless-steel tanks. They were sealed shut after the building inspector showed up and nearly had a coronary, since anything that lets in both air and light doesn't conform to code. I don't know how my mother talked him into it but we didn't have to spend the extra money to brick them up or even paint them over as long as they remained permanently closed.

The windows were too narrow for me to climb through, and even if I could shimmy through the opening, I'd be doing a swan dive from two stories up onto drought-hardened terrain. But if I could prop our twenty-foot extension ladder below the window and then break the glass with my cane, at least I'd be breathing oxygen instead of CO_2.

My vision was improving and the huge steel tanks became looming shadows lining the far wall. The ladder should have been hanging from an oversized set of hooks on the adjacent wall, near the hoses. I hadn't noticed if it was there when the lights were on. If it was gone that was it. I'd be dead when someone finally found me in the morning.

I knew from Jacques's repeated lectures that one of the early symptoms of CO_2 poisoning was anxiety. Later came dizziness, confusion, and finally loss of consciousness and death. Already the room seemed stuffy. Wasn't it too soon for that to happen? God, who knew?

The anxiety had started.

I walked slowly toward the wall using my cane to orient myself as a blind person would. The extension ladder was exactly where it belonged on the hooks. I leaned my cane against the wall so I could use both hands to get it down, just like Jacques and the crew always had. I don't know why I assumed it would practically float into my arms but it was heavier and more unwieldy than I'd bargained on. My bad foot buckled as I jerked the ladder up and over the hooks. It slipped out of my grip, crashing onto the concrete floor. By some miracle it missed landing on my feet. I could hear my heartbeat in my ears, feel it pulsing behind my eyes.

I half-dragged, half-shoved the ladder along the floor until I was below the bank of windows. Dizziness seeped into my brain. I bit the back of my hand until it hurt to keep from screaming.

I'd read stories about people who found some kind of superhuman strength that enabled them to pick up a car or move a collapsed wall because it was a matter of life or death. Wherever that burst of strength came from—divine intervention or adrenaline-fueled fear—I picked up the ladder and placed it against the wall like it was suddenly made of balsa wood.

The metal latch in the extension mechanism clanked against the rungs as I pulled on the rope. The ladder grew toward the window like Jack's beanstalk. I heard the lock snap into place and tied off the halyard. Then I hung my cane on one of the rungs and gripped the sides of the ladder. My hands were so sweaty they slipped.

I am, unfortunately, acrophobic. An accident involving me and a rickety tree house when I was eight. I wiped my wet hands on my skirt and looked up. The windows seemed to float above me. I shook my head and blinked hard until they finally stopped moving. Then I put my foot on the first rung—and climbed. After a couple of rungs I hooked my cane over my arm so I wouldn't keep bumping against it. I'd made it to the fifteenth rung before the cane hit the side of the ladder. It slipped, ricocheting off one of the steel tanks before clanking on the concrete below. I rested my head against one of the rungs and sobbed.

CO_2 pools in low places. The top of the ladder was better than the bottom and I was nearly there. There was no climbing down to get the cane. I counted four more rungs, then I was at eye level with one of the windows and moonlight was glinting through the caked-on grime. I rubbed the glass with my hand even though I knew there would be nothing to see except a field leading to the woods. This was the far side of the building. Anyone who strolled by below was somewhere they didn't belong.

My head ached. Concentrating was a chore. Open the window. That's all I had to remember. Just one thing.

I banged on the glass with my fist but it might as well have been steel. Nothing moved. I tried the joint between the glass and the frame, running my finger along the caulked seal.

The caulk was old and brittle and there was a piece missing. I dug at the hole with my fingernail and another long chalklike piece fell out. My breathing was more labored now but I kept pulling at new ragged edges, as more and more caulk broke off. CO_2 poisoning is supposed to leave an acid taste in your mouth. By the time I finished mine tasted of blood from biting the tip of my tongue.

I pushed on the glass again, willing it to move. It was stuck as firmly as when I'd started. The window was caulked on the outside, too.

I thumped the glass again with my fist, this time beginning in the lower right-hand corner and working my way around the perimeter of the window. If there was one spot where the caulk had fallen out, maybe I could shove the glass out of the frame. I heard a small crack and something gave way. I pounded some more.

The glass swung like a hinge, about two inches out of the frame. I put my mouth and nose to the opening and gulped fresh air. My head throbbed and my heart felt like there was a vise around it, but at least I wasn't going to die yet.

In the distance, music from the jazz concert floated across the sultry stillness and the cicadas sang to me. There were no other sounds. I was alone.

Unless whoever kicked that brick away from the door was still around. If I called out now he'd know I was alive. Then he'd come back and rattle the ladder until I landed like Humpty Dumpty on the concrete floor below.

I clung to the window ledge and listened to a jazz riff that sounded like someone trying to sound like Mangione. All I had to do was stay here until morning when Quinn or Hector opened the door to the barrel room and discovered me perched atop the ladder like a bird in a treetop. Guarding a warm room filled with tanks of very expensive vinegar.

I hooked one arm through the rung of the ladder and held on to the windowsill with the other. And waited.

The voices came after what seemed like hours. At first I thought I was dreaming them. Then they grew closer. Coming my way.

"I can't imagine what happened to her." Kit, sounding worried. "We agreed to meet at the villa at eight-fifteen."

"Hey!" I shouted. "Look up! I'm here!"

"Why in the hell don't I hear the air conditioner and the equipment?" Quinn was with her. "Something's wrong. I've got to get inside and find out what's going on. Come on! Let's go!"

Their voices grew fainter as they moved away from under the eaves. I saw—or maybe hoped for—darker shadows in my line of vision that meant they had moved to where they could finally see the sliver of my barely opened window.

Quinn's voice again. "Holy shit, look up there! There's a window open. Someone's in there. With the power off the place will be full of carbon dioxide. Run!"

"Yes," I shouted uselessly. "I'm in here. Please come get me!"

I suppose, in retrospect, Quinn did the right thing taking care of the wine first before he got to me. The lights came on and the air-conditioning started with a roar. The fans began whirring and I blinked in the hard, sudden brightness.

The door opened and I heard Kit scream my name.

"Kit! Don't move," Quinn ordered. "Let the CO_2 clear out first."

The ladder shook as Quinn climbed toward me. I clung to it, white-knuckled, too scared to look down where Kit stood twenty feet below, praying I wouldn't fall off in the process of being rescued after the near-death miracle of surviving poisoning by carbon dioxide. He stopped just below me and put an arm around my waist. He smelled of perspiration and something tropical, like coconut. "Are you strong enough to climb down on your own if I stay right here with you? I don't think the ladder's sturdy enough for me to carry you and I don't want to find out the hard way."

"I'll be all right."

"Take your time."

We went down slowly, and then he jumped off a few rungs from the bottom and reached up and pulled me into his arms like he was grabbing a sack of potatoes. "Let's get her out of here," he said. "She looks like a ghost."

He carried me outside and set me down on the grass.

"Is she going to live?" Kit asked.

"She'll be okay, but she's probably got a headache the size of Pittsburgh."

"Why are you talking about me in the third person?" I mumbled. "I can hear what you're saying."

"Hush," Kit said. "We probably ought to get her to the hospital."

"She doesn't want to go to the hospital," I said. "And she means it."

"Don't be silly," Kit said. "You've got to let someone check you out."

"No! I'll be fine."

"Well, then, you're coming home with me," Kit said.

"No, she's coming home with me." Quinn stood up. "Keep her quiet. I'm going to call Hector and get him to stay here tonight in case there are more equipment problems."

"Lucie," Kit said urgently after Quinn left, "do you know how lucky you are to be alive? Jesus Lord. What are the odds that your power and your backup would fail at the same time?"

I tried to sit up on my elbows but my head felt like Fourth of July fireworks exploding and the ground started to spin so I lay down again. "They didn't. Someone shut down the power and the generator. Then they put the lock through the hasp so I couldn't open it from inside."

"Oh my God."

"Where was Quinn when you found him?"

"You don't think Quinn . . . ? Oh, no. Not him." She put her hand on my forehead, checking apparently for a fever or signs I was delirious. "I ran into him as he was coming back from the Ruins. I'd been looking for you for a while. I saw the look on his face when he realized what had happened. He was trying to calculate how long it had been since he was last there, when he knew the power was on. It wasn't him."

I tried to sit up again and groaned.

"Lie down," she said. "You're not going anywhere."

"Unless I roll away. I get vertigo just being two inches off the ground." I lay on my back again. "When you called you said you had something to tell me."

"It can wait."

"Maybe not."

"I found out who tried to buy the vineyard from your father."

"I already know. Mason told me tonight."

"I think it stinks."

I made one more attempt to lever myself to a semi-sitting position. The aurora borealis was still going on inside my head, but I was lucid enough to figure out that we weren't talking about the same thing. "What stinks?"

"Building a Civil War theme park. Here, of all places. It's disgusting."

"What are you talking about? The Blue Ridge Consortium offered to buy it, presumably to turn it into parkland, not theme-park land. Besides, who would want to build a Civil War theme park here, anyway? How dumb can you be to invent something when you've got the real McCoy?"

"That's not what I heard," she said. "Leland was approached by someone on behalf of a group of developers. They want to get in under the radar, get the land first. Then they'd work on bribing whoever they needed to in Richmond to get the zoning laws changed."

"How do you know about this?"

"I'm a reporter. It's my business to know."

"Well," I said, "it doesn't matter anymore, anyway. The vineyard's not for sale."

"They'll buy something else. You're not the only fish in the pond."

"The Blue Ridge Consortium will stop them, once they get wind of it. Besides, who do you know around here who'd like to have their farm back up on a theme park?"

"Don't be naïve," she said. "For enough money some people will do anything." I opened my mouth to reply, but Kit shook her head. Quinn was walking toward us. She said in a low voice, "Don't say anything about this. For once in my life, it would be nice to have a scoop and not get beat by the *Post*."

I nodded as Quinn reached us. "Hector's on his way. I found him talking to Eli when they were clearing up after the concert." He leaned down and scooped me up. "Put your arms around my neck."

He was settling me into the front seat of his Toyota when a black Corvette pulled into the parking lot and Hector got out.

"Stay here," Quinn ordered, "while I talk to Hector."

Eli said he wasn't coming to any more festival events because of some deadline at work. At least, that was his story. Why did he change his plans?

"Do you still think Eli's involved in this?" She read my mind.

"He wasn't supposed to be here tonight. I want to talk to him."

"About what? Maybe trying to kill you tonight in the barrel room? Come on, Lucie," Kit said. "I think we ought to get Bobby over here."

"Absolutely not . . . I need to talk to Eli, Kit. It'll turn into a three-ring circus when Bobby gets involved."

Quinn's footsteps crunched on the gravel.

"Tomorrow," Kit said. "I'm calling Bobby tomorrow. At least tonight I know you're with Quinn."

"Give me twenty-four hours. Then I'll call Bobby myself. I promise."

She nodded imperceptibly as Quinn said, "All right. It's all set up with Hector. Why don't we get out of here? We've got harvest again tomorrow morning."

Kit left in the Jeep before we did, driving fast enough to churn up a cloud of dust. Her way of letting me know she was not happy with the way our conversation had gone. The Toyota started, sounding like a dentist's drill that just hit something bad.

I leaned my head back against the vibrating seat. Who tried to kill me tonight?

Someone who knew his way around the winery and how to work all the equipment. Eli?

Not him. He was too concerned about any more "accidents" happening at the winery and what it might do to discourage prospective buyers. However much I stood in his way, he wouldn't have picked the winery as a place for yet another murder.

Then who?

Quinn? He could have shut the power off, then gone back to the concert. Maybe Kit met him on a return trip to the barrel room, double-checking to make sure I was dead and his "concern," as Kit called it, was part of the ruse. Now he was adamant that I go home with him, instead of her.

Hanging out at Mom's Place watching Angela, he could have gotten to know Sara Rust. Sure. He could be a suspect.

And now here I was going home with him. Alone.

Maybe I'd just played right into his hands.

CHAPTER 23

Quinn's cottage was on the same dirt spur as Hector and Sera's place, about a half-mile in the other direction. The last time I'd visited, Jacques lived there.

Quinn hadn't left any lights on and, with the heavy tree canopy overhead, no ambient light permeated the woods. His cottage seemed smaller than I remembered, but perhaps it was the deceptive way places have of shrinking when memory is finally confronted by reality, as though you're looking through the wrong end of the telescope.

He stopped the car. "I'll come 'round and get you."

"I can manage."

"No, you can't," he said. "I found your cane on the floor in the barrel room. It's got a big dent in it. You can't use it the way it is. Hector said he'd try to straighten it out, but he's not sure he can do it without breaking it. You got another one?"

"No."

"Then sit still. I don't need you falling on your face." He sounded annoyed, more than anything else.

He nudged open the screen door with his foot and flipped on the light switch with his elbow. We were in the middle of the living room. It was as soulless as a hotel room. This was a man without a past or a present.

"You take my bed," he said. "You'll be comfortable there."

"I wouldn't dream of inconveniencing you."

"The sheets are clean. I've been sleeping at the summerhouse. Or at Angie's."

"That's not what I meant."

"Nevertheless, I'd prefer to have you there."

"In your bed."

"I was thinking more in terms of you not being on the couch because it's in a room with a door to the outside."

"You think I might run away?"

"I think someone's looking for you," he said. "At least this way, they'd have to get past me first."

He spoke in his characteristically blunt and unemotional way so it was hard to tell if he considered being my human shield as part of the maintenance responsibilities that came with his job or if he really cared what happened to me. Either way, his words were disturbing.

Quinn shifted my weight in his arms. "I need to set you down. My arm is going to sleep. Let's get you into the bedroom."

"I can walk."

"You couldn't even sit a while ago without getting dizzy."

He carried me into the bedroom, a real monastic cell, and set me down on the bed.

"You want a drink?"

"What have you got?"

"Whiskey."

"No wine?"

"I've got wine. You look like you could do with something stronger."

"Carbon dioxide does that to me. Okay, then. Whiskey's fine."

The whiskey was somewhere in the living room. I could hear him rummaging around and then the sound of glasses clinking together. He showed up with two glasses and a bottle of Jack Daniel's. He poured two shots and handed me one of them.

"I figured you take it straight," he said.

"Do I look as bad as that?"

"That foot must really bother you at the end of the day. It looks pretty twisted. I'm sure it hurts."

I must have shrunk back against the headboard as though he'd just seen me naked. "I don't really think that's any of your business."

Outside the bedroom window a flash of silver light illuminated the silhouettes of trees and bushes. I jumped.

"Calm down. Storm's a long way off. We won't get any rain tonight." As if to validate his statement, distant thunder rumbled like muffled drums. "Not until tomorrow or the day after. Give me your foot, Lucie. I've had some training in this."

I shifted on the bed so that my left foot was tucked underneath my right leg. "If you mean you've been practicing back rubs on Angela, thanks, but I'll pass." There was no way I was going to let him touch my foot. He'd have to look at it. I managed fine by keeping it hidden under a dress or long pants. To display it, in all its misshapen deformity, made me feel like Superman without the cape and special suit.

"I was talking about medical training. Therapeutic massage." He reached over and slid my dress up my leg. "Come here. Give me your foot. I won't hurt you."

I had to look away while he did it, but he was right. He knew what he was doing.

"Why did you change your name?" I asked abruptly.

On cue, the thunder crashed around us. He looked at me in the washed-out light, his face all angular planes and dark shadows. "What are you talking about?"

"Isn't your real name Paolo Santori?"

"Legally. But I'm not real big on Paolo. It was my old man's name."

There was another crack of thunder, but this one was so close it sounded like a cannon going off in the front yard. I sloshed whiskey down the side of my glass and caught the drip with my finger, licking it.

"What happened in California?" I asked.

He reached for the bottle and poured us both refills. "How'd you hear about that?"

"Leland had a copy of the *San Jose Mercury News* among his papers. Surely you didn't think I wouldn't find out. Why didn't you say something?"

He walked over to his dresser and opened the top drawer. For some reason, my heart started doing the war drum thing again. Then I saw the box of Swisher Sweets and resumed breathing. He removed a cigar and came back over to the bed. "Hand me that ashtray, will you?" he said.

It was on the bedside table, next to me. I gave it to him. He fished a lighter out of the pocket of his camouflage trousers. He lit up, walked over to the window, and stared outside. Lightning flashed and the lights went out briefly and came on again.

"I never kept it a secret."

"Did Leland know?"

"Of course. I told him up front."

"What did he say?"

"He said he appreciated my honesty. Most people would have tried to cover up something like that."

It was also true that when Leland checked his references, he would have found out anyway. Maybe Quinn was just trying to get in front of a bad situation. Besides, the "honesty" remark didn't sound quite like Leland, a man who had his own reputation for playing fast and loose with the truth. "Can I ask you something else?"

"Fire away. You seem to be on a roll tonight."

I ignored that. "Did you know about Leland before you applied for a job here?"

"What about him?"

"His past was a bit . . . shaky. He had some questionable business partners. And you seem to know a lot about our financial problems."

He swung around. "Meaning what?"

The lights went out again but this time they didn't come back on. Quinn was silent.

"I think we just lost power." My voice sounded small.

There was a metallic click and then a flash of fire. He held his lighter aloft. "Yeah, this time for real. I've got candles." He sounded mad.

He left the room holding his lighter like a torch. I heard the front door open and close. Where did he keep his candles? In the bushes? I sat in the dark as a bead of perspiration ran down my cheek.

The front door opened and closed again. The living room glowed faintly orange and he walked back into the bedroom, shielding a candle against air currents with one hand. "I just tried to call Hector on my mobile. He must have turned his off and the phones are out. I think I'd better go back over there and see if the generator came on. You're coming, too. I don't want you here by yourself."

"I can walk to the car."

"You can hopscotch for all I care. Come on, let's go. I've got a flashlight by the front door."

I walked unsteadily to the car. Neither of us spoke on the drive back to the vineyard. The thunder rumbled more quietly now than before and the lightning zigzagged in the distance, toward the west and the mountains. He pulled into the parking lot. "Stay here," he said. "I'll be right back. You'll be all right for a few minutes. Lean on the horn, if you need me."

He took the flashlight, then sprinted up the stairs in the direction of the loggia and the barrel room. He disappeared out of the swath of light made by the car headlights and I was alone. I switched on the radio and hit the button until I got to WLEE.

Greg's voice. " . . . has been real hard on the local economy. One of the worst droughts on record."

"Well, it's too late for me," a male voice said. "I sold my cattle last week. Nothing for them to eat. They were starving to death."

"I'm sorry to hear that, Ron," Greg said.

"You and me both."

"Looks like we're not going to get a break from the heat any time soon," he said. "The National Weather Service is predicting more hot, dry weather for the next few days."

What weather forecast was he listening to? It was big news that we were finally in for some rain. Unless, of course, he'd actually had this conversation with Ron some other time.

He was rebroadcasting an old show.

"I know," Ron was agreeing. "A hunnert and thirty days with no rain. A record."

"Look, how about I play something by Art Pepper for you? 'Here's That Rainy Day.' We can always dream, right?"

"You dream, son. But, sure, I like old Art. Dedicate it to Mandy, would you? We'll be married thirty-four years tomorrow."

"That's great, thirty-four years. Okay, Mandy, here's Art Pepper with Gerry Mulligan playing 'Here's That Rainy Day.' Happy Anniversary from Ron. This is WLEE in Leesburg, Virginia, and you're listening to *Knight Moves*."

I saw headlights in the rearview mirror of Quinn's car just as the haunting sexy sound of a sax began to wail. The driver wasn't coming to the winery. It sounded like the car was heading toward the house. There weren't too many engines that purred like that.

Eli's Jag.

I slid over to the driver's seat of the Toyota, put it in gear and backed out of the parking lot. By the time I got to the house, the Jaguar was parked next to the front door. The power was out here, too. Inside the house was black as a coal mine. My flashlight was still in the picnic basket where I'd left it since my trip to the Goose Creek Bridge with Kit. Quinn had taken his with him. I waited until my night vision adjusted to the gloomy foyer. A beam of light played upstairs. He'd come prepared.

I climbed the stairs quietly, holding the railing with both hands since my cane was gone. I heard him in Mia's room and the sound of opening and closing drawers. I stood in the doorway and watched as he pulled a small bundle of letters out of the drawer to her nightstand.

"Do you mind telling me what you're doing?"

He let out a yelp as he shot up from where he'd been kneeling in front of the nightstand and whacked his knee on the corner of the open drawer.

"Jesus H. Christ, Lucie! What are you doing, sneaking up on me?"

I walked over to him, limping heavily without my cane. "What's that?"

"None of your damn business." He jerked his hand out of my reach and an envelope slithered out of the package he was holding and fell to the ground. He shone the flashlight around our feet. "Damnit."

"It's probably under the bed. We've got spiders, by the way. Want to get it?"

His fear of spiders was legendary, as bad as my fear of heights. "You made me drop it. You get it."

"Give me the flashlight. I can't see a thing."

I held on to the bed and knelt on my good leg. The envelope was addressed to Greg Knight and the return address was from Brandi Simone. Eli helped me up and I gave it to him. "Are all of those envelopes full of letters she wrote him?"

"I have no idea."

"How did you know they were here?"

"Mia got them."

"From Greg?"

"In a manner of speaking."

"She stole them from him?"

"They belong to Brandi."

"What's in them?"

"I have no idea," he repeated. "They're private."

"He was blackmailing her, wasn't he?" I said. "What did he want from her?"

"Look," he said, "she's having false labor again. I've got to get back home right away."

"What are you talking about? Haven't you been here all night?"

"I came from home," he said stiffly.

"You were at the jazz concert."

"So what? It's a free country last I checked. I stopped by, then I went home."

"She sent you back to get these letters, didn't she?"

"No, I'm psychic. I knew they'd be here."

"They must be pretty important. Aren't you going to look at them?"

His voice was harsh. "I don't think that would do a damned bit of good. They're ancient history."

"You really love her, don't you?"

"You have no idea, babe," he said. "Not a clue."

Then he brushed by me and I heard him clatter down the stairs. A minute later, the Jag's motor leaped to life and roared away.

I groped down the stairs hand over hand, clinging to the walnut banister. Two thirds of the way down I knew someone else was in the foyer standing in the shadows.

Waiting for me.

CHAPTER 24

—✺—

"What are you doing here?" Quinn's disembodied voice came from somewhere near the front door. A flashlight swept the room like a semaphore until he spotlighted me. In the unexpected brightness I missed the next stair. My bad foot twisted and buckled.

"Oh, for God's sake." He crossed the room and took the stairs two at a time. "You are going to break your stupid neck. What is it with you tonight?" he demanded. "And, no, I don't mind one bit that you borrowed my car. I enjoyed the moonlight walk over here except for being nearly run over by your brother, who acted like he was driving the home stretch of the Indy 500."

"I saw Eli drive past the winery while I was waiting for you. I followed him."

"You are one weird family. What was Eli doing here at midnight with all the lights off?"

"Retrieving something that belonged to Brandi."

"It couldn't wait until morning?"

"No."

"You know, to hell with you." He sounded furious, all of a sudden. "You can stay here by yourself and wait until the power comes on for all I care. I'm leaving."

He started down the steps again.

"Wait! Please! Where are you going?"

"The summerhouse. I need some sleep. You probably ought to get some, too. I'm sure your favorite hammock's free. Here." He tossed the flashlight to me. "Take this. I don't need it. No one's trying to kill me. I'll be fine. Thanks for asking."

He strode over to the door to the veranda, flinging it open and disappearing outside. I limped after him but the darkness had already swallowed him up.

"Wait! I'm coming with you!"

No answer. By the time I reached the summerhouse he was standing outside, arms folded, staring stonily at the night sky. He didn't turn his head or acknowledge my arrival.

At least now I knew why he was spending his nights here. A telescope sat on a tripod, aimed at the skies above the Blue Ridge. On one of our old wooden tables was a collection of magazines. *Star Gazer.* An astronomy magazine.

"Astronomy? You come here to look at stars?"

"Got a problem with it?" he snapped.

"Uh, no."

"The leaf canopy's pretty dense at the cottage. The view is much better here."

"I guess it would be."

He held the door for me and we both went inside the summerhouse. "You are one royal pain in the ass sometimes, you know that?"

"I could say the same thing about you."

I shone the flashlight around the room. When my mother was alive we'd used the place all the time for dinner parties and as a quiet retreat to get away and read. It had been filled with plants and more of her white wicker furniture, but now everything was heaped in a corner and it had become another storage depot for beach paraphernalia, a couple of garden hoses, Leland's golf clubs, and two graying Adirondack chairs.

Quinn went over to the golf bag and pulled out one of the clubs. "I think something's probably living at the bottom of that bag, but why don't you use this temporarily as a cane?" He handed me the golf club.

"Thank you."

"And now," he said, removing his shirt, "I'm going to sleep. Good night, Lucie." I would have expected a tattoo of a hissing serpent or something with thorns woven through it like I'd seen on the beach in France, but he'd stripped off most of the usual jewelry so all he wore was a plain gold cross on a heavy chain. He was no Greg, and of course he was about twenty years older, but he looked good, considering.

He saw me staring. "Now what's wrong?"

"I hope that's as far as you're going to go."

"Nope." He unzipped his pants and pulled them off. He was wearing a pair of plaid boxer shorts. He sat down on an air mattress. "This is as far as I'm going to go. See you in the morning."

"Where am I supposed to sleep? I'm not sleeping in one of those Adirondack chairs. It's like sleeping on a wooden airline seat."

"You can have half the mattress if you like. There's room." He turned over and closed his eyes. I waited, debating an uncomfortable night of sitting in the chair or part of a musty air mattress with a half-naked man I had practically just accused of trying to kill me. "Aw, for God's sake, lie down, will you? I don't bite."

"All right, but I'm sleeping in my clothes."

"Honey, I don't care if you sleep in a suit of armor. Lie down and let's get some sleep. We're getting up in less than three hours."

I settled next to him on the far edge of the mattress, my back to his back. I heard his breathing lengthen and grow more measured.

"Are you still awake?"

"Aw, jeez." He rolled over on his back. I turned around and faced him, leaning on my elbow. He looked sideways at me. "What?"

"That newspaper article said they'd never recovered any money from the winemaker."

In one swift movement he stood up and went outside to the telescope. I could see his silhouette through the screen door as he bent over and squinted through the eyepiece. "Ever look at the stars, Lucie?"

"Um . . . sure. Not through a telescope."

"I thought I was going to miss 'em tonight, but now the moon has set." He paused, to adjust one of the eyepieces. "We can see the Perseids."

"Oh?"

"You know what they are, don't you?"

"One of the summer constellations?"

He shook his head and rummaged for something on the table near the stack of magazines. "They're a meteor shower. Yesterday and today are the only days they're visible this year. They were beautiful last night." I heard the crackling of cellophane as he unwrapped a cigar.

So he'd been here last night.

"Come here." There was a small flash of fire as he lit up. I went out and joined him. "They're not as spectacular as the aurora borealis, but they're really something. First, I want you to look up in the sky."

I obeyed as he sketched with his cigar the outline of the three stars that made up the Summer Triangle above us, then made me look through the telescope at the swath of light, like an explosion, that passed through the band of stars.

"What is it?"

"The Milky Way. Actually all the stars you see in the sky belong to the Milky Way. It's just that when you look along the edge of the galaxy, you see thousands more stars than by looking above or below it. Now here . . . look . . . the Perseids."

It was, as he said, like watching fireworks. "It's beautiful. Does it happen often?"

"Every August."

"Too bad I never saw it in France. There wasn't much light pollution where I lived. The sky was always full of stars and they seemed so close it was like I could grab a fistful and pull them down."

"Lucky you. You could have seen the Perseids if you'd looked on the right day and time. A change in longitude doesn't change the night sky from one place to the next. A change in latitude does. You were about the same latitude in Grasse that we are here."

He smoked his cigar and we sat, side by side, in silence. Then he said, "I hope Allen Cantor rots in jail. As for what happened to the money he stole, who knows?"

"You had no idea what he was doing?"

"No," he said. "Though I'm sure you don't believe that."

"How could somebody you were so close to deceive you so completely?"

"Happens all the time, sweetheart. What's the saying? 'Regret is insight that comes a day too late.'" He stood up. "Come on. It will be light in two hours. We still have harvest in the morning. I think we should sleep."

He was already awake and dressed when I opened my eyes. "Power's on. I can see lights coming from the house. I'm going to get some breakfast. You want something?"

I leaned on the golf club and stood up. "I need a shower and a change of clothes."

We split up when we got back to the house. He headed for the kitchen and I went upstairs. When I joined him later, he'd brewed a pot of coffee and was in the middle of cooking something on the stove.

"What's that?"

"Omelet. Want some?"

"What's in it?"

"Whatever you had in the refrigerator. Salsa. Goat cheese. Tuna."

"Maybe I'll pass. Is there any bread?"

"Nope. You're pretty cleaned out. It's the omelet or nothing."

It actually wasn't that bad. While we were eating he said, "I called Hector while you were upstairs. He says everything's quiet. We only lost power for an hour, so at least the generator wasn't running all night."

When we finished eating I took our plates and stacked them in the kitchen sink. "Let's get over there," he said. "You ready?"

I picked up the golf club where I'd propped it against the wall.
"Yes."

We walked out the front door. The Toyota was right where I'd
parked it. The air felt different and the sky was overcast. He looked
at me and raised his eyebrows. "Car keys?"

"What?"

"You drove here last night."

"So I did. I left them on the dresser in my room. I'll get them."

"No, I'll go." He stared at the sky. "It's going to rain."

"Feels like it."

"I'll be right back. Why don't you practice your golf swing while
you're waiting?"

"Ha, ha."

He disappeared inside the house. I swung the golf club absently,
then stopped and looked at the dirty white ceiling of low cloud
cover in the early morning sky. It was definitely going to rain. We'd
have to work fast to get rest of the Chardonnay picked.

"What's the matter?" He reappeared with his keys. "You look
upset."

"I think I'm starting to get a headache. It's definitely going to rain."

"What are you, a human barometer or something?"

"I need some aspirin."

"Let's get over to the winery. I've got some in my office." He
started the Toyota. We pulled into the parking lot. The only other
vehicles there were Hector's pickup and Bonita's Corvette. "Why
don't you go see Hector and check things out?" Quinn said. "I've
got to run back to my place for a minute. These clothes could walk
by themselves. I'll be right there."

I found Hector, looking sleepy, sitting on a stool in Quinn's lab
in the barrel room. "Morning, Lucita." He stretched and yawned.
"The crew's on its way. César went to get them. We'll start picking
then, though I'm gonna let César take over for today. I'm going
home to get some sleep."

"Do you know how many men we've got coming?"

He picked up a piece of paper and squinted at it. He patted his shirt pocket absently and frowned. I watched him reach for the reading glasses on the counter and put them on.

I'd left those glasses here last night when the power went out. Hector thought they were his.

"Looks like we got eight men."

"Those glasses," I said quietly. "I guess they really help you read, don't they?"

He looked up from the paper, over the top of the glasses. "Oh, I can still read some stuff real good," he said. "But not small print. Maps. Menus. Anything with little writing." He took off the glasses. "These are pretty strong, though. All those drugstore glasses look alike until you put them on."

"They're not yours?"

"Nope."

"Can I have them, please?"

He looked puzzled, but passed them over to me. "What's wrong, Lucita? Where are you going?"

"To return them to their owner," I said. "I know who they belong to."

CHAPTER 25

I left the barrel room and walked along the courtyard loggia toward the parking lot. I knew who. I didn't understand why.

A man who had everything.

As I rounded the corner I nearly collided with him. He was dressed immaculately as always, even at this hour of the morning.

He looked astonished to see me. "Why, hello, sugar," he smiled. "I wasn't expecting to find you here."

When Eli and I were kids, we used to fry marbles in an old cast-iron skillet, then pour ice water over them. The sudden temperature change would make them crack inwardly. The marbles were broken, but not shattered.

Looking into his familiar eyes I thought of those marbles. "That's because you thought I'd be in the barrel room, where you left me last night. You're the one who locked that door and shut off the electricity and the generators," I said.

"I don't know what you're talking about."

"Yes, you do, Mason. You tried to kill me and you were coming back just now to make sure I was dead." I held out the reading glasses. "These are yours, aren't they?"

His face was like granite. "Where did you get them?"

"From Sara Rust. You must have dropped them when you were searching her house. That's why you arrived so early at the concert last night. You couldn't read the small print on your ticket so you thought it started at six thirty, not seven thirty. Why, Mason? Why did you do this?"

He slipped the gun out of a holster under his jacket as easily as if he'd been reaching for his starched handkerchief. "I wish you hadn't done this, sugar. Now I'm going to have to do something about it. Let's go."

Mason went hunting every year with the Romeos. He was a crack shot.

"You wouldn't." He'd burped me as a baby, maybe even watched when my mother changed my diaper. I wasn't fooling him.

"No one's coming. I know Hector's in the barrel room. And I saw Quinn leave about five minutes ago. So we haven't got much time. Now move. I don't want to shoot you here." He motioned for me to walk in front of him to the parking lot.

The silver Mercedes was parked next to Bonita's Corvette. "Get in," he said, "and don't do anything stupid. I don't want blood all over my car."

I got in the car. He leaned over me and pulled something out of his glove compartment. Plastic handcuffs. "Put your hands out."

He cuffed me and we drove out of the parking lot, headed for Atoka Road. We passed the turnoff for Quinn's cottage. No sign of the Toyota.

"He'll be a while," Mason said. "He's got a few things to untangle."

"What did you do to him?"

"Nothing."

My voice shook. "Why are you doing this? Are you trying to buy the vineyard yourself? What do you want it for? You already own a palace."

"You wouldn't understand."

"How do you know?"

He glanced over at me, with his most ruthless and pitiless courtroom eyes. "Because you've never been a success. Nor any of your family."

I held up my hands, manacled in the plastic handcuffs. "What a shame I'm not as successful as you are. Look where it's brought you."

I shouldn't have goaded him. He had that gun.

"Shut up!" He reached out and slapped my face hard with the back of his hand. My head jerked backward. We had reached Atoka Road. He put on his left turn signal, though there wasn't a soul in sight. Law-abiding citizen kidnaps niece at gunpoint. At least he wouldn't be cited for a traffic violation.

He drove through Atoka in silence, then turned onto Mosby's Highway.

"I thought we'd take a little drive to the Goose Creek Bridge," he said casually. "Since it's one of your favorite spots."

I'd never thought of him as sadistic before. He was enjoying this.

"Who was in the SUV, Mason?"

He didn't even flinch. "Someone who owed me a favor. He's not in jail like he oughta be."

"And I was the favor. Was he supposed to kill me?"

He said, coolly, "It would have been an unexpected bonus."

I shivered and stared at the man who used to bounce me on his knee. "Does Aunt Linda know what you're doing?"

He glanced over at me and those eyes shut me up immediately.

Another blinker signal and we turned smoothly onto the gravel road that led to the Goose Creek Bridge. It was too much to hope that there would be someone there, picnicking at dawn. "Get out."

I opened the car door and stepped out. He let me keep the golf club. It didn't help much with the plastic handcuffs.

"Move."

"Then take these handcuffs off," I said, "or you can carry me."

"Don't be a fool."

"The ground's uneven. It's hard enough using my cane, but nearly impossible with this golf club. Come on, Mason. Do you really think I can run away?"

He hesitated, then reached in his pocket and pulled out the key.

I held out my hands as he unlocked them and yanked them off my wrists. For a moment he seemed unsure what to do with them. Then he opened the door to the Mercedes and threw them on the passenger seat.

"Walk to the bridge."

I walked as slowly as I could, even stumbling a little, but he was only going to believe so much ineptitude. Besides, who was going to find me here?

We finally reached the arched stone bridge. The air was heavy with the scent of honeysuckle, as it had been when I was there with Kit . . . when? Two nights ago?

"Okay." He gestured to the parapet. "Climb up there. You're going to jump."

"You are out of your mind. There's no water." I didn't move from the gravel path. He was about ten yards away from me.

"You're too distraught to notice. The vineyard has no future. Everyone in town knows you and Eli are battling over money because you're broke."

"Everyone in town knows I'm not suicidal."

"You're dependent on painkillers since your accident and it's changed you. You became despondent when you found out your ex-lover was screwing your sister. You're still in love with him, but he's rejected you. Unfortunately, he finds you repulsive, with your twisted foot and that pathetic limp." He added cruelly, "You're ashamed of your deformity."

I should not have been surprised that his fine, courtroom mind would have thought everything through so coldly and thoroughly. But his viciousness stunned me.

"I am not ashamed of anything. And I'm not in love with Greg Knight. You must be getting senile in your dotage, Mason. In addition to being very farsighted."

It was stupid to continue to taunt him when he clearly had every intention of making sure I was dead before he climbed back in his Mercedes. I half-expected him to raise the hand with the gun and aim. Instead, he looked perplexed and then I knew why. He'd been getting his information from Greg, who was probably too vain to admit I'd rebuffed him.

"Why do you believe everything he tells you?" I said. "You were with him last night. You went to that concert to see him, didn't you? And afterward he never went to the radio station. He replayed an earlier version of his call-in show. I heard him tell someone that the drought was going to continue for the next few days. But it's going to rain today, isn't it? He's done this before. He can be in two places at once. Probably figures he's got a rock-solid alibi for anything and no one will catch on." Mason's face, normally so inscrutable in the courtroom, gave him away for once. "Was he blackmailing you, like he was blackmailing Brandi?"

He didn't answer.

"What dirt did he have on you, Mason? Did you bribe a judge? Lie under oath? Cheat on your taxes?"

"Shut up!"

I read somewhere that someone who was on the verge of committing murder enjoyed bragging about their accomplishments to their victims, probably because they were the only audience they could count on not to rat them out. He stood there with the gun and slowly raised his arm. I closed my eyes. He was going to shoot me now.

"He thought he could manipulate me."

I opened my eyes. "But you were too smart for him, weren't you?"

"Don't you dare patronize me."

"What happened?"

Mason's jaw worked and for the first time since we'd embarked on this little adventure, he looked like he was ashamed of something. "It happened years ago."

"What did?"

"Jimmy fixed my car one night after I had a small accident. Made it as good as new. It wasn't the Mercedes. I had a Cadillac in those days. Greg happened to be around. He must have been about ten or eleven. Jimmy did me a little favor because I helped him out more than once, but the kid didn't have the class of the old man. When he got older he realized what had happened."

"Did you hit somebody?"

"It was an *accident!*" He sounded genuinely anguished. "It was raining, about ten o'clock at night. I didn't even see the woman on the bicycle. It was a deserted stretch of Bull Run Mountain Road. Hell, there were no streetlights, not even a sliver of a moon. It was dark and she was wearing dark clothing. I thought I hit a deer. That's why I didn't go back. I was on my way to your house. I was supposed to take your mother to the hospital. She'd gone into labor with Mia."

I swallowed hard. "Then what happened?"

He looked off toward the hills, like he was trying to recall. But I think it was probably because he was trying not to cry. "Jimmy found a piece of her dress in the undercarriage of my car. I never knew. By that time, I'd heard about the report of a Jane Doe found in a ditch on Bull Run Mountain Road. They had no clue who did it. Nothing to trace it to me."

"Except that piece of her dress."

He looked at me. "You have to understand, sugar. I have done a lot of good in my career. I have helped so many people. I have made it a crusade to do *pro bono* work for those people, most of whom would never have been able to hire a lawyer of my caliber."

"What people?"

"She was Mexican."

"I see."

"I'm glad," he said, "because let me tell you, I have repaid my debt to society. And it's been far, far better this way than if I'd been behind bars."

"Of course."

"You do see, don't you?"

"Yes." I swallowed. "So what did Greg want from you?"

He smiled a rictus smile. "To be rich. To be like everyone else he grew up with. He hated it that Jimmy was a grease monkey. He knew that was his future, too. Hell, he's not that smart. Just barely got through college without flunking out. He was too busy screwing girls and partying to really learn anything. But he wanted your house. More specifically, he wanted your land."

I was stunned. "He has no money."

"No, but I do. He knew your daddy was broke. He figured he could pick the place up for a song, then flip it and make a bundle." He added, acidly, "I would have recouped my original investment of course. It would have cost me nothing."

"He was going to sell to a group of developers who want to build a Civil War theme park. That's how he was going to make a bundle."

Now he looked surprised. "Who told you that? The Eastman girl." He spoke with the same kind of venom as when he had talked about my "deformity." "I'll handle that."

"Leave her alone. She hasn't done anything. She doesn't know any of this."

His laugh was unpleasant. "Don't worry, sugar. I don't resort to something this extreme unless the situation warrants it."

"That's a relief."

"Don't you smart-mouth me or I'll shoot you in the one good leg you've got left. If the fall from the bridge doesn't kill you, you'll bleed to death."

"You mean, like Leland?"

He looked momentarily startled, then he smiled. "Poor old Lee. If only he'd gone along with me, none of this would have happened. It all would have been peaceable. He'd have his money and we'd have the land."

"Were you with him that day?"

"I was."

"You killed him."

"Now, honey, don't you go sayin' things like that," he drawled, like I'd just said a cuss word and he was trying to make me mind my manners. "Your daddy died in an honest-to-God hunting accident."

"You're lying. You shot him."

"Lucie love, I'm warning you. Let me put you right on this. Lee asked me to go along with him to shoot a few of those pesky crows that were eating your grapes. What happened was he got tangled up in a trellis wire while he was sneaking up on some danged bird. He should have known better than to have his finger on the trigger. Damn thing went off and he shot himself. Unfortunately, he bled to death before anybody could get to him in time."

"You left him there to die."

He looked at me severely. "I had to protect my reputation."

"Of course you did."

"You're sassing me again, sugar. I don't like that." He waved the gun at me. "I'd hate to have to really shoot you. You know I'm against handguns except for legitimate hunting purposes. Plus I didn't bring the silencer."

I almost said "what a pity" but that fell in the category of sassing him and I wasn't sure how much patience he had left. "What happened to Fitz?"

He almost spat. "That was Greg."

"Greg killed Fitz?" I stammered.

"Had to. Fitz came upon him when he was at the winery that night. He figured everyone would be at Lee's wake and he wanted to go through things in case Lee had been sloppy and left anything around that might get back to him. So he made it look like a robbery, guessing you'd think it was one of your migrant workers."

"I met Greg leaving the wake as Eli and I arrived. What did he do, rebroadcast his show that night, too? Until somebody figured out it was an old show, it looked like he always had an alibi, didn't it?"

"He did have it all figured out," Mason said. "He shacked up with Mia and screwed her until he got her to see reason about agreeing to sell your land. Then he had Brandi work on Eli. He had some old letters she'd written him. She wanted him to pay for the abortion and I guess he finally coughed up a little something."

"Abortion?"

"Yes," he said, "they had quite the fling."

So Brandi wasn't faking her difficult pregnancy. "That's sick."

"He's not a nice guy," Mason said. "Then you came home. Greg was getting tired of Mia anyway, so he decided to work on you. He bet he could get you to go to bed with him within a week. But you wouldn't cooperate, would you? I think he really wanted to do this without it getting messy."

"It got messy enough that you tried to set Sara Rust's house on fire so you could get rid of the records from Knight's Auto Body."

There was a distant rumble of thunder. It could have come straight from hell. "Aren't you the clever girl," he said. "Guess we're going to get that rain, aren't we?" He motioned with his gun. "Let's get on with it. I don't want to get this suit wet."

"Don't do this. You haven't killed anyone. Don't."

"Don't be difficult, sugar."

"I'm not jumping."

"I'm going to have to shoot you, then."

"Then do it."

He raised his hand and aimed. I looked away.

"Goddamnit, Lucie! Jump!"

I looked over at him. He was furious.

"No."

"Then I'll have to make you."

It's still hard to remember precisely how it happened, but he did make a lunge for me. I swung the golf club at him, as hard as I could. The hooked end caught his hand, knocking the gun out of his grip. He yelped with pain and staggered to regain his balance. But I think those nice wing tips must have been brand new, because he slipped on the gravel like it was greased. He stumbled forward and pitched toward the low wall. God help me, but I swung at him again. He went over the ledge head first. His scream reminded me of the Wicked Witch of the West as she melted to her death.

I got to the parapet and looked down. He lay crumpled, face down in the dry creek bed. He'd landed among some river rocks. I was sure he was dead. If we got the kind of rain that the skies seemed to be promising, there'd be water flowing there again and maybe it would wash him downstream toward the Potomac.

I got back to the Mercedes, hobbling as fast as I could across the rough ground. There had been a car phone on the dashboard. I didn't remember him locking the doors. Not only was the car unlocked, he'd left the keys in the ignition.

I took the phone out of the cradle and punched the button with the little green telephone on it. Greg's name flashed on the display. I hit the button again and the LED display flashed that it was calling his number.

He answered instantly. "I'm leaving the house. I'm finished with the gasoline. You got rid of her, didn't you?"

I disconnected.

CHAPTER 26

I jammed the phone back in the cradle. The Mercedes started like a charm as the phone rang again. Greg, calling back.

The ringing stopped and the message icon blinked a few seconds later. How long did I have before he wondered why Mason wasn't answering the phone? I backed out onto Mosby's Highway and raced for home. When I finally looked at the speedometer, it read eighty. Sixty in the Volvo and you'd need a chiropractor. I slowed to fifty to take the turn onto Atoka Road.

A wispy column of smoke floated upward as I turned onto Sycamore Lane. Was I too late, or would I meet him head on as I drove toward the house? He said he was leaving.

The taillights of Hector's blue pickup, fishtailing as it churned dust, were disappearing down the road that led to the house as I headed toward the divide at the sycamore tree. At least help was on the way and Hector and the others knew about the fire. In the distance, sirens sounded faintly along with more thunder. But no rain—yet.

Highland House was made of stone and stone doesn't burn. They'd probably said that when Sheridan's men burned the Ruins. That fire had left . . . ruins.

I turned left at the divide toward the winery. Greg's convertible sat in the handicapped spot in the parking lot. He'd put the top up, probably on account of the expected rain. I parked and got out next to his car and saw a gun on the passenger seat. He'd locked the doors.

Wherever he was—the villa, the barrel room—I probably didn't have much time before he returned. I lifted the golf club over my head and swung hard at the canvas roof. It bounced with such kick-back my arms nearly came out of my shoulder sockets and I staggered backward.

I needed something sharp. Mason's car keys were attached to a slender silver monogrammed case. I opened the case. A nail file.

I jabbed at the plastic back window and made a small puncture. From small things big things come. I continued stabbing. The sirens grew louder as I worked, until finally the trucks screamed up Sycamore Lane.

The hole in the window was now wide enough to put my arm through. Unfortunately I needed the arms of a chimpanzee to reach the gun. I tried the golf club, angling like I was trying to hook a fish. Then I heard him behind me. He yanked me off the car and threw me to the ground. The golf club remained stuck in the plastic at a crazy angle.

"My car! What did you do to my car?"

I landed hard on my elbows and skidded in the brittle grass. What was it about men and cars?

"Fixed your air-conditioning." I wasn't as intimidated by him as I'd been by Mason.

He unlocked the car with his sensor and got the gun. Then he shoved the golf club through the hole so it came at me like a spear. I ducked and it hit the ground next to me. I grabbed it and pulled myself up.

"Move." He picked up what looked like a metal strongbox that had been on the ground next to him.

"Where are we going?"

He seemed to be thinking. "The barrel room."

"No."

"I'm not asking. Move." He gestured with the gun. "What's Mason's car doing here? Where is he?"

"Dead."

He stopped walking. "You're lying."

"Why don't you go see for yourself?"

"I will," he said, "when I'm done with you." This time he shoved the gun into my ribs. "What happened?"

I had known him since I was six years old. We'd played together, studied together, and made love together. Unlike Mason, he'd really killed someone. Fitz. He wouldn't hesitate to use that gun.

Maybe I could stall for time. Maybe they'd put the fire out right away at the house and someone would come back to the winery. "He fell off the bridge at Goose Creek. What's in the box, Greg?"

The gun was in my ribs again. "Shut up and get going."

We had reached the door to the barrel room, which was ajar. When they took off for the house, closing up was probably the last thing on anyone's mind. He opened the door. "After you."

We went inside and he frog-marched me down an aisle between rows of stacked wine casks, stopping at the far end by Jacques's workbench. The tools, usually neatly hanging on a pegboard above the bench, were heaped on the floor. The wine barrel with my mother's painting of the vineyard's logo was in pieces, the staves splayed open in a tidy circle.

"Why did you destroy that barrel? That was my mother's artwork!"

He said nothing, but his eyes roamed over me, then swept the room. He hadn't figured out what to do with me.

"That strongbox was in the barrel, wasn't it?" I said. Maybe I could get him to talk and use up more time. "How did you know it would be there?"

"My old man designed the box for your mother. I was there when she asked him to do it."

"You knew it was here, all these years?"

"Not exactly. Fitz told me." He paused. "Well, actually he told you."

The only conversation I'd had with Fitz had been when we were alone, outside on the porch at Hunt's Funeral Home.

"You couldn't have heard! You left as I was coming in!"

He shrugged again, looking disarmingly sheepish as he smiled. "Funny, isn't it? I left my blazer over the back of a chair upstairs. It had my wallet, my key card to get into the studio—everything was in it. I didn't plan to eavesdrop, but I guess I got lucky." He laughed lightly. "I practically dove into the bushes when Eli slipped out the front door. You heard me, you know, but you were so intent on what Fitz was saying, and hell, he was half in the bag so he told you it was a cat."

"So you knew he was going to the winery?"

He spread his hands apart, the gun in one, the strongbox in the other, still smiling with that "boys will be boys" kind of rogue's pleasure. "What can I say? Lucky break."

"Not for Fitz it wasn't."

"Don't start with me." The smile disappeared. His handsome face still reminded me of something from a Roman coin, but now I knew which god he resembled. Janus. The two-faced one. "I guess we'd better get this over with. Give me the key, Lucie."

"Whatever is in there won't mean anything to you."

The strongbox must have been heavy, because he set it down on the workbench. He flexed his fingers, then caressed the barrel of the gun almost lovingly. Those hands had once touched me like that.

"How do you know?" He pointed the gun at me. "Bang. It was the only painting she signed on the back, not the front. She also added the drawing of the vineyard logo and those vines. Her signature was a duplicate for what was on that wine barrel, right down to the logo." He pointed to the destroyed cask. "Anyone would have figured it was just a fancy way of signing her name. But then I got hold of my old man's invoices. Your mother told him she needed a box that would protect the contents from damage against damp if it was stored at a constant temperature of around fifty to fifty-five degrees."

I shuddered. "Here."

"Bang, bang."

"Please stop saying that."

His smile was like an ad for toothpaste. "So I assume what's in here is that necklace that belonged to Marie Antoinette," he said, almost casually. "Or else your mother went to a lot of trouble for nothing."

"Whatever is in there doesn't belong to you."

"It does now. Give me the key or I'll shoot you."

"No."

After what he did to Mia, I should have expected what came next. He raised his arm and clubbed me on the side of the head with the butt end of the gun. My brain exploded and I fell against the workbench. He frisked my pockets and pulled out Fitz's key.

"Why did you make me go to all that trouble, sweetheart?" He sounded genuinely disappointed. "Don't make me do that again. Now let's see what we have here."

The necklace, even more exquisite than I remembered, flashed brilliantly as he pulled it out of the box. "Christ," he said. "I guess I hit the jackpot. And what else is there?"

He held up a stack of letters tied together with a blue satin ribbon. I'd seen charred remains of a ribbon like that in Fitz's fireplace.

"Whatever's in here must be pretty important to hide them away with these rocks. Why would anyone want to hide a bunch of old letters? What's in them, Lucie? You know, don't you? Some skeleton in the Montgomery family closet?" He didn't have to move too many muscles for that smile to turn ugly.

"Go to hell."

He threw the bundle in the air with one hand and caught it easily. "Guess I'll have to hang on to these. I bet they'll come in pretty handy if I need to do any more motivating."

I lunged for him again. I heard the crack as the gun connected again to the side of my head. I hung on to the workbench because the room started spinning.

"I'm getting tired of hitting you." He sounded weary. "Let's get this over with. Move. Over behind those big tanks. It'll take longer for someone to find you there." He grabbed me roughly by the arm and shoved me. "Get up. Get going."

The gun was in my ribs again. I staggered, leaning heavily on the golf club, as we walked around the corner to where we kept the ladder and the hoses. Quinn, or probably Hector, had put the ladder back on the hooks after I'd used it last night trying to break out of the place. But one of the hoses was on the ground, which was unusual. Among other things, it was a safety hazard. I stumbled around the mass of coils, avoiding the spots where the concrete was still wet.

With the air-conditioning on and the fans blowing, the concrete should have been dry. I glanced again at the nozzle, which had an automatic shut-off. Maybe they'd left so fast on account of the fire that the water was still on. If so, the pressure would have built up inside the hose.

I dropped the golf club and it clattered on the concrete floor.

"What are you doing?" he snapped. "Pick that thing up."

I would only have one chance. I bent to get the club and reached, with my other hand for the hose. I twisted the nozzle so it was aiming at him and pressed the trigger. The water hit him right in the eyes. He yelled and fell back, temporarily blinded, waving the gun in my direction. I was nearer to him than I'd been to Mason. I hit him full in the face with the golf club. He screamed again, a high-pitched keening sound and blood spurted from his mouth and coated his teeth. The gun flew out of his hands and bounced off a wine barrel, landing somewhere out of sight.

It was my lucky day for men wearing the wrong shoes. Greg turned toward the noise of the gun hitting the floor and slipped on a wet patch of concrete. He lost his balance as his legs went out from under him and banged the back of his head against the metal corner of a stand of wine casks. He hit the floor, moaning, with a hand covering his mouth.

To get the gun meant walking past him and risking the chance that he could still knock me down or else circling the long way around the wine casks and letting him out of my sight for a few seconds. I chose the latter, scanning the floor, the adrenaline jolt of my little victory mutating to fear. He'd begun moving as soon as I did. I heard him scrabbling around like a crab.

His hand was on the gun before I could pick it up. I brought the golf club down hard, for a second time, and connected with his wrist. He yelped again and I thought I'd stopped him, but he just reached for it with the other hand, now completely covered in blood from his mouth. He aimed and squeezed the trigger.

I closed my eyes. Somehow he missed me. The bullet hit a wine cask, which sprang a leak like a geyser, shooting red wine over both of us. He slumped to the ground and the gun fell from his hand. I hooked the golf club around it and putted it to where I could pick it up.

He was unconscious, but breathing.

Quinn got to us even before Bobby and Hector arrived. Greg was lying in a pool of wine. I looked at the cask. Merlot.

"You okay?" Quinn scooped me up in his arms. "You're a mess."

"You always have something nice to say about how I look," I mumbled.

He looked at Greg. "Bad year for Merlot, hunh?"

I thought about the necklace as he carried me outside. "Maybe. But things might be improving. It might be a good harvest after all."

"That so?"

"You promised you'd stay through harvest."

"I'll keep my word."

"What about afterward?"

He set me down carefully on the grass and touched one of my bruises. I winced. "Sorry," he said. "What did your man Jefferson say? 'I like the dreams of the future better than the history of the past.'"

"The history of the past is finished," I said.

"Glad to hear it," he said. "You need to move on."

FIRST IN WINE

For nearly four centuries—since the first colonists arrived in Jamestown in 1607—Virginians have been making wine. Elated to discover abundant wild grapes growing on the shoreline of the James River, the settlers took only two years before they produced their first harvest. The results, unfortunately, were less than stellar as the native American grapes produced wine that tasted and smelled like wet dog.

By 1618, the Jamestown settlers abandoned local grapes and began importing French vines—and French winemakers. But these delicate vines, known as *vitis vinifera,* weren't well suited for the heat, humidity, and pests found in Virginia. The vines either died or didn't bear fruit. Nevertheless in 1619 the House of Burgesses—stubbornly determined to cultivate a home-grown wine industry—passed a law requiring every male colonist to plant twenty vines. For every dead or non-fruit-bearing vine, the fine was a barrel of corn. Not surprisingly, the House of Burgesses acquired a lot of corn.

Over the years the Virginia legislature continued unsuccessfully to foster a wine industry, even as tobacco was becoming the true cash crop. More than 150 years after Jamestown, Thomas Jefferson, one of Virginia's most famous native sons, tried to grow grapes at his beloved Monticello. Convinced Virginia had the right soil and climate for producing grapes that would rival European wines, Jefferson died without seeing his dream realized.

Yet his fellow Virginians persisted, and by the 1800s cross-pollination between European *vitis vinifera* and American grapes created the first American hybrids such as the Alexander, Norton (a Virginia native), Catawba, and others. However, the Civil War, which was hard fought on Virginia soil as nowhere else, caused many vineyards to be destroyed or abandoned. Shortly afterward California wines arrived on the scene and rapidly cornered the lion's share of the U.S. market. It took Prohibition, arriving in Virginia three years before Congress made the U.S. a dry country in 1919, to finish off what little was left of the industry.

The mid-1970s saw a renaissance in grape planting in the Commonwealth thanks to new success growing French hybrids such as Seyval Blanc, Vidal Blanc, and Chambourcin, along with agricultural breakthroughs finally allowing *vitis vinifera* grapes to flourish in Virginia. In 2004 the state government in Richmond produced a strategic blueprint for the industry that traces its lineage directly to Jefferson's long ago dreams. Known as Vision 2015, the goal is to establish Virginia—already a serious contender in national and international markets—as a producer of world-class wines.

Thomas Jefferson would be proud.

ACKNOWLEDGMENTS

I owe an enormous debt of gratitude to Juanita Swedenburg and the late Wayne Swedenburg, owners of Swedenburg Estate Vineyard in Middleburg, Virginia, for the hands-on experience, technical help, and insight they gave me while researching this book. It goes without saying that any mistakes on matters involving wine or the workings of a well-run, small vineyard are mine. Gordon Murchie, president of the Vinifera Winegrowers Association, also provided assistance with historical information.

I hope the good people of Loudoun and Fauquier Counties will forgive the liberties I took with geography—especially re-routing Goose Creek and playing a bit fast and loose with county boundaries—in that beautiful region of the Commonwealth.

Special thanks to Tony and Belinda Collins for an introduction to and education on Virginia's 90+ (and growing) wineries—and for plying me with reading material and good wine over the years.

Cathy Brannon, Debbie Gador, Catherine Kennedy, and Leslie Shepherd read and commented on early drafts of this book. I am also indebted to Donna Andrews, Carla Coupe, Laura Durham, Peggy Hanson, Val Patterson, Noreen Wald, and Sandi Wilson.

Thanks especially to Sarah Knight and Brant Rumble, my editors, and heartfelt thanks to Dominick Abel, my agent.

Finally, it's an oft-repeated truism that although writing is a solitary pursuit no writer works in a vacuum. If it were not for André, Peter, Matt, and Tim, nothing I do or say would matter as much.

ABOUT THE AUTHOR

Ellen Crosby is a freelance regional reporter for *The Washington Post* and a former Moscow correspondent for ABC News Radio. Her first novel, *Moscow Nights,* written while living in London, was published in the United Kingdom and is based on her experiences working in the former Soviet Union. *The Merlot Murders* marks her American debut, and takes place nearer her current home in Virginia's historic horse and hunt country. She's married and has three sons. She is currently writing the sequel to *The Merlot Murders*.

Visit her website at www.ellencrosby.com.

Printed in the United States
By Bookmasters